*Property at the
Garden Gables Inn*

'At times Burke's writing and atmosphere remind one of William Faulkner; at other moments Raymond Carver. I cannot think of much higher praise that can be accorded a novel'
Marcel Berlins, *The Times* Metro

'Although the novel's tone is elegiac and aches with an excruciating sense of despair, it's Robicheaux's humanity which shines a light through the room and invests the book with a life-affirming quality. *Purple Cane Road* is undoubtedly Burke's best novel yet, an ambitious work which blurs the boundaries between so-called "serious" literature and crime fiction' *Crime Time*

'This is prose that cuts straight to the heart, summoning a wonderful parade of damaged humanity in its wake'
Maxim Jakubowski, *Guardian*

'I think of no other writer today who captures the American ___ with such eloquence and sympathy'
Susanna Yager, *Sunday Telegraph*

'James Lee Burke is a writer to be remembered' *USA Today*

'James Lee Burke has a sophisticated and brilliantly expressed vision of humanity and one can see, smell and taste the America of which he writes' *Times Literary Supplement*

'The book makes straight for the heart of American darkness, and the fact that it achieves a kind of redemption . . . marks it out as a triumph' *Mail on Sunday*

'Burke writes prose that has a pronounced streak of poetry in it'
New York Times

By James Lee Burke

DAVE ROBICHEAUX NOVELS
The Neon Rain
Heaven's Prisoners
Black Cherry Blues
A Morning for Flamingos
A Stained White Radiance
In the Electric Mist with Confederate Dead
Dixie City Jam
Burning Angel
Cadillac Jukebox
Sunset Limited
Purple Cane Road
Jolie Blon's Bounce
Last Car to Elysian Fields

OTHER FICTION
Half of Paradise
To the Bright and Shining Sun
Lay Down My Sword and Shield
Two for Texas
The Lost Get-Back Boogie
The Convict and Other Stories
Cimarron Rose
Heartwood
Bitterroot
White Doves at Morning
In the Moon of Red Ponies

James Lee Burke is the author of twenty-three novels, including thirteen featuring Detective Dave Robicheaux, and a volume of short stories. *The Lost Get-Back Boogie* was nominated for a Pulitzer Prize; *Black Cherry Blues* won the Edgar Award in 1989; and *Cimarron Rose*, Burke's first novel featuring Billy Bob Holland, won the 1997 Edgar Award. In 1998 *Sunset Limited* won the CWA Macallan Gold Dagger for Fiction. James Lee Burke divides his time between Missoula, Montana, and Louisiana.

JAMES LEE BURKE

TO THE BRIGHT AND SHINING SUN

PHOENIX

A PHOENIX PAPERBACK

First published in Great Britain in 2003
by Orion

First published in the USA in 1971
by Charles Scribner's Sons

Fourth impression

Reissued 2005
by Phoenix,
an imprint of Orion Books Ltd,
Orion House, 5 Upper St Martin's Lane,
London WC2H 9EA

A CIP catalogue record for this book
is available from the British Library.

ISBN 0 75284 268 4

Printed and bound in Great Britain by
Clays Ltd, St Ives plc

www.orionbooks.co.uk

This book is for my mother,
Mrs James Lee Burke, Sr.,
of Houston, Texas,

and for my uncle and aunt,
Mr and Mrs Oran Burke,
of Baton Rouge, Louisiana

Come all you fellers, so young and so fine
Don't seek your fortune in the dark and dreary mine
It'll form to a habit and seep in your soul
Till the stream of your blood is black as the coal.

There's many a man I knowed in my day
Who lived but to labor his whole life away.
Like a fiend for his dope, a drunkard his wine,
A man can have lust for the lure of the mine*

Merle Travis

TO THE BRIGHT
AND SHINING SUN

chapter one

Three men and a boy sat in the dark in a battered 1958 Ford on a shale road that wound along the base of the mountain. One of them smoked a hand-rolled cigarette in the cup of his hands, bending down his head below the level of the windows whenever he drew in the smoke. The first leaves were shedding from the trees, and they rattled dryly along the road in the wind. Around the curve of the road was the coal tipple, huge and looming over the railway tracks that led past the mine opening down towards the switch where the C & O made up the long freight cars that would eventually take the coal to Pittsburgh. The boy, Perry Woodson Hatfield James, sat in the back seat with one hand gripped tightly under his thigh and the other over his wrist. He could feel the sweat form under his arms and run cold down his sides. He believed that if fear had a smell it would already have soaked through his clothes and permeated everything in the car. He could smell it in himself every time he took a breath. It was a rancid odor, like something dead in the sun. Big J.W. and Little J.W. sat in the front, immobile against the glow of the moon except when Little J.W. bent to smoke off the cigarette. They were half brothers, both fathered by a North Carolina moonshiner who was killed at the age of seventy-six in the dirt streets of Harlan while giving whiskey free to the miners when John L. Lewis first organized the coal fields and the National Guard was sent in by the state to shoot down a man who tried to stop a scab from crossing the picket.

Big J.W. wore a tin hat down low on his forehead, and his skin was grained with coal dust, rubbed so deep around the corners of his eyes that it looked like a burn. The faded pinstriped coat he wore over his overalls was stretched almost to tearing across his angular shoulders, and the knobs on his wrist looked like white bones sticking out of his sleeves. His teeth were yellow and long, and his fingernails were as thick and hard as tortoise shell, broken to the quick and colored with blue-black half-moons. His wife cut his hair with a straight-edged razor, and it hung unevenly over the back of his neck like a girl's. Little J.W. was a small round man with a hard, little, round stomach that pushed against his work trousers. He was thought to be an invaluable man in the mines because he could go a half mile up and down a narrow shaft on his hands and knees like a groundhog. His soft, brown eyes and quiet mountain accent caused few people to pay any particular attention to him except when there was an explosion or cave-in down in the hole and somebody was needed to crawl through the fallen limestone and timbers to some gas-filled pocket deep in the earth where no sane person would go. But those who knew him well realized that he was a much more dangerous person than Big J.W., and when set in motion he would go at something or someone with the quiet rage of a hot iron scorched across wood. Once, he and an uncle argued while drinking, and after the uncle drew a knife, Little J.W. hit him six times in the head with a poker and threw him off the front porch of the company cabin into the yard. 'Pull a knife on me, will you,' he said, the poker still in his hand. 'Pull one against your own blood, will you. Well, if you get home by yourself that's all right with me, and by God if you die out here in the lot that's all right with me, too.'

On the back floor of the car, under a blanket, were a leveraction 30-caliber Winchester, a double-barreled twelve-gauge with the barrels sawed off two inches in front of the chambers, fourteen cans of dynamite, three primers, and a four-hundred-foot spool of cap wire. The boy also knew that each of the three men with him carried a .38, since they would no more leave home without it than they would without their trousers.

'It ain't we got to blow it,' he said. 'Maybe just set it up on the mountain and push some rock down on the hole.'

'I done told you, honey,' Big J.W. said. 'We're a-blowing that tipple right over on the moneyman's head. We didn't risk no year in Frankfort breaking open the shack just to move some rock around.'

'Moon's a-setting,' Little J.W. said.

'Get them charges out, Perry,' Bee, the man next to the boy, said. He was the boy's uncle, a tall man who had to stoop slightly so his head wouldn't hit the top of the car. Like Big J.W., he wore overalls, with a leather belt around his waist, and a suitcoat and a cloth slug cap on his head. Years ago he had lost his dentures, and his mouth was collapsed in rows of thick creases around his lips. His gums were blackened from the wad of snuff that was always under his tongue. During the forties he did two years in the Kentucky penitentiary for shooting a company deputy, and because he had refused to name any of the other men who shot three more company men in the same battle, he was made a business agent for the United Mine

3

Workers when he was paroled. He rasped and coughed into his sleeve. He'd had silicosis since he was twenty-five from working in the mines before the companies had been forced to put ventilation systems in the shaft.

'What if them scabs is there?' Perry said.

'They're a-going right with it,' Big J.W. said. 'They can steal food out of a man's mouth down in hell if they've still a mind for it.'

Bee tore the blanket off the explosives and guns. 'Now you build them charges,' he said. 'By God, there ain't nobody saying a James or a Hatfield puts a scab before a workingman.'

The boy screwed the cans end to end, tightening each socket securely. He built the charges in cylinders of four cans each, with a primer on the butt end of each row. The sweat on his hands was cold against the metal. There's enough here to put half the mountain down in the holler, he thought. Them four hundred feet of wire ain't even going to give us running distance. We'll be a-setting here with rocks big as cars coming down on us. I seen them drop a charge like this on Black Mountain in Harlan once, and the trees and rocks burst all over the sun. The dust stayed black across the crest of the ridge until twilight when it started to rain. He wished he was back home in the cabin now, with the dry poplar logs and huge coal lumps burning in the blackened sandstone fireplace. He was too afraid to care whether he worked union or not. Maybe the operator ain't wrong, he thought. Maybe he can't afford to pay scale, and it ain't nothing but trouble to push union in the coal field. We was doing all right with what they was giving us. Twelve dollars a day is more than we're a-getting on the picket. There wasn't no shooting and no company men coming around the houses asking where the men was

4

at the night before. We didn't have nobody cutting off our charge at the store. And on Saturday afternoon a feller had a hard dollar in his pocket to ride the bus into Winfro Valley for the Barn Dance that's over the radio.

Then he felt an old secret shame inside him at his fear. His people had been against the operator since his grandfather had had his mineral rights stolen out from under him for fifty cents an acre by a New York sharper – an eastern feller, with a gold watch that must have cost a hundred dollars hanging on his vest, his grandfather had said. He set down at your table and told ye how good your fatback and greens was and how the half dollar would pay the county tax and said the land wasn't good for anything no way. Bought up the whole holler for no more than the price of that train ticket from New York. And didn't tell nobody that what ye signed give the operator the right to do whatever he wanted to the top of the land. They could tear away the mountain and let it slide all across your tobacco crop, there wasn't nothing ye could do about it except go to work for him.

Perry knew that no James or Hatfield in his family had ever been afraid of operators, company thugs, strikebreakers with their axe handles, or even the National Guard. His grandfather said he was related to Frank James, the outlaw who hid out in the Cumberland after robbing a bank with Jesse over in West Virginia, and his mother was a direct descendant of Devil Anse Hatfield, who killed McCoys all over Pike and Logan counties. His family had been union people even before John L. Lewis and the CIO organized the coal field. They had fought side by side with the organizers from the National Miners Union before the Great Depression, when the man who breathed the word 'union' was fired from his job, evicted from his company-owned cabin, maybe run out of the county by the sheriff, and sometimes shot and thrown down the hollow.

'It's dark enough now,' Big J.W. said. 'Hand baby brother up the shotgun.'

Perry gave Little J.W. the sawed-off double-barrel and watched him break open the breech and plop two shells into the chambers. Little J.W. rolled down his window and held the shotgun outside against the door.

The entrance to the mine was a dark, square gap in the face of the mountain. Farther down, a huge slag heap was smoking in the cold. Since the time he was a small child Perry could not remember ever having been near a mine without smelling the odor of burning slag. It was a fire that never went out because its source of fuel was never stopped, and the air around his home always had the same acrid stench to it. The coal from the tipple spilled across the road into a black slide and down the gulley into a stream. Next to the road a discarded sign on a wooden stick, left from the day's picketing, was propped at an angle against a rock. It read in crude, hand-printed letters THIS MINE UNFAIR IT DON'T HIRE UNION MEN.

'They didn't leave no guard,' Little J.W. said.

'Watch that opening. Them scabs might be a-drawing right down on my windshield now,' Big J.W. said. 'Remember when they shot up Noah Combs? He never knew where they was at till he was right up on the shaft.'

Bee took the .38 special from the bib pocket of his overalls and let it rest in his palm against his leg. Big J.W. drove past the tipple a hundred yards and stopped the car under an overhang of pine trees. The base of the burning slag heap glowed red in the breeze.

Down in the hollow Perry could hear the bats squeaking through the darkness as they swept in circles over the creek.

'Don't do no talking when we're out of the car,' Big J.W. said. 'And if you see a scab, drop him fast before he gets off a shot. He hits one of them primers and they'll have to scrub us off the mountain.'

The four of them got out of the car onto the road. The wind against the sweat on Perry's face made him cold. He and big J.W. each carried two sticks of charges; they held the spool of cap wire between them with an iron pipe stuck through the center. They moved up the mountain towards the tipple, over the scattered lumps of coal and slag. The rocks rolling down under their boots and hands sounded to Perry like an avalanche crashing into the hollow. There ain't no sense in it, he thought. You ain't got to blow half the county to let them know he wasn't working for no one-twenty-five. There ain't going to be no work anyhow when the tipple goes.

Before they got to the base of the tipple, Little J.W. and Bee dropped to one knee and pointed their guns to each side of the structure. Bee held his .38 straight ahead of him, with his left hand gripped around his wrist to steady his aim. The boy and Big J.W. moved up to the steel stanchions sunk in concrete that supported the weight of the tipple. Perry's fingers felt thick and uncoordinated as he and Big J.W. placed the charges around a stanchion on the downhill side of the mountain and wrapped them securely with baling wire. Big J.W. pulled the end of the cap wire loose from the spool and carefully set the small, plastic tube of gelatin detonator across a primer head and wound it over with electrician's tape. Then he took the spool of wire and made two turns around the bottom of the stanchion and tied a sailor's bowknot in it so that the tube of gelatin would not pull loose when they strung the wire downhill.

Big J.W. grabbed the boy's arm hard and pulled him into a crouch beside him. Several rocks rolled past them from above. They waited in the dark, hardly breathing, while the bats squeaked and whirled above them. Little J.W. and Bee looked like carved soldiers, frozen in their positions. Run now, the boy thought. Drop the wire and take off across the road into the holler. It ain't cowardice to run from getting shot at. People in wars do it. They didn't say nothing about shooting. It ain't fair to get shot at when you ain't got a gun.

'Set, boy,' Big J.W. whispered fiercely, his hand tightening on Perry's arm.

'We can't even see them. They'll tear us up soon as we get in the open.'

'Shut.' This time the hand clenched so tightly over his arm that the boy thought his blood veins were pressed flat against the bone.

They waited five minutes under the tipple, each with his hand squeezed hard on the iron bar that held the spool of wire, the slag cutting into their knees. Perry felt that even if a small rock was set in motion by the point of his boot a volley of shotgun and rifle fire would open up that would blow him backwards like a pile of rags onto the road.

'Start stringing it,' Big J.W. said. They crawled down the mountain between the two other men while Big J.W. pulled the cap wire off the spool with one hand and laid it out evenly behind them. Bee's extended arm was as rigid as a thick piece of wood as he kept his pistol pointed towards the top of the rise, his jaws sucking slowly on the saliva-smooth lump of snuff in his mouth. He started to cough once and pressed his palm across his face, spitting tobacco juice all over himself in a dry rasp. Perry knew that somewhere up there in the dark a man had the V-sight of a carbine lined in on the nape of his neck, and involuntarily he kept touching the back of his head with his hand. I wouldn't be afraid if they give me a gun, he thought. Them company guards ain't likely to stick to a fight when they get shot back at. Big J.W. wouldn't be a-grabbing on to me like he was something unless he had that special in his pocket.

He felt that a gun would be like a piece of magic in his pocket. He knew the heart-pounding and heavy breathing would stop if he could feel a .38 stuck hard down inside his trousers with the hammer on half cock. A gun was something smooth and lovely that fitted into the curve of a man's palm as though it were an extension of his arm. You could hold scabs and company deputies at a distance with it, and you didn't have to be afraid of a man letting off a shotgun at you from the dark opening of a mine shaft. Noah Combs wouldn't have been shot up if he'd had his revolver in his hand rather than in his glove compartment when the company guards hit him from both sides of the road.

Perry and Big J.W. made the road and strung out the last of the wire to the automobile. Big J.W. unlatched the hood, raised it carefully, and pulled the cap off of a sparkplug. Little J.W. and Bee moved backwards down the mountain, with their guns still pointed in front of them. The mountains looked cold as iron. The black trunks of the trees and the sharp rock walls of the cliffs were beginning to coat with ice. The boy's feet felt like stone. J.W. opened his pocketknife and shaved off the insulation from the end of the cap wire.

He pulled the wire apart in two sections and wrapped the exposed metal strands around the head of the sparkplug and replaced the rubber cap.

It ain't too late, the boy thought. Run on down the road as far as you can get and it ain't a part of you no longer. Stringing the wire didn't hurt nobody. Get across the ridge into the next holler and it's them burning out the operator. You didn't have nothing to do with sending that spark up to the charge. They ain't going to send a feller to Frankfort for laying some wire down a mountain when it would have got done if you was there or not.

He put his chafed hands down deep inside his pockets and felt his fingers come out through the worn lining against his thighs. His long, straw-colored coarse hair was damp with sweat, even in the wind. The women in his family said he looked like a Hatfield, because at sixteen he was already taller than most of the men in the hollow where he lived. They said his eyes were like a Hatfield's, too, washed-out and pale, as though he were looking at you from under water. The pupils looked like pieces of burnt cinder. He was always able to pass for several years older than his age, and he had been working in shaft mines since his fifteenth birthday. His hands and the hard, bone places in his face had already begun to take on the black discoloration from the coal dust. In a few more years his face would look like Big J.W.'s, with the grit from the coal seam ground deeply into the pores, and no amount of scrubbing with the hard, skin-blistering soaps they sold at the company store could get rid of it. His clothes, made of different fabrics and belonging to at least two generations of the James family, were faded and patched and without any resemblance of a crease in them from being washed in boiling water and left to dry over a rick fence behind the cabin. The old suitcoat his father had given him was too large for his shoulders and it hung limply against his back. The work shoes he wore were hard as brick from walking through water every day at the bottom of the hole, and they had rubbed a ring of callus around his ankles. He looked as though he were made of sticks; but his long arms could swing a pick harder than a grown man, and he could work two shifts in a row in the mine when other men wouldn't stay sixteen hours in the hole even for double time.

'What we got to blow it for?' he whispered. 'They'll find the charge and know we wasn't fooling with them.'

'Because the operator don't sign a contract till it starts costing him money,' Big J.W. said.

'There's somebody moving around on that ridge,' Little J.W. said, the sawed-off double-barrel hanging loosely by his side. 'Knock the fire out of their ass and let's get off this mountain.'

'Get ready to pull that wire, baby brother,' Big J.W. said. He got into the front seat to start the engine, and the other three crouched behind the far side of the automobile.

They ain't got no sense, Perry thought, his head pulled down between his knees. We'll get buried under all that coal and rock. There won't even be no way to tell who we was when they dig us out.

As Big J.W. turned the ignition and pressed the starter, the boy leaped to his feet and ran for the far side of the road, towards the slope that fell off into the hollow. He heard the car engine gun and looked over his shoulder to see the tipple explode in white and yellow flame. The noise was as if God had crashed every lightning bolt He owned into the side of the mountain. The roar of sound and the heat rushed over him and beat against the walls of the hollow. In that instant when the flame ripped over the black sides of the tipple, he saw a man's silhouette stand out sharply on top, and then the whole structure erupted in pieces of torn metal into the sky. Years later, he would never know if he actually heard a scream in that ear-splitting second or if something inside him was screaming. Slag and coal and rock clattered down on the automobile and broke both front windows. Little J.W. and Bee were hunched over on the ground, with their hands over their heads. A twisted spar whistled through the air like a cannon ball, cutting through the tops of two maple trees. The air became black with coal dust. As the last echo of the explosion began to thin in the distance, the boy could hear the leaves from the trees settling to the ground around him.

Little J.W. ran to the hood of the car, pulled the cap wire loose from the sparkplug, and threw it behind him on the ground.

'Get that boy out of there,' he yelled.

Perry felt a pair of hands on each side of him grab his arms and pull him towards the car. He choked on the coal dust when he breathed. It seemed that the mountain with the jagged hole torn in its side was spinning rapidly around him and was about to crash in an avalanche over his head. He thought he was going to be sick, as though he had drunk too much corn whiskey on an empty stomach. Then he felt the movement of the car jolt him against the seat, and he knew he was roaring down the mountain, because he could see the trees change shape in the moonlight through the spiderwebbed cracks in the front windows.

chapter two

The hollow where Perry lived looked like any other in the Cumberland range. A creek wound out of a cut in the mountain and washed over the smooth pebble bottom and grew larger from the small drainages flowing into it from the springs up on the hillside. The walls of the hollow rose straight up into the clouds, with dark holes in the cliffs that were left from when eastern Kentucky was covered by an inland sea. Along the slopes above the creek were small, three-room cabins, the green and white paint blistered and flaking, and each had an identical small porch in front, a stone chimney, and an outhouse like an upended matchbox in the back. The hollow was the type of place the state tourist bureau would have photographed and put on the cover of a vacation brochure to advertise the scenic loveliness of the Cumberland Mountains and the simple life of the mountain people except that long streams of garbage were strewn down from the front of the cabins into the creek, wrecked cars – some upside down and gutted by fire – lay in front yards, and by the dirt road that led into the hollow were a school bus without wheels and several shacks made of crates, cardboard, logs, and tarpaper. In front of each shack dirty children with mucus dried on their faces played with rusted barrel hoops and tin cans. The fences all had clothes laid over them to dry in the wind, and in some places rotted mattresses, bed-springs, piles of car parts and tires, were heaped at the side of the house.

The mining company had once owned all of the hollow and the cabins and people in it, but through the years some had been able to buy their house from the company; others had been laid off or crippled in cave-ins and had been forced to leave and build a shelter out of whatever discarded material they could find. The property the company still held title to was not maintained, because a miner who didn't like what he was given could get out and look for a job driving a cab in Ohio. This hollow, along with almost every other settlement on the Cumberland plateau, had at one time or other been called a depressed area by either the state or federal government; but nothing ever changed greatly. More men were laid off the job because of automation or a decrease in the demand for coal; there was more garbage down the mountainside each year, more strip mines tore great pits in the top of the mountain, more tobacco crops were ruined from the yellow rainwater that seeped down over the exposed coal; and more people learned how to lie to the county relief worker when he made his monthly visit and asked if the man of the house was still gone and not contributing to his family's support.

In Perry's hollow a man had one of three kinds of support – if he had any at all. He could work in the mines, but it was getting harder every year to work union and get a decent scale. There were machines now that did the work of a hundred men with picks and mattocks, and the strip- and truck-mine operators could tear the earth away with bulldozers, explode the bared seam with dynamite, and pick up the great hunks of coal with machines, using only a handful of men as a crew. And if a man worked for the small operator, he crawled through badly ventilated shafts on his hands and knees, clawing the coal loose from the wall in a bent position, and the little money he made wouldn't pay the charge at the store at the end of the month. Also, he could have a shaft ceiling come down on top of him, and no one would be responsible for either his hospitalization or the support of his family, because he had no welfare card and no union disability fund.

So if a man didn't work in the mine, he made whiskey in a rock house, a shallow limestone cave in the base of the mountain, where he had a supply of water from a spring and there was a heavy cover of trees and brush over the entrance. If he made good whiskey that took its 'bead' from the corn and not from several sacks of sugar poured in the mash to hurry the fermentation, he could sell it in Detroit to the syndicate for as much as fourteen dollars a gallon; but he still had to split with the transporter, who had to run it across two state lines and risk not only arrest by federal law officers but by county deputies, who would stop a runner on his way back from the sale, take him before the local justice of the peace, and fine him every dollar they found taped under his dashboard. The moonshiner also knew that the A.B.C. (Alcohol Beverage Control) would eventually get him, break up his cooker, thumping keg, and mash barrels with axes, and chop his fifty-dollar condenser coil into pieces. The A.B.C. used airplanes now, and they could spot a wisp of smoke from a rock house miles away or a trail worn by the mules through the trees where there should have been no trail.

If a man had no support at all, he could receive as

much as two hundred and fifty dollars a month from the federal government as a 'happy-pappy' – an unemployed father. The happy-pappies in the hollow picked up paper and raked leaves for the Forest Service, cleaned the cinders from barbecue pits in recreation areas, and sometimes cut grass along the new interstate highway. Most of these men were either old or partly crippled. In the morning, when the sun broke over the edge of the mountain, an old army flatbed two-and-one-half-ton stake truck would grind down the road and pick up the men sitting on their front porches. They each carried a paper-sack lunch with pork chops and bread inside. When the truck was full, it would move back out of the hollow into the national forest, where the men spent most of their day. They always looked like part of an army of refugees, with their legs hanging over the tailgate of the truck and their scythes and shovels held in the crook of their arms.

Perry waited for the clerk to sack his groceries in the small clapboard company store and then asked for the charge slip to sign. The store smelled of the oil that was spread on the door to collect the dust. The walls of the building looked as though they would cave inward from the weight of canned goods stacked on the shelves. The clerk was a balding man with thin grey hair above his ears who had gone to college a year at Richmond. He made seventy-five dollars a week to keep books and inventory, and to close a miner's account when the word came down from the company. People in the hollow treated him with the type of respect that comes from fear; he could use words they didn't understand, and anything he said was always backed by some power of money and authority down in Harlan or Sterns. He pulled open a drawer under the counter and thumbed through the stiff pieces of cardboard that separated the stacks of carbon charge tickets held together with rubber bands. He popped the edge of a file card with his fingernail and knocked the drawer shut with the flat of his hand.

'It says you're in arrears and you ain't working at the mine anymore,' he said.

'There ain't nobody working at the mine now. It's shut down,' Perry said.

'I'm just going by the record. You didn't pay all of last month's bill, and the timekeeper ain't carrying you on the pay sheet.'

'I don't care about no pay sheet. They won't let us go down till we get an election.'

'Who won't let you go down? There's a full crew going into the hole every day.'

'That's them scabs from West Virginia. There ain't nobody from around here going through that picket.'

The clerk leaned against the counter.

'Your credit was good here while you were charging against your salary at the mine,' he said. 'You don't work there any longer. You already owe me money that you can't pay, and you can't buy groceries on money that you're not about to have. Do you understand that?'

'We was good enough to buy here till we ask for a white man's wage.'

'You can make twelve or fifteen dollars a day anytime you want to carry a shovel instead of a sign, son,' the clerk said.

Perry left the sack of groceries on the counter and walked out of the store onto the slanting wooden porch, where two other men from his mine were sitting on steps, chewing tobacco and spitting on the frozen ground.

'They taken away your charge, too?' one of them said.

'The bastard wouldn't give me two dollars' worth of pork chops and a loaf of bread.'

'He ain't a-giving anything to nobody,' the man said. 'They'd let that food go sour on the shelf before they'd give it to the likes of us.'

'Maybe somebody ought to spread a little coal oil on his place one night,' the second man said.

'It's too bad he wasn't up on the tipple with that scab when them boys blew it the other night,' the first man said. 'They couldn't find no part of that feller. They say that charge must have pushed the nails in his boots plumb up through his head.'

'I'll see you fellers around,' Perry said.

'Where you looking for work?'

'They say them truck mines over in Letcher is a-hiring,' he said.

'There ain't no operator taking men from our mine. They figure somebody might drop something extra down the hole one night.'

Both of the men laughed. Perry walked down the rutted road towards his cabin. The sky was covered with snow clouds, and there was a haze over the mountains in the distance. The first light snow from last night lay powdered in the pine and beech trees. As Perry started the climb up the slope to his cabin he felt the sharp air burn down in his lungs. A flight of geese flew high overhead in a V-formation. He could hear their faint honking through the cold. But they ain't going to set down around here, he thought. There ain't nothing good going to happen around here this year. Bee and J.W. seen to that. They're going to shut us out of work and starve us right out of this holler if they don't put us in the pen first.

The incline before his cabin was covered with tin cans, rusted tangles of wire, automobile parts, and garbage. The green and white paint on the building had long since weathered to the dark color of slag smoke. The rick fence had fallen down in places, and the clothes his mother had put out in the morning to dry on the rails had been blown to the ground by the wind. His younger brothers and sisters were playing inside the wheel-less wreck of a 1946 Chevrolet in the side yard. There were six children besides himself, all younger than he, and he had once had an older brother, who was killed in a barroom knifing in Cincinnati. The children all had dirty faces and colds, and their clothes were more patched and wash-faded than his. The smallest one, Irvin, had had tuberculosis when he was two, and the doctor in Richmond, who had kept him in his clinic for two weeks without taking a fee, said the child needed to be in a hospital for several months; but Perry's father never had the money, and there was no charity hospital in any county close to their home. So Irvin was four now, and the fact that he had once had tuberculosis and had needed a hospital was something the parents pushed off into a dark corner of their minds, and in the cabin no one mentioned anything about it except that Irvin had once been 'sick.'

The front of the cabin was covered with broken bits of harness and rope hung on wooden pegs, dried coon skins, cane fishing poles stacked against the wall, tattered quilts that Perry's mother had laid across the porch rails to air in the wind, wagons for the children made out of apple crates and rollerskate wheels, and fish scales, dried like pieces of broken razor blade and ground into the wooden planking.

Perry's father sat in a straight-back chair in front of

the fireplace, with his great square hands spread out on his thighs. His shoulders and back and the bend of his flat stomach were as rigid as the chair he sat in. His clear blue eyes and the sharp mountain features of his face made him look like a man in the prime years of his life, but on one side of his chest was a cavity that sunk back to the bone as though he had been struck with a sledge. Ten years ago he had been working across the line in Virginia in a hot coal mine where there was gas always in the shaft, and when somebody had lighted a cigarette during the lunch hour an explosion thundered through all the corridors and blew the elevator cage straight out of the hole. The pinning in his shaft gave way, and he lay two days in an air pocket under a mound of rock and coal before a rescue team got to him.

His hair had always been wavy and brown, and he had combed it straight back with a short bob on the nape of his neck. But now the hair had begun to thin and turn gray, and from his temple one lock always hung in the corner of his eye. But he was still a handsome man, with a high, straight forehead and a row of even teeth that looked like new enamel; and his wife said that as he grew older he looked more like the picture of Frank James he kept locked in a tin box on the top shelf of his closet. The picture had been given him by his grandfather, and it had a round gilt frame and showed Frank James with a Confederate tunic on his shoulders and a gray officer's hat above his pale, classic features. Once a man from the University of Kentucky offered Perry's father one hundred dollars for it, but he would no more have sold it than he would have sold part of his birthright.

Perry's mother looked older than her husband. Her skin had once had the smooth glow of a lilac petal, but now it was rough and creased around the eyes, and her hands were almost as calloused as a man's. Like most women on the Cumberland plateau, she came to flower before she was twenty, and by the time she had reached thirty, her hips were widened from childbearing, there was a stoop to her shoulders, and the hours of work that started before sunrise and sometimes ended late at night had wasted her body. Once she had loved the square dances and dinners on the ground at the dollar fishing lake on Saturday night, when all the women talked about their children and traded jars of preserves and listened to the fiddle and banjo music coming over the lake while the men, in straw hats, stood around the hoods of automobiles, chewing ten-cent cigars and drinking somebody's best corn whiskey; but with the years and the harder times she had settled into a resignation that was neither boredom nor determination, but an acceptance of her life as another mountain woman who would never have enough food to cook for the number of people at the table, never have enough money at the end of the month for new clothes, or even a chance to see a place like Cincinnati, where whole blocks stayed lighted all night and people never seemed to want for anything.

'Where's the groceries at?' Perry's father said.

'They won't give us no more charge,' he said. 'They ain't a-selling to nobody that don't scab for them. They ain't going to give nothing to anybody without work, and they ain't going to hire nobody from our mine.'

'They done it like that to me and Bee in 1930. Sent a company man down here with a pistol to run us out. By God, a dozen of us picked him and his little Ford up and throwed them both in the honey hole. They couldn't burn the smell out of that car with a blow torch.' The old man laughed, then pressed his hand to the cavity in his chest. 'He had it all over him. He tried to fire his pistol, but the barrel was clogged with it. The outhouse must have been setting thirty years over that hole.'

'You reckon there's any work over in Virginia?'

'I don't want you in none of them gas mines,' Perry's father said. 'My boy ain't a-getting buried five miles down because a fool wants to smoke or somebody jumps a spark off the wall. A man don't know what it's like to lay in the dark for days with the whole earth crushing in on you. There ain't no man should have to go through that. Rocks covering you all over till there ain't no feeling in your body. Just laying there sucking at the little bit of air you can get. Even God ain't got a right to do that to a man. You forget about anything over there in Virginia.'

'We ain't got any food, Daddy,' Perry said.

'We got what the government give us,' his mother said. 'We'll make do with what we have.'

'That ain't enough. We couldn't hardly make do when I was working,' Perry said.

'We can't take no more loss in this family,' she said. 'Your brother run off just like you want to. He said there was big jobs up in Ohio. Then we didn't even know he was dead till the police sent us a wire.'

'The mines is going to open up again, anyway,' his father said. 'And they're going to put union men down in the hole working scale. They ain't beat the union here in ten years.'

'They ain't going to hire me. It don't matter if we win our election or not,' Perry said.

'There ain't a man working in this holler that ain't been on a job at sometime or other when somebody shot up some company men. They done their share of it to us, and we done it right back,' his father said. 'If

22

they tried to keep out every man that worked around a blowed tipple, they wouldn't have nobody to bring up their coal.'

'What are we going to do when there ain't none of that government food left?' Perry said.

'We always got through before. The Lord ain't ever let us starve,' his mother said, almost believing the old Church of God axiom that she always told herself when times became so bad that she saw no way out of them. She went to the wood-burning stove and lifted the iron cover off the fire with a small handle. The flames leaped out through the open hole. She dropped a handful of dried twigs into the fire, replaced the cover, and pushed a caldron of string beans and a bit of ham over the heat. The water that had been carried from the well stood in a wooden bucket on the drainboard. She dipped water out of it with a ladle and poured it into the soup.

'It ain't going to end with cutting off our charge. They're going to do everything they can to run us out of the holler. I know it,' Perry said. 'I been feeling it all day.'

'They can't do nothing they ain't already tried,' his father said. 'They taken the land from your grandfather, and after that we learned the way they worked. They try to run Jameses or Hatfields off and there won't be no coal moved out of this county.'

'Daddy, it don't work that way no more. They got machines now that eat up a whole seam and dump it in the cars with just one man setting up on it. Twenty of us can't do the work in a day that them machines does in an hour.'

'Machines don't matter,' his father said. 'The union ain't a-going to let its men get run off to make more money for the operator. Them machines has got to have men to run them, ain't they? A machine can't set a charge and tamp it down so the whole mountain don't cave on your head. There's got to be men down in that hole.'

'That ain't the point,' Perry said. 'They just ain't got no use for us except working dollar and a quarter for the independents.'

'They taken care of Bee, didn't they? They give him a job in an office when he couldn't work no more.'

'That's because he could put a bunch of them in the pen if he told what he knowed about that shooting,' Perry said.

'Son, right or wrong, we ain't got no chance against the operator without the union,' his father said. 'They got our land for hardly nothing. They ruined the ground for growing anything. They give us shacks to live in, and they paid us in scrip so we couldn't buy from nobody excepting them. They taken all they could get and they never give nothing back. I put twenty-seven years in the hole, and I didn't get out with nothing except a check for part of the doctor bill.'

Outside, the winter sun began to set over the mountains. The rays struck across the crest and reflected bright scarlet against the snow clouds banked in the east. The creek was filmed with ice, and occasionally a wood duck would dip out of the twilight and hum low through the hollow and splash into the water. The wind blew cold down the mountain and beat against the walls of the shack.

One by one the children came in from playing inside the ruined car and sat down by the long plank table near the stove. The first ones in always sat on the bench closest to the warmth. Their cheeks were chapped from the wind. Their mother poured the soup of string beans and ham into their bowls and tore a piece of bread in half for each one of them. The largest portion of soup was given to Irvin, because his mother believed that enough food was cure for any type of sickness, and somewhere inside her she was never able to forget the voice of the doctor in Richmond who said the boy should be put into a hospital.

After supper Perry went into the small room where he and his brothers and sisters shared a large iron bed broken in the middle and a pallet on the floor. In the cold months Irvin and the two other small children slept next to Perry in the bed for his warmth, and the other three curled together on the pallet. On a wooden shelf nailed against the wall was Perry's Indian arrowhead collection. He had over one hundred spear and arrow points, tomahawks, hatchets, banner stones, pipes, awls, bits of pottery, beads, and part of a flintlock rifle with the inscription 'London England 1799' cut on the barrel. He picked up some arrowheads in his hand and felt the cool smoothness of the flint in his palm. He had dug them all from rock houses where the Cherokee and Shawnee used to camp when they followed the buffalo down the Warriors' Trail, which later became the Wilderness Trail, through Cumberland Gap into Virginia. He had found more Indian artifacts than anyone else in his hollow. He knew how to look for the smoke-blackened roof of a rock house, the few small pieces of broken flint on the surface of the soil, the smooth, hollow places in the bed of the rock where the Indians ground corn, and he would spend days sifting the dirt by the handful through a wire screen until he reached the charred cinders of a fire and knew that he had found the remains of an Indian camp.

The next day at sunrise the county sheriff's car

stopped on the road at the bottom of the mountain in front of Perry's cabin, and the sheriff, a man of over three hundred pounds, with emphysema, toiled his way up the slope to the front porch. He was breathing hard, whistling down in his throat as though he were suffocating, when he knocked on the door.

'What you want him for?' Perry's father said.

'This ain't no arrest, Woodson,' the sheriff said. 'I ain't got a warrant and the boy don't have to come. We think we cotched one or two of them that done it, and I just want to talk to him if you'll let me.'

'I ain't saying I hold with killing a man, but that tipple wouldn't have been blowed if they'd paid them boys what was fair,' Perry's father said.

'Well, like I said, Woodson, I ain't going to do nothing to him.' The sheriff's short breath steamed off in the cold. 'I'll take him on down to the county seat to talk a minute, then I'll bring him home.'

'Who you brung in for it?'

'It might be one of the J.W. brothers. I ain't saying yet.'

'There ain't a court around here a-going to hold them guilty for it. Besides, my boy ain't got nothing to do with the J.W.s excepting he works at the same mine with them.'

'You know I don't take no sides in what goes on at the mine,' the sheriff said, 'and it ain't none of my business what the court does. Now you can let me have Perry for an hour, or I'll go back to the judge and get a warrant on him, even though I don't want to do it.'

Perry rode with the sheriff back down the bad, tar-covered road through the hills to the county seat. As he sat in the car he watched the beech and white oak trees sweep by overhead and wondered if it was not all a lie and the sheriff was going to send him off to Frankfort in manacles on the first train out of town. The steep cliff walls of the hollow loomed high above him like a prison. He wondered how many years they could give him in the penitentiary. They had put Bee away for two years just for wounding a man, and the company people even tried to have Noah Combs sent up after he was shot to pieces. I couldn't take no prison, Perry thought. It must be just like the mine caving in on you, with no air to breathe. I rather they set me in the electric chair than put me away in one of them places.

Almost every building in the county seat was painted green and white except the sandstone courthouse and jail and the company district manager's house, a blue and white mansion built among shade trees on top of a hill overlooking the town. The small, private clinic, run by a doctor who had received most of his education at a city college in Cincinnati, had broken windows and screens, and the foundation had settled at an angle. The store fronts along the main street were grimed with dirt, and men in overalls, brogans, cloth caps, miners' helmets, and old army clothes stood on the corners in front of the saloons and pool halls. Because it was Saturday and the men were in town to drink up all the money they had, their women sat with the children in junker cars parked along the curb, and they would remain there all day and into the night, breast feeding, changing diapers, and rocking the infants to sleep until the men walked unsteadily back to the cars, telling how Jake McGoffin or Wilson Pruitt was cut up in the pool room; and then they would drive the fifteen or twenty miles back into the mountains.

The inside of the courthouse smelled strongly of urine. There was no bathroom in the building, and parents often let their children relieve themselves in a darkened corner. The finish was worn off the plank floors, the plaster had fallen out of the ceiling in places, and the glass windows in the office doors were filmed with dirt. The county had no full-time elected officials because the tax revenue was never enough to afford them, so the sheriff, the clerk of court, the county judge, the justice of the peace, and the tax assessor all worked two or three days at the most and made up the rest of their income in any way they could, which meant that every moonshiner, bootlegger, union agent, or company official usually delivered money in one form or another to the courthouse.

Big J.W. and Little J.W. sat on the straight-back wooden chairs inside the sheriff's office, smoking hand-rolled cigarettes. A deputy, without a uniform and wearing a World War I service revolver, sat on a window ledge, watching them. Big J.W. had his tin hat slanted down over his forehead, and he smoked bent over with his forearms propped on his knees. He cleared his throat and spat on the floor, then rubbed the saliva into the wood with his boot. Little J.W. looked as passive and immobile as a piece of dough. His soft eyes stared straight ahead, and he would do nothing more than nod when the deputy or his brother spoke to him. When he finished his cigarette he ripped the paper back along the seam and rubbed the tobacco between his palms into the waste basket, as though he were grinding some fierce energy out of his body.

Later, the sheriff and Perry came into the office. Perry sat on a bench against the wall, his cloth cap in his hands, and looked at the floor.

'All right, I ain't even going to talk about a murder,' the sheriff said. 'We'll put you down for illegal possession of dynamite and destroying property and say that man up there was an accident. Involuntary homicide. You didn't even know he was there. But you ain't walking off from it free.'

'We done told you. We wasn't nowhere near that mine,' Big J.W. said.

'And you don't know nothing about breaking into that dynamite shed, either, do you?' the sheriff said. He sat his huge weight on the corner of his desk. His face flushed with the effort of talking.

'That's right, Sheriff. You just picked up the wrong boys,' Big J.W. said.

'Somebody seen four of you riding up towards that mine,' the sheriff said. 'You was one of them, Perry, and I have a notion that other one was Bee Hatfield.'

Perry felt something drop inside him. 'They give me a ride home the other night. That don't make me guilty of nothing,' he said.

'So the J.W.s is running a jitney service, is that it?' the sheriff said. 'You all was just riding up and down the mountain at night carrying people home.'

'Lookie, sheriff,' Little J.W. said. He peeled the dirt from under his fingernails with a small penknife. 'All you got is somebody seen us in a car up in the north part of the county. That don't mean nothing, and you know it and we know it. You could just as well bring in anybody that worked in that mine. So there ain't no use in us setting around here a-wasting your time.'

'I'll decide whose time you're wasting,' the sheriff said. 'Anybody could have blowed that tipple, but it was one of you and by God I'm going to prove it. This ain't the first time you been in on closing a mine. Three mines you worked in have been dynamited or somebody's got shot, and my county ain't going to turn into no war like Harlan or Pike. I don't know what part you had in it, Perry, but I guarantee you these men won't get you nowhere but on a cooling board or in the pen.'

Little J.W. folded his penknife in his palm and sucked his teeth.

'Now I give you an out,' the sheriff said. 'You can get off with maybe a year in Frankfort, but if you just set there and tell me you ain't done nothing, I'm going to press for murder.'

'We got no more to say, Sheriff. Either turn us out or put us in a cell,' Big J.W. said.

'What about you, Perry? Are you a-letting these men put you up in Frankfort with them?' the sheriff said.

'I don't have no hand in what they do,' he said. 'I told you they rode me home, and anything else they done ain't my business.'

'A dead man ain't your business?'

'Them scabs knowed what they was doing when they hired on that job,' Perry said.

'All right, I ain't holding none of you now,' the sheriff said, 'but that don't mean you and me is finished. J.W., you and your brother better not let me catch you even spitting on a sidewalk. You give me any cause and I'll put you in jail and leave you there, and the county judge ain't going to let you out on no habeas corpus. Perry, I'll take you home because I promised your daddy.'

'I reckon I'll stay around town a while.'

Perry walked out onto the square with Big J.W. and Little J.W. The sidewalks were crowded with people who had come into town for Saturday afternoon. Women dressed in faded, old clothes, thin cotton coats, scarves, and some with men's shoes on, stood in front of the company stores looking at the cheap goods they could buy on credit if their husbands were working. There was a roar of noise from the taverns and pool halls on the side streets, and in places traffic was blocked because someone in a rusted Ford with smashed fenders would stop his car and begin talking with people on the sidewalk. Next to the courthouse was the one-story sandstone jail built in 1890; several men looked out through the bars and called to friends passing by. Farther down, people were lined up outside a tin warehouse, where they received their surplus government food – peanut butter, canned meat that tasted like paper, shortening, powdered milk and eggs, and flour.

'Honey, you just keep remembering there can't nobody shut that jail house door on you unless you open your mouth,' Big J.W. said.

'And that's something you ain't going to do,' Little J.W. said.

'I didn't tell him nothing, did I?' Perry said.

'He'll be back after you again when we ain't there,' Big J.W. said. 'Then you might reckon you can do better for yourself by testifying for the company.'

'I ain't that kind.'

'If you are, you better not let us catch up with you,' Little J.W. said.

'I ain't telling the sheriff nothing, because I ain't going to be around here,' Perry said.

'Where do you think you're going?' Little J.W. said.

'I might go over in old Virginia and get me a job where I ain't got to worry about pickets and sheriffs and going to the pen. So let me be.'

Perry crossed the street into the traffic and left the two men on the corner staring after him. He felt a relief at getting away from them. There was always something in Little J.W.'s voice that was like the edge of a well-honed knife. Perry walked across the square, past the taverns, the feed and hardware stores, the small Church of God tabernacle, which had been converted from an old barbershop, past the drunks in overalls and brogans who stood in front of the open poolroom that always smelled of flat beer, talcum, tobacco spittle, greasy food, and unwashed bodies. Next to the pool hall was the 'jenny-barn,' a bar that had girls working upstairs. He could hear the music of the string band through the doorway. The fiddle, mandolin, bass, dobro, banjo, and guitar blended together in an old Bill Monroe bluegrass song:

> *Run, ole Molley, run*
> *Tenbrooks is going to beat you*
> *To the bright and shining sun.*
> *Out in California where Molley done as she pleased,*
> *Came back to old Kentucky,*
> *Got beat with all ease.*
> *Tenbrooks uas an old gray mare,*
> *He rode that shaggy mane,*
> *Run all around Memphis,*
> *He beat the Memphis train.*
> *Go catch ole Tenbrooks*
> *And hitch him in the shade,*
> *We're going to bury Molley*
> *In a coffin ready made,*
> *In a coffin ready made, Lord, in a coffin ready made.*

The state employment service, along with the county welfare department, was located in a run-down clapboard office with a cracked front window. Perry had been there once before to apply for unemployment compensation, but he was told that he was ineligible because he was on strike and was therefore out of work by choice. Most of the people in the county thought of the state employment agency as a joke; there was no work outside of the mines, and if the agency did not exist, the people who worked there would also be unable to find a job. The waiting chairs and all the desks were empty except for one, where a middle-aged woman sat filling out forms about non-existent job placements and filing them in a box for the state inspector. She was a stranger to the county, from somewhere up north, with an accent that no one could recognize or place.

'I don't want to take up none of your time,' Perry said. 'I'm looking for a job somewhere that ain't around here.'

'Fill out a card with your employment history and I'll help you in a minute,' she said.

'Is there any jobs or not?' he said.

'Well, there might be, but you do have to fill out the card.' She smiled at him pleasantly. She wore glasses tied to a ribbon around her neck, and her skin was smooth and white as though she had never had to boil clothes clean in a vat or cut wood by hand for her stove. She wore a woman's suit, something Perry had never seen before.

He printed his name in large, crooked letters on top of the card, then pushed it and the pencil towards her. His face reddened slightly.

'I can't write,' he said.

'All right. Then let's not worry about that now. What kind of work have you done before?'

'I cut tobacco for a half cent a stick, and I been down in the mine the last year. But I don't want no job here. I want to go over in Virginia or maybe up in Ohio. It don't matter what kind of work I do.'

'You know it's hard to find a job today unless you have some kind of skill or education. Did you ever think about finishing your schooling?'

'A feller don't make money while he's setting in a schoolhouse,' he said.

'Did you ever hear of the Job Corps?' she said. Her strange, quiet accent made Perry drop his eyes to the desk when she spoke. She took a booklet with a blue, white, and red shield on the cover out of the drawer. 'In Job Corps you can finish your education and learn a trade, and they'll pay you thirty dollars a month, put twenty-five in the bank for you, and send fifty dollars home to your family.'

'That's like them three-C camps where my daddy was. They don't do nothing but work on the forest.'

She leafed through the booklet and showed him pictures of boys studying in classrooms and welding shops, working on automobile engines, operating bulldozers and highway graders and printing presses, learning how to cook in large restaurants and how to repair electronic machinery. 'You can take up any of these things and maybe get a high school degree, too,' she said. 'They'll give you new clothes to wear, and they'll pay your travel home for vacation after six months.'

'There ain't nothing wrong with what I got.'

She reached over and touched his forearm with the softness of her palm. He felt the blood come to his face. He wanted to look over his shoulder to see if anyone was watching him and this strange woman.

'Son, there's nothing wrong with your clothes,' she said. 'You just give yourself a chance for a little better opportunity than your parents had.'

'Where's these camps at?' He avoided her eyes and held his cloth cap tightly in his hands between his knees.

'They're all over the United States. You might go to California or Texas or even up to Vermont.'

34

'I don't want to go to none of them places.'

'How about the Smoky Mountains in North Carolina?' she said. 'You wouldn't be too far from home in case you wanted to come back.

'I ain't worried about that. How much is the bus fare to get there?

'The government takes care of all your travel expense. You'll ride the bus to Lexington, and somebody will be there to put you on the plane.'

'I ain't getting on no airplane,' he said. 'You'll have to chloroform me before I get on one of them things.'

'You just sign your name on this card,' she said.

'All right. But by God they ain't putting me on no plane.'

chapter three

From the airplane window he saw the late sun reflected like pools of fire on the clouds above North Carolina. The land was flat and distant below him, cut into brown and green squares, with small red barns and white farmhouses close to the road. Over the plane's wing he could see the Smoky Mountains rise up against the brilliance of the sun's reflection in the east. It was the biggest range he had ever seen, much bigger than the Cumberland in Kentucky and Tennessee. There was a blue haze over the mountaintops, and in some places it was raining down in the hollows. It was a place so wonderful and huge that it could not have things like strip mines, smoking slag heaps, rivers filled with sulphuric acid, and whole mountainsides that had eroded into the hollows. Then the plane turned and dipped for the approach to the Asheville airfield. He grabbed the back of the seat in front of him, shut his eyes tightly, and felt his heart beat inside his chest.

'Do you feel ill?'

He didn't open his eyes, but he knew it was that stewardess again. She had tried to give him some type of pills twice before on the flight.

'No, I ain't sick. Why you keep asking me?'

'We'll be there in a few minutes,' she said.

He thought he was going to faint when the plane

started its descent. The sweat broke out on his hands and face, and his lungs felt as though he had held his breath for two minutes. It's going to crash right into one of them mountains, he thought. That pilot said we was going over four hundred miles an hour. There ain't nothing that can touch the ground that fast and not tear us all apart. He opened his eyes and saw the countryside getting closer, flattening out before him, and the tops of houses and trees rushing under the plane. Then he saw the long, white strip of concrete runway rise up suddenly from the ground, and he felt the impact reverberate through the plane as it touched down. He leaned back in the cushions of the seat and rubbed his wet palms against his work trousers.

Perry found eleven other Job Corpsmen waiting inside the airport, each wearing a blue, white, and red card pinned to his coat. There were four Negroes, two Mexicans, and an Indian in the group. A man in a Forest Service suit and two boys his own age dressed like soldiers were with them.

'This tall one must be the last of the bunch,' one of the boys in army clothes said. 'All right, you guys, everybody on the bus. Get moving, too, if you want to eat tonight. Where you been, anyway? We've been waiting for you two hours.'

'I was on the airplane. Where's it look like I been?' Perry said.

Outside, they got into a green and white government bus, and the Forest Service man handed out sack lunches of ham sandwiches and fried potatoes. The bus moved off through the late afternoon traffic and then began the climb into the mountains. Perry walked to the back of the bus and looked out the window at the sprawling area of the city in the twilight. The buildings downtown rose out of the purple haze, huge green and red neons blinked on and off over large stores, and long lines of new automobiles stretched endlessly along the highway. Then as the sun set beyond the mountains, the city looked like a shower of light spread across the valley, and he smelled the cold air through the window and the scent of pine and spruce along the roadside. In the dark interior of the bus, he felt he was very far from the J.W.s, the county sheriff, the man on the coal tipple, and the company men who would be around his father's cabin – and there was no way they could touch him now.

One of the boys in army clothes stood up in the aisle with one hand against a metal bar for support. He had a dark, Latin face and black hair that was oiled and combed straight back over his head. There was a deep scar across his chin and part of his lip, and he had a cross with three rays emanating from it tattooed between the thumb and first finger of his left hand.

'We're glad to have all you guys in Job Corps,' he said. 'It's a straight outfit, and we've got the best guys and best camp in the states. If any of you are carrying a shank or anything else you're not supposed to have, you can drop it off at the administration building before you get your linen. If we catch you with it later, you'll get your bus ticket and sack lunch back home.'

'Who's that feller shooting off his mouth?' Perry said to the boy next to him.

'They say he's what they call a work leader,' the boy said. He was a thin, pale boy from Mississippi, with long brown hair over his ears. He wore a hand-knitted sweater that had holes at both elbows. 'They give a feller twenty extra dollars a month for getting up to leader, and he don't have to pull K.P. or work on clean-up.'

'Well, I ain't come here to be no janitor,' Perry said.

'Everybody gets along here,' the boy in army clothes said. He had a New York accent, hard and clipped. 'We don't allow no fighting, and any guy that don't work pulls extra duty on the weekend and loses his pass to town for two weeks. Play it straight and you get the best deal in the country.'

'Do all them fellers carry on like that when they give them some soldier clothes?' Perry said.

The camp was located high in the mountains, ninety miles from Asheville, near a blue lake that was frozen around the edges. The pines and silver-leaf aspens grew back beyond the sandy stretch of lake front, and the green camp buildings were set up on blocks in a large clearing in the forest. The buildings were all prefabricated and made of tin, and icicles hung from the eaves in the cold moonlight. Perry walked with the other Corpsmen over the frozen ground covered with pine needles to the administration office, where they were issued starched fatigues, leather boots that laced above the ankle, black Air Force dress shoes, Eisenhower jackets, Navy denims, slickers, long underwear, sheets, blankets, and shaving kits. Perry carried all his issue piled in his arms. Then they walked back out into the dark, along a worn dirt path through the trees, and into one of the barracks.

The barracks was a flat, oblong building separated by a single corridor and with rows of partitions on each side. Each partition had in it two bunks, foot and wall lockers, night stands and writing tables, and all the wood and metal gleamed softly from the light overhead. Perry and the boy from Mississippi were assigned bunks next to each other, and they set about putting their issue in their lockers and making their beds.

'You guys better learn how to stretch that blanket

tighter than that,' a Negro boy said from across the hall. He was dressed in soiled pink slacks, tennis shoes with white athletic socks, a denim shirt with the sleeves cut away, and a white sailor's hat with the sides pulled down over his ears. 'If a quarter don't bounce on it at morning inspection, you'll be pulling extra duty tomorrow night.'

'What's this extra duty about?' Perry said.

'You get it for screwing off,' the Negro boy said. 'They give you all the dirty details, like scraping the ice off the sidewalks or cleaning the crapper.'

'I ain't a-cleaning no toilet,' Perry said.

'Man, where did you get that crazy accent?'

Perry closed his foot locker and straightened up. 'You got something to say about the way I talk?'

'Look, cool, you got to learn around here when another dude is just jiving you. We don't have no beefs. Everybody in this barracks is soul brothers. All the guys that thought they were bad ass have been kicked out.'

'I come here to go to school, not for no trouble,' Perry said. 'I had all I wanted of that back home.'

'You're talking soul now,' the Negro boy said. He put a thin cigar butt in a cigarette holder and lit it. 'You dudes get finished and I'll take you over to the chow hall. After you eat we got a movie in the rec room.'

The mess hall was immaculately white. The serving counter was made of glass and stainless steel, and the cooks and K.P.s wore laundered white uniforms and tall caps. Perry went through the serving line with the other new Corpsmen, who were all eating late, and filled his tray with steak, potatoes and gravy, a bowl of soup, string beans cooked with bacon and tomato sauce, ice cream covered with pineapple, and milk and coffee.

'Soul, you eat like food's going out of style,' the Negro boy said to him.

Later that night after the movie was over, Perry lay in his bunk under the blankets in the dark, smoking a hand-rolled cigarette. His body was almost too long for the bunk. Through the frost-covered window he saw the full moon in the clear sky above the mountains. The wind scratched the tree limbs across the tin roof of the barracks, and somewhere in the distance he heard the thin whistle of a train echoing through the hollows.

'Put out that damn cigarette before the resident worker comes down here,' a voice said out of the darkness.

He dropped the cigarette into a butt can on his night table and lay back against the pillow. Maybe it ain't such a bad deal, he thought. That ranger said we could buy eighty-five dollars' worth of store clothes when we been here a month, and I can get into that welding and heavy equipment class. Six months of that and I can get one of them three-dollar-an-hour jobs running a cat in Cincinnati. At least it's a lot better than working around the likes of the J.W.s. Then he felt himself pulled into sleep, and he thought once that his bunk dipped towards the earth like an airplane.

The next morning, as the sun broke above the top of the mountain range, Perry lined up with two hundred other Corpsmen by the flag pole, while a man in a Forest Service uniform called muster. The boys who were attending class that week were dressed in street clothes, and the others had on their army issue jackets, snow boots, and fur-lined Korean War caps that tied around their ears.

Perry was assigned to the work crew that cleared trails and maintained the recreation areas in the forest. After one hour on the detail he threw his chain saw on the ground and refused to work until he was allowed to see the camp director.

'That ain't no different than the three Cs,' he said. 'I can cut trees down back in Kentucky and get more money for it. I come out here to learn machinery, because that's where the good jobs is at.'

The director was a middle-aged man, an ex-forest ranger, with steel-rimmed glasses and a soft pink face. His collar was unbuttoned and his tie was pulled loose from his throat. The veins in his wrists were purple like a woman's.

'We don't put any of the Corpsmen into a vocational class until you've been here a month,' he said. 'That's because some of the boys leave during the first few weeks, and we don't have time or enough instructors to start teaching people who aren't going to stay.'

'They told me at the unemployment office I could go right into a trade.'

'Well, you can't. So you can go back to your crew and wait it out for three weeks or we can send you back to Kentucky.'

'I didn't say nothing about going home. I just didn't see no sense in doing the same work my daddy is and not getting nothing for it.'

'You go back to your crew and do what the work leader tells you, and I promise you'll be in the heavy equipment class,' the director said. 'But I'm going to give you four hours' extra duty for refusing to work this morning. Do you think that's fair?'

'No sir, I don't, but I'll pull it just the same as long as you put me in that class.'

Perry lost his first weekend pass and spent Saturday afternoon washing the camp buses in below-freezing weather. The water coated and froze on the windows even before he could rub the rag over them. By five o'clock he was numb with cold. There was a film of ice on his trousers where the water had splashed on them, and he had lost the feeling in his fingertips. He resolved that nobody was ever going to get him on the Saturday afternoon punishment detail again. It took him fifteen minutes under a hot shower before he felt the warmth begin to come back into his body, and then he fell into his bunk and slept until he heard the boys who had been into town weave through the corridor, carrying a drunk by his hands and feet.

The next week Perry went back to his work crew and felled trees with the chain saw, cut them into sections for burning, cleared brush off the trails, ripped roots loose with the pick, and cleaned out the soot and ashes from barbecue pits in the recreation areas in the forest. Most of the boys on the crew were either new in camp or ones who could not learn in a vocational class. There were also some who had been put out of vocational training by the instructor and were being considered for dismissal from the camp. During his first day on the crew Perry saw one Corpsman, a big Georgia cracker from Macon, turn the blade of his chain saw against a rock and tear out all the teeth so that he could take the truck back to the tool shed for another one. Instead, the work leader made him walk the six miles back to camp with the saw.

It was cold working out on the trail. Perry wore his long underwear, two pairs of trousers, an army flannel shirt and a sweater, boots with rubber snow shoes over them, and a fur-lined coat; but by noon the cold would always seep into his body, and his feet would become brittle and stay that way the rest of the day. The crew was too far from camp to return for the noon meal, and the cooks made up sack lunches for them; but the meat always froze in the sandwiches unless the boys put them under the hood of the truck for the heat.

During the first two weeks on the trail Perry gained six pounds. After a while he didn't mind the cold anymore, and some days the sun would shine down out of a clear sky and reflect like gold off the mountaintops and off the snow on the branches of the evergreens. The shadows of the spruce and fir would fall blue on the ground. He loved the sweet, burning resin smell of the beech wood when the chain saw cut through it. There were deer, grouse, rabbit, and bear tracks in the snow, and once when they were working by a natural rock bridge that arched over a stream, he could see rainbow trout lying in the swirling eddies behind the rocks, their tails fanning the water as they waited for food to come downstream.

Every other week Perry sat in the education building in a classroom that was decorated like the inside of an elementary school. There were geography maps on the wall, mathematic charts of basic addition and subtraction, the letters of the alphabet in bold, black print on individual cards, and reading machines that flashed cartoons and simple words on a white screen. Perry's first textbook was a cardboard primer with stick figures and six letters of the alphabet. He felt ashamed in front of the other Corpsmen when he was assigned to the special class for nonreaders, and he told the instructor that he could read as well as anyone in the camp.

'Read the title off the book in your hand,' the instructor said.

'I ain't interested in learning nothing but running

them machines, mister,' Perry said. 'We had books like this in the first grade.'

'How can you operate a machine if you can't read the book that tells you how to do it?'

'I can tear down an air hammer, and I didn't learn it from no book.'

'Can you read an engineer's manual about a piece of equipment like that twenty-five-thousand-dollar bull-dozer out there?' the instructor said. 'Or a blueprint that tells you how much grade and fill to cut on a highway job?'

'Double O Cool, you sweat everything too much,' the Corpsman in the next desk said to Perry. It was Popcorn, the Negro whom he'd met in the barracks his first night in camp. 'I been in this class three months, and I'll probably still be here when they kick me out after my two years. And, man, believe me when I say that half the studs in this place couldn't tell the difference between the men's and women's rest room unless somebody pointed them at it.'

Perry spent eight hours a day in the reading and math classes, and filled his Big Chief notebook with simple words scrawled in his childish handwriting: *I am a pin, I am a man, I am an ant, I am a tin can, The tin can has an ant in it.* It always took him several minutes to write one sentence, squinting with one eye at each letter as he tried to hold the pencil correctly in his hand. He felt that writing words was the most difficult thing he had ever attempted. The words would never shape themselves the same way they looked in his primer, and his fingers would cramp and ache from the effort. But he worked hard every day, sometimes through part of his lunch hour, and at night he took his book of stick figures and simple captions to the barracks and read it in bed before the resident worker turned out the light. In a few weeks' time he went through eight books of the primer series, and he could recognize most of the words that the instructor flashed on the white screen with the reading machine.

After his first month on the trail crew the work leader recommended Perry for a five-dollar merit raise, and he was promoted to Corpsman first class, one step below an assistant work leader. Also, the director kept his word, and Perry was transferred to the heavy equipment class, where he began learning how to operate a bulldozer, a highway grader, a back hoe, a fork lift, and a dragline. At the end of the day his clothes were always covered with grease from the engines. The instructor made the new boys in the class swamp the blade on the dozer, cleaning the dirt free with a shovel and do all the lubrication on the other machines, which meant climbing under them on the frozen ground with a hand-soiled diagram of the bearings, and squeezing the hand-pump into the sockets while the grease ran back into their faces. The worst detail was to change the oil, because as soon as the nut was unscrewed from the pan the oil would usually pour all over the Corpsman who was under it.

During his second week in the class the instructor told Perry to climb up into the double operator's seat of the bulldozer with him. Perry snapped the canvas safety belt over his waist, and they moved out along a flat stretch of red clay road through the forest. Perry learned how to control each of the treads with the levers and to turn the machine around by throwing one track into reverse while the other was in forward motion. Once, he lifted the blade too high so he couldn't see in front of him and ran into a thick pine trunk. His head banged into the side of the cab from the impact and his tin hat cut the bridge of his nose.

He put his coat sleeve across his face to catch the blood and tried to back the machine off the tree. He gave it too much gas, pulled one lever too far back, and the bulldozer spun around in a half circle, the engine roaring and the treads ripping brush and small trees from the ground. Then Perry dropped the blade too fast and shattered a Forest Service trail sign into splinters.

'Look what you done,' another Corpsman yelled at him. 'You run over my chain saw. There ain't enough left of it to put in a paper bag.'

The saw was flattened into the clay, the parts twisted and smashed as though they had been beaten with sledge hammers.

'What was it doing in the middle of the goddamn road?' Perry said.

'If I'd known you was running that dozer, I wouldn't be nowhere on this mountain,' the other Corpsman said.

'By God, you get up here and run it, then.'

'All right, you guys knock that crap off,' the instructor said. 'James, get over there and clean up all that brush and burn it in the stream bed. Then pick up what's left of the saw and throw it into the truck. Tonight we can explain to the director how we ran over the only chain saw laying on the ground in North Carolina.'

'Does that mean I don't get no more chance on the machine?' Perry said.

'No, it means that you try to do things on your own before you ask an older man a question.' The instructor had his machinist's goggles pulled up on his forehead. His face was red from the cold in the thin light through the trees. The skin around his eyes was white where the goggles had been. 'Once you learn a little patience and stop trying to do everything in one day, you'll be a good heavy equipment man. But I ain't going to let you tear up my machine because you have to show these other boys something. The next time you do something wrong, you pull the key on the ignition and let me get you out of it. We lost a chain saw this time, but it could have been some boy's foot, and I ain't going to spend three days making out accident forms for the Forest Service because somebody didn't have enough sense to know the difference between asking a question and being a fool.'

'I wasn't trying to show nobody nothing,' Perry said.

'Son, you've got an engine running in you all the time. You're the type that can't be second best at anything, and you're out to prove it even if you have to run over yourself doing it.'

'When can I get back on the dozer?'

'That's just what I mean,' the instructor said. 'You haven't asked me yet what you did wrong. All you can think about is making that machine do what you want it to without learning how to do it right.'

'All right, I ain't a-giving you cause to get on me again. You say frog and I'll say how high.'

'Go back to the oiling detail for the next two days and we'll talk about it then,' the instructor said.

'I already been on it a week.'

'Boy, I just said frog.'

That weekend Perry took his first town pass into Asheville. He had washed and starched his dress khaki uniform by hand in a tin tub of water in the shower and had pressed the creases in it as rigid and sharp as a knife blade. The barracks resident worker, a retired Navy enlisted man, had shown him how to spit shine his black shoes, and Perry spent all of Friday evening burning the old polish off the leather with a match and then rubbing wax and saliva into the rough grain with a woman's nylon stocking. He buffed the toes until he could see most of his body reflected in the shine. He stood in front of the full-length mirror in the shower and looked at the sharp cut of his uniform, his black tie tucked inside his blouse, the Job Corps shield sewn on his sleeve, and the pale area around his ears and the back of his head from the haircut one of the Negro boys had given him for a quarter. And he had fifteen dollars' pay in his pocket, money that he could spend in any way he wished, without having to worry about buying food or paying off the charge at the company store.

He ate eggs and sausage in the mess hall and signed out at the administration building. The leave bus was packed with Corpsmen, some dressed in uniforms and others in the street clothes they had been issued after their first month in camp. The day was cold and bright, and the fir trees were a violent green against the snow. The horses in the fields had ice in their manes and tails, and their breath fogged in the air. In the distance at the far end of the hollow Perry could see the small log cabins with wood smoke rising from the chimneys, and occasionally he would see deer tracks wandering through a clearing in the trees on the mountain.

The resident worker parked the bus at the Y.M.C.A. in Asheville. In minutes the bus was empty and all the Corpsmen had disappeared into the busy traffic of Saturday afternoon. Perry and L.J., the boy from Mississippi, walked along a crowded sidewalk on a side street and looked at the rows of bars, secondhand stores, tattoo parlors, cafes that sold fried chicken and catfish, three-dollar hotels, and hillbilly dance halls.

Many of the people on the sidewalk in that part of town were dressed like the mountain people Perry knew back in Kentucky. The men had on worn, shiny suitcoats over their overalls, and their women wore thin cotton-print dresses and hand-knitted sweaters that always looked shabby and never fitted them quite properly. Through the glass window of a tavern Perry saw women sitting at the bar sipping beer and highballs, something that he believed women did only in the jenny-barn.

'Look at that feller getting a tattoo,' L.J. said. His uniform was too small for him, and his thin neck stuck up out of the collar like a turkey's. 'That needle is hopping up and down on his arm like a sewing machine.'

'Listen to that music across the street. Buddy, that sounds like home. Let's go over and get us a beer.'

'They ain't going to serve us. Besides, we won't get in nothing but trouble there, anyhow.'

'A twenty-cent beer ain't going to hurt you, is it?' Perry said. 'We'll get a table in back and I'll do all the buying at the bar. They give me my union card when I was fifteen because I looked twenty-one. These people can't tell no different.'

'There's always some feller cutting on somebody else in them places,' L.J. said.

'This ain't Mississippi. It's a city. We ain't going to have none of that here.'

'I'll wait outside. You go on in.'

'No, we ain't a-doing it that way. Come on.' Perry took L.J.'s arm and they crossed the street through the line of cars. The noise was loud from the barroom door as a drunk walked out into the street. 'Go get a place over in the corner and I'll be there in a minute,' Perry said.

'Let's get out of here, Perry.'

'They'll think you're a soldier. The whole town is full of them. Go set down now and stop a-worrying.'

He went to the bar and ordered two draughts in glass mugs that were filmed with ice. The tables were filled with men and women who drank straight shots of whiskey with beer chasers. On a raised wooden platform at the back of the dance floor was a country string band. One of the musicians lowered the microphone, and the fiddler played 'The Orange Blossom Special' directly into it.

A man at the end of the counter passed out and shattered a bottle on the bar rail. Perry worked his way through the tables until he found L.J. sitting far back in the shadows, his face nervous and afraid.

'Look, Perry, my people is hard-shelled Baptists,' he said. 'If my daddy knew I was in a place like this and drinking, he'd wear me out with a belt. Once he caught my brother with some homemade wine, and he almost never turned loose of him.'

'Remember what they told us back at camp? You ain't a boy no longer with your daddy to tell you what to do. Drink your beer and we'll buy a big dinner.'

'I ain't throwing my money away in a place like this.'

'Well, I didn't work two weeks for fifteen dollars so I could waste it, neither,' Perry said.

Two hours later he was drunk. His tie was pulled loose from his collar, beer was spilled down the front of his shirt, and the color had gone from his face. The whites of his eyes looked yellow in the barroom light. He danced with several women, but he didn't know how to lead or make his feet follow any sort of pattern, and he backed one girl into a table and knocked over several glasses. He sat in his chair, a dull expression on his face; his shirt sleeve lay in a puddle of beer.

'You wore out all my patience,' L.J. said. 'Let's get out on the street and get something to eat.'

'Go on by yourself.'

'I can't leave you alone in here. Somebody'll tear you up.'

'I been drinking corn whiskey since I was fourteen, and there ain't nobody yet that had to take care of me.'

'You see all them fellers that just come in? They're just looking for somebody to grab hold of.'

'By God, they ain't running me off. My mother's people was Hatfields and the rest of us is related to Frank James. Back home we'd take fellers like that and stick their head in the honey hole.'

'Keep fooling with them women, and there ain't none of that going to help you,' L.J. said. 'If you was sober enough to see what you was dancing with, you wouldn't touch her unless you run castor oil and turpentine through it first.'

'Where's those fellers at that wanted trouble?'

'You're going to get us in jail, and then they'll throw us out of camp. You want that to happen to us?'

'We're on pass. What we do in town ain't any concern of theirs,' Perry said. 'What did them fellers say to you?'

'God darn it, I ain't setting still for any more of this. We're leaving.'

But Perry had already ordered another draught beer and a shot of whiskey. An hour later he vomited on himself in the men's room. His head was spinning and he couldn't walk straight. He walked unsteadily to the bar with his trousers unzipped and tried to buy a beer to get the bad taste out of his mouth, but the bartender refused to serve him. L.J. took him by the arm and guided him outside into the street. The sun had begun to set over the buildings, and the wind blew like ice against their faces. Perry slipped once on the sidewalk and fell into a parking meter. The side of his head struck the metal pole, but he felt only a dull numbness from the blow. The street and the store fronts looked dirty in the half-light of the late sun.

'Stand up straight. I can't hold you,' L.J. said.

'You ain't got to.' Perry pulled loose from him and stumbled out in the street through the traffic. He heard cars slamming to a stop and horns blowing as he tried to walk in a straight line. The vomit had frozen on his shoes and trousers. He tripped over the curb and walked along the row of buildings, keeping one shoulder always close to a wall. I don't need nobody to take me home, he thought. They ain't seen the day that somebody had to pick up after me because of whiskey. The warmth of the alcohol began to wear off and he felt the cold reach inside his body, then he realized that he had left his coat in the bar; but he couldn't remember how many blocks he had walked down the street or even where the bar exactly was.

There was a policeman on the corner directing traffic. Perry began to wish he had stayed with L.J. He knew that he would never get across the street under the policeman's gaze without getting arrested. He stood in front of a tattoo parlor, balancing himself on his feet, and he felt the eyes of the people passing on the sidewalk boring into his face. He opened the door of the tattoo parlor and almost fell inside. A muscular sailor with his shirt off sat on a stool while a man dressed like a horse tout worked on his arm with the needle. The walls were covered with brightly colored designs of American and Confederate flags, knives dripping blood, dragons and snakes curled around

Marine Corps and Navy emblems, nude women, inscriptions to mother, crosses, and the face of Christ.

'I'll be with you in five minutes, soldier,' the man with the needle said. He wore a green and black checkered shirt buttoned at the throat without a tie, and pointed patent leather shoes. There were red and blue blood veins in his cheeks.

Perry sat in a chair against the wall and began belching. He reached into his shirt pocket and counted out his money. He had five soiled dollar bills left, which was all he would have until the next pay day two weeks away. He tried to remember why he had come into the tattoo parlor, but his mind wouldn't clear and he looked at the designs through one squinted eye. He began to smell the odor from his clothes in the heated room. Then the sailor was gone and Perry was on the stool, pulling off his shirt.

'You sure you want a tattoo?' the man said. 'I don't like to work on a man while he's drunk and have him come around about it the next morning.'

'What do you think I come in here for? This don't look like the bus depot, does it?'

'Okay, soldier, what do you want and where you want me to put it?'

'I ain't no soldier. Give me a tattoo just like that Job Corps shield on my shirt sleeve.'

'I got to have a pattern. Pick out something up there on the wall.'

'What's wrong with Job Corps?' Perry said.

'I've tattooed just about half of the marine base, and I have all the customers I need. I do the best work in Asheville, and if you want to argue with me you can go up the street to one of those parlors that'll give you blood poisoning in your arm.'

'Put one of them big Confederate flags on me with United Mine Workers of America under it.'

The man washed the upper part of Perry's arm with warm water and soap, and rubbed a cotton pad soaked in alcohol over his skin. His arm was cool as the alcohol evaporated, then he felt the needle go into him and burn as though someone held a lighted match to his body. The pain seemed to run up through his shoulder and into his groin. The blood broke to the surface in small drops and ran down his elbow. The man stopped for a moment, wiped his arm clean, and then continued. It took forty-five minutes for the man to finish the tattoo because he had to change ink three times to fill out the Confederate flag, By that time Perry's arm had gone numb. The man cleaned the tattoo once more with alcohol and rubbed ointment over it.

'It'll scab over and stick to your clothes a little bit the first week,' he said. 'Just don't pick at it and you'll have a good-looking tattoo the rest of your life.'

Perry tucked his shirt into his trousers and gave the man his last five dollars. He walked out into the dark street and felt his arm stiffen and begin to ache in the cold. The traffic had thinned and the policeman was gone from the corner, and Perry made his way across the street and walked towards the Y.M.C.A. parking lot. Snow flurries spun through the air and stuck damply in his hair and shirt collar. He wanted to get another drink, but he didn't have a quarter in his pocket. He didn't know the time and he wasn't sure whether or not the bus had already left for camp. He began to feel a sense of fear at the thought of being left in the city with no money and nowhere to go. Just like L.J. said, he thought, they'll put me in the jail house and leave me there. Vagrancy and drunk, thirty days.

The people at camp won't even know where I'm at. Then they'll put me down A.W.O.L. and kick me out of Job Corps.

Perry rounded the corner, his arms straightened out by his sides in the cold wind, and saw the bus in the parking lot. There was nobody in it except one Corpsman in back. Perry pushed in through the folding doors and then slammed them shut with the big lever attached to the bottom of the dashboard. He walked down the aisle, holding on to the tops of the seats to keep his balance. It was cold even inside the bus. He could still see his breath in the air.

'All root, all reet, Double O Cool is back on the scene and balling,' Popcorn said from the back seat. He had on a lavender sports jacket and slacks, his frayed tennis shoes, and his sailor's cap pulled down over his ears. He drank out of a bottle of muscatel wine. 'Man, you look like a disaster area. Are they playing World War II down the street? Blue face, bloody arm, that good yellow vomit smell in the air. Baby, you have arrived in technicolor.'

'Let me have a drink.'

'Be careful with it, soul. They run airplanes on this stuff.'

Perry took a long swallow out of the bottle. The wine tasted like hair tonic and wood alcohol.

'Take it easy,' Popcorn said. 'You don't want to barf your groceries twice in one night. Who put the shank in your arm?'

'I got a tattoo. It cost five dollars.' Perry rolled up his sleeve carefully. The blood had frozen to his sleeve.

'That's what we call a bad news flag back in Cleveland,' Popcorn said. 'Like what all those studs wave around in the air down in Alabama while they're playing Dixie on a black man's head. What's that say under it?'

'United Mine Workers. I worked a year and a half under ground before I come here.'

'Don't go showing off that thing to any of the black guys tonight after they've been drinking.'

'Lookie, I don't show off nothing to nobody, and I ain't got any bad feelings towards any feller in this camp. We ain't got many colored people around home, and I don't know much about them. So a flag like this don't have that kind of meaning to me.' Perry drank out of the bottle again and passed it to Popcorn.

'You know you got real innocence, Double O. You're so way out that the studs back in Hough wouldn't believe there's whites like you around. But you got something bothering you all the time, and you're not going to make it in Job Corps unless you get that block of concrete off your head.'

'I ain't got nothing bothering me.'

'You're not talking to the heat on the corner. I've heard you saying things in your sleep. Then sometimes you stare at a wall like you've just fixed.'

'What did I say?'

'It don't matter to me what you've done. Back home the only thing we have for the law is a finger, because the law is Mr Skins with his blue uniform and a billy club.'

Perry took the bottle back and upended it. He felt himself begin to grow warm again. 'If I had the police after me, I wouldn't be a-setting in no government camp where they could come grab me whenever they had a mind to.'

'You're putting yourself on, not Popcorn. I know where you got those snakes. I was in on something once just like you were. When I was fourteen we had a rumble with some white hoosiers in the next welfare project. We told their warlord to come into our territory for a truce. I led him up the street behind a store, and the rest of the guys got him. He was the toughest stud they had. He put my brother's eye out with a chain and cut up two other guys the week before. I watched them while they stomped him all over the alley. That poor cat tried to run and they kicked his balls in. He even got down and begged before they all put their shanks in him. I was so scared and sick watching it that I puked all over myself and then got the dry heaves right there in the alley. I couldn't get rid of seeing that cat beg until my mother took me to the wig mechanic. Even then, it took me a year to put the snakes back in their baskets.'

'I didn't want to do it,' Perry said. 'We didn't know there was somebody up there on the tipple. Then I heered his scream come roaring out of the fire. He stood out like lightning was racing over his body. He wasn't nothing but a West Virginia scab, but we didn't have no need for a killing.'

'It happened, though, didn't it? And it could have been you that got it instead of him or it could have been me in that alley instead of that hoosier. You didn't plan it, but that's the way it went. Man, don't you know that you can't pull the strings all the time?'

'That feller probably had people somewhere, even if he was a scab. They never found enough of him to tell who he was.'

'So you're going to worry about it until they put the net over you and carry you off to the monkey farm.'

'I don't want to talk about it no more.'

'All root, Double O.'

Perry looked out the window and saw fifteen Corpsmen and the resident worker headed down the street towards the bus. The resident worker had rounded them up out of the bars during the last hour, and most of them were drunk to one degree or another. Their shirts were pulled from their trousers, their hair was down in their eyes, two of them had to be carried, and the Indian boys were yelling like Apaches in a grade-B movie. A Negro boy climbed up on a tall embankment and acted like a human sled with another Corpsman on his back. They swished down the slope through the snow and landed on their heads in the middle of the sidewalk.

After everyone was on the bus, the resident worker turned on the overhead light and stood at the front of the aisle. Some of the Corpsmen had already passed out in the seats.

'You guys are going to get it for this,' he said. 'I'll have each one of you chipping ice for the next two weeks. Close that window!'

'James is going to toss his cookies again,' Popcorn said.

chapter four

After they arrived back at camp the resident worker
and three other Corpsmen had to carry Perry to the
barracks. He was sick all day Sunday with a hangover,
and he lay in his bunk, shaking with nausea and a
throbbing headache. He tried to eat at the evening
meal, but he couldn't swallow any of his food and had
to return his tray, still filled, to the K.P. window.
Monday morning at roll call he was released from
education and was told to report to the administration
building for a board of review. Outside the director's
office a dozen other Corpsmen sat on wooden benches
waiting to be called in. They were either boys who had
been drunk on the bus or the ones who had already
been assigned to the trail crew for disciplinary reasons.
Ain't this a bunch to get yourself in with, Perry
thought. There ain't one of them that's hit a lick since
he's been here, and they got me right with them.

The director called Perry into his pine-paneled office
that smelled of linseed oil and cigar smoke. Three
other foresters and the head of the education program
sat in leather chairs, with note pads in their laps. Perry
sat down in front of the desk and looked at the floor.
He wished that he had put on his class-A uniform that
morning instead of fatigues. He began to imagine that

his tattoo was bleeding again and showing through his shirt sleeve.

'You know why you're in here, Perry?' the director said.

'Yes, sir.'

'I mean, do you know that we're considering expelling you from Job Corps?'

'You give me warning the last time I was in here.'

'How do you feel about your conduct?' one of the other foresters said. His voice was level with no accusation in it.

'I done wrong and I didn't act no better than them people in the jenny-barn. I give my word to the director and the heavy equipment instructor that I wouldn't cause no more trouble. But I done it anyway. I'm sorry for it, and there ain't much more I can say.'

'Did you know that both your math and reading teachers recommended you for assistant work leader?' the director said. 'Your vocational instructor told me that you'll be the best man on his detail once you learn that you can't be first in everything in a few weeks. You wouldn't be here unless we had something we could teach you.'

'I come here because I know I can't do nothing but common labor in the mine and cut tobacco. I don't want to go back to none of that. Mr Henson got on me for tearing up your trail sign and running over the chain saw. He put me back on the oil crew, and he was right in doing it. But I worked hard for him, and he says he'll put me back in the dozer seat next week.'

'What about getting drunk in town?'

'I ain't a-touching no more whiskey or wine while I'm at this camp. I figure it's already cost me enough trouble.'

'Do you think you can start playing by our rules and not your own?' the director said.

'Yes, sir.'

'How do you feel about Job Corps?' the other forester said.

'I never had no better chance at anything.'

'All right, we're going to keep you,' the director said. 'But I'm giving you two weeks' restriction to camp. No football games, no trips to the roller rink, not even a hike in the woods. And eight hours' extra duty and a five-dollar fine for losing your jacket. Do you think that's too rough to take?'

'No sir, but I rather you give me more extra duty instead of docking my pay. The fifty dollars the government sends home ain't enough to help my family as it is. My daddy's a happy-pappy, and what he brings in don't hardly pay the credit at the store.'

'You were willing enough to spend all your money on liquor.'

'That's because I was drunk and set on seeing how much of a fool I could make out of myself. But I ain't going to have no more chance to waste my money in the saloon, because you ain't catching me in Asheville till I get my air ticket back home.'

The director gave Perry five more hours' extra duty instead of the fine. Perry worked the entire thirteen hours off in one week by trading K.P. duty with another Corpsman every night. He usually caught the pots and pans detail, the worst in the kitchen, and he would stand behind the receiving window, in the steam from the electric dish washer, and clean the spilled food and wet cigarette butts from the trays. During his restriction he was allowed no farther from camp than the front road, and he was not even allowed to go into town to buy his eighty-five dollars' worth of civilian clothes. He had no money for cigarettes, toothpaste, or razor blades, and he spent his weekends in camp with the few other boys, shooting pool, ironing shirts for a dime apiece, or rolling cigarettes with a hand machine for two cigarettes a pack.

After his restriction was over he went on recreation trips only to the football game against the rural high school in a small town at the bottom of the mountain, or to the twenty-five-cent roller rink on Tuesday nights. He began sending half of his pay home, and he could usually earn two dollars on Saturday or Sunday by pulling someone's K.P.

A month later a letter of commendation was put in his government file by the director. Perry received a carbon copy of it on Forest Service stationery with a large Job Corps seal under the letterhead, and he had to have one of the instructors help him read some of the long words.

One afternoon on a hike after Indian artifacts two Corpsmen had separated from the group and had crawled up on a flat ledge overlooking the hollow. They couldn't find their way back down and began calling for help; but no one could determine where their voices came from because of the echoes. Then one of them flashed a signal in the sun with a tin mirror. Both boys were two hundred feet straight up a cliff. They were pressed out flat on the rock, their white and drained faces sticking out over the edge. The resident worker tried to go after them, but he was an older man from New York, much out of condition, with a heavy roll of fat around his stomach, and he slipped on a loose rock twenty feet above the ground and landed on his back, scraping the skin off the side of his face. Perry took the rope from him, looped it crossways over his shoulders, and climbed up the face of the mountain. By instinct he always placed his foot in the right crevice and pulled his weight up on a root or protruding rock that would not give. He knew how to pause when the rocks rolled out from under his foot and showered down the mountain, and how to make his fingers dig into places where the only opening was a small split that had been caused by the expansion of the ice. Just before he reached the top of the cliff, there was a cave that cut back into the mountain and an area of completely smooth surface below it. He had both feet on a three-inch ledge. He jumped upwards with all his strength and caught the edge of the floor with his fingers and pulled himself inside. He strung out twenty-five feet of rope and tied a heavy oak branch to the end of it, then threw it on top of the cliff to the other two Corpsmen.

'Knot it around something that don't pull loose,' he said.

'I ain't going down on that thing,' one of the boys said.

'By God, you're going down or I'll leave you here and you can freeze to death before the ranger crew finds you. Now tie it down and get your ass moving.'

Perry threw the rope in a long arc down into the hollow. The other Corpsmen looking up at him were small figures against the late winter green of the brush and the patches of snow on the ground. The rope swung back and forth in front of the cave.

The first Corpsman came down past Perry hand over hand, his face bloodless with fear.

'Wrap your legs in that rope,' Perry said. 'If you slip, just hold on, even if you burn your hands off.' He watched the first Corpsman, who had his eyes shut, work his way down far below him. The heavily wooded hills and the creek that wound through the hollow looked miniature in the distance.

The second Corpsman would not leave the ledge. Once, he took hold of the rope and crawled backwards over the edge until just his feet protruded into space; then he climbed back again and lay out flat, shaking, against the rock shelf. He was a slight boy of sixteen who had been in camp one week, and his face had the frightened, empty expression of the retarded.

'I can't come up after you. There ain't no way for me to get over the ledge,' Perry said. 'Slide on down to me, and I'll get under you and we'll go down together.'

'We'll smash all over the rocks.'

'No, we ain't. Remember what they told you when you come into camp? This is a man's outfit and you got to act like one. Now get on down here.'

'I got sweat all over me. I can't hold onto the rope.'

'I can hold both of us if you let go. You can't get down no other way, and you might as well set your mind to it. Keep your eyes shut and let your legs come down on my shoulders. Goddamn it, boy, climb down off there and let's go get us some dinner.'

The second Corpsman inched backwards and began to slide down the rope. Small rocks rolled out from under his body. The knuckles in his hands were as white as bone around the rope. Perry grabbed onto the slack, held it taut until the boy reached the opening of the cave, and then swung out and caught the boy's legs over his shoulders. They worked their way down together, the rope biting into their hands, while their own weight swung them hard into the face of the mountain. Both of Perry's elbows were bleeding, and he had a cut in his scalp just above his hairline. Later, the camp doctor picked out the pieces of rock from the wound with tweezers and put four stitches in his head.

A week after he received his letter of commendation, Perry was promoted to assistant work leader with a fifteen-dollar raise in pay. In the next three months he advanced to the regular reading program and was able to read most of the words in a newspaper. He had gone through subtraction, addition, and fractions and the instructor moved him up to decimals. As an assistant work leader he supervised a crew of trainees in the bulldozer class, checked out all the chain saws, picks, and axes from the tool shack, and saw that the machines were oiled and gassed after morning roll call. His body had filled out and toughened, and his skin had the rough tan that comes from working outdoors in the reflection of the sun off the snow. He had his hair cut every two weeks, and even on the work detail he wore starched khakis.

The vocational instructor told him that in another three months he would know enough about heavy equipment to get an apprentice's book in the union, and Perry began to plan for the day he would go to Cincinnati and get a job that paid three dollars an hour. He could not imagine that a man could make twenty-five dollars a day, or even more if he worked overtime. He didn't believe anyone except coal operators could have so much money. It was enough money to have a house with plumbing, like at camp, or to take Irvin to a good doctor, a specialist, or to buy an electric icebox and fill it with more food than his family could eat. And there would be money left over for motion picture shows on Saturday afternoon, new clothes for his brothers and sisters, and maybe a car to drive down to the Winfro Valley Barn Dance. There would be no more company shack on the mountainside, no more string beans and ham hock every night for dinner, no more smell of the burning slag heap in the air.

Spring came to the Smoky Mountains with thunder showers every afternoon. The snow melted off the ground, except for the shaded areas under the timber, and the new grass was a light green against the hillsides. In the morning water ran down off the mountain and collected in pools on the blacktop roads, and then evaporated like steam in the sun's first light. One day the dogwood suddenly bloomed, and the blue-green of the spruce and the fir trees was broken by a spray of white flowers. The temperature still went below freezing at night, and the edges of the streams were coated with ice, but the days became warm and clear, and hawks flew high above the mountains in the bright sky. The farmers began plowing in the hollows to plant their tobacco, and there was always a smell of new earth and guano in the air.

A rainstorm broke one afternoon when Perry was clearing a road through the woods with the bulldozer. He took his slicker from behind the operator's seat, slipped it over his shoulders, and pulled the machinist's goggles down over his eyes against the rain. It swirled under the roof of the cab into his face. In a half hour the ground was drenched, and the wet clay flew through the air from the dozer's treads. Perry lowered the blade and pushed a pile of stumps and tree limbs over the edge of the cliff into the riverbed below. He backed off, raised the blade, and two other Corpsmen cleaned it off with their shovels.

'Shut it down and let's go back to the truck,' one of the boys said. It was the big boy from Georgia, named Birl, whom Perry had seen turn his chain saw against a rock four months earlier. His wash-faded fatigues had turned dark olive from the rain. The water spilled down over the brim of his cap. He had been put on the brush detail for fighting, and he was scheduled for a board of review the next week.

'Mr Henson said we don't quit till five. He wants this road cleared down to the blacktop,' Perry said.

'I got enough sense to come out of the rain, even if he ain't.' One of his eyes squinted when he looked at Perry. He was powerful all over, and the muscles in his arms and thighs were tight against his clothes. His face was white with no tan, and there were deep pock marks in his cheeks. Red clay was splattered over his rubber boots and trousers. Some of the boys in camp said he carried an Italian switchblade inside his boot.

'I'm just telling you what Mr Henson said. If you want to holler about it, you can go on back there and talk to him,' Perry said.

'That work leader badge don't allow you to work us like riggers.'

Perry pushed the throttle in and cut the ignition. 'You ain't a-working for me. I'm just doing what I'm told. I don't like setting out in the rain no more than you do, but we're still going to run this road straight out to the blacktop.'

'Why don't you go fuck yourself, hillbilly?'

'Lookie, I ain't taking that from you or no other man. You got this detail because you beat up on a feller a foot shorter than you. I wouldn't give twenty-five cents for a bag full of your kind. Back in Kentucky you wouldn't even be a good scab. The likes of you stand in the welfare line and bitch about somebody not giving you a chair to set in.'

'Why don't we take it back in the woods?'

'You pull that knife on me and I'll whip it all over your head.'

'No knife. Just fists and feet,' Birl said.

'You better shut your mouth and start picking up that brush and throw it down the holler.'

'I think you got that yellow feeling down inside you, James.'

'You done it then, buddy.' Perry set the brakes on the bulldozer and jumped down from the cab. The mud and water splashed over his slicker. Birl stepped back, his one hand rolled into a fist by his side. 'No, there ain't going to be no fight,' Perry said. 'We're a-going to see Mr Henson.'

'You think you can take me down there?'

'I know I can.'

Birl reached down inside his rubber boot and switched open a long, double-edged Italian knife. The handle was made of bone. He held the blade out before him, moving it from side to side.

'I warned you, but you wouldn't pay me no mind,' Perry said. He pulled a ballpeen hammer from the seat in the dozer cab and raised it up to the level of his shoulder. Lightning crashed across the sky and struck against the mountain on the far side of the hollow. The rain beat into their eyes. 'You know what I can do to you with this? Your head won't be nothing but a cracked flower pot. Throw it on the ground and get moving down the trail.'

'Look, James—'

'I mean now, goddamn it. Get rid of it. You taken enough of my time already. I ain't working after five on this road because of you.'

The boy dropped the knife on the road and walked back down the trail. Perry threw the hammer into the cab and followed him. The faint afternoon light glowed through the heavy timber and fell onto the pine needle-covered floor of the forest. Mr Henson was operating the back hoe with a crew of Corpsmen on a clay bluff high above the river. The hoe dug into a trench and lifted out a load of wet earth and broken tree roots. Some of the Corpsmen were shaking from the rain and the cold. Mr Henson put his machine in neutral and let it idle when he saw Perry and Birl come towards him.

'Why ain't you all back on that dozer?' he said.

'He don't want to work and he pulled a knife on me,' Perry said. 'I ain't going to have him on my detail no more.'

'Where's the knife?' Mr Henson said. There were beads of water on his goggles.

'It's a-laying back on the trail, but it don't matter because he won't have no chance to use it. I'm putting in my report with the director so they can pack his sack lunch and get his bus ticket ready.'

'He come at me with a hammer,' Birl said.

'I done it after he opened up that gut ripper. And I liked to split his head open, too.'

Mr Henson climbed down from the back hoe, pulled off his cloth gloves, and lighted a cigarette. The rain drops spotted the white paper. He smoked evenly for a few moments and spit the pieces of loose tobacco off his tongue. 'One of you other boys run back and find that knife and bring it to me. Perry, put the tarp over your machine and bring the truck around to pick up the crew. We ain't going to get anything done in this rain.'

'You ain't heard what I had to say,' Birl said. 'Do I get kicked out for having a shank when another man picks up a hammer at me?

'Did you refuse to work?'

'I told him there wasn't no sense in standing out in the rain. You just said the same thing, didn't you?'

'But I didn't say it to you,' Mr Henson said. 'When one of my work leaders tells you to get on it, that's just like you're hearing it straight from me. I don't know for positive who pulled the hammer or knife first, but every time I've had you on my crew you've given me trouble, and I've had my fill of it.'

'You mean in this outfit a man gets a pay raise and one of them badges for copping out because he ain't got enough balls to step it off in the woods.'

'I'm going to do you a favor, son,' Mr Henson said. 'Get on the truck, set still until we get back to camp, and I'll make sure you're on your way back to Macon tomorrow. Keep bothering me and I'll put you and James in the woods by yourselves for fifteen minutes, and then I'll come pick you off the ground and carry you to the truck.'

Perry drove the canvas-covered van through the mud, and the Corpsmen threw their chain saws and tools inside and climbed up over the tailgate. A pool of water had collected in the center of the tarp, and it sagged heavily between the wooden ribs that arched over the back of the truck. One of the boys pushed a hoe handle into the hard lump, and the water sluiced down in streams onto the trail. Perry got down from the cab and let Mr Henson get behind the wheel for the drive along the blacktop back to camp.

'You can ride up here, and one of the others can get in back,' Mr Henson said. 'I don't want to stop on the road and have to pull you boys apart.'

'There won't be no need for that,' Perry said. He pulled himself over the tailgate and sat back against the wood siding of the truck. The rain streaked in and spotted the boards. He unlaced the leather thongs on his work boots and rubbed the chafed area around his ankles, then he took out his package of Bugler tobacco and papers, and rolled a cigarette.

Most of the boys were exhausted. Their clothes were soaked through to their long underwear, their hair and faces were flecked with mud, and their hands were pinched and wrinkled from being wet all day. They smoked quietly, passing cigarette butts to each other, and occasionally one of the Indians spit a stream of tobacco juice over the tailgate. Birl sat against the cab, with his long legs spread out before him, and stared sullenly at Perry.

'I'm going to fix your ass for this, James,' he said.

Perry said nothing. He finished his cigarette, peeled the paper back along the seam, and let the tobacco spin out in the wind current.

The rain had washed down the mountain and covered the sidewalks in camp with mud. Huge pools of water lay in the low areas, and the thunder rattled the tin buildings. The Corpsmen returning from their work details ran towards the barracks in their slickers and rubber boots. Lightning had struck a tree and dropped it across a power line, knocking out half the lights in camp. After the crew had unloaded from Perry's truck, he drove it a half mile down the shale road to the equipment shed, locked the ignition keys in the maintenance shack, and walked back through the driving rain to the administration building. It took him twenty minutes to write out a five-sentence incident report in large printed letters; then he took it in the director's office.

'Are you sure you didn't pick up that hammer first?' the director said.

'No sir, he pulled the frog sticker when I told him to take his bitching to Mr Henson.'

'Do you have a witness?'

Perry's clothes dripped water onto the carpet. His face was drawn with fatigue. 'Yes sir, but if you got to call him, this badge you give me don't mean much.'

'The other man has a right to a hearing, too.'

'He don't have no rights after he tries to cut on a man. The rule says a Corpsman caught with a weapon gets put out the same day. When you made me assistant work leader, you said you'd back me all the way as long as I kept straight. Well, I done it.'

'I don't think you ever forget anything that's said to you, do you?' the director said. 'I accept your word and I never doubted it. But there are things we have to go through that you don't understand before we put a boy out of camp. Go change clothes and get down to the mess hall before they close the line.'

Outside, Perry pulled his slicker up over his head and walked along the smooth clay trail through the pines to the barracks. He pulled off his wet clothes, wrung them in the washbasin, and stuffed them into his duffle bag. He showered with hot water, washed the mud out of his hair, and rubbed down his body with a towel. The Confederate flag on his arm was a brilliant blue and red against the paleness of his skin. He dressed in the brown slacks, soft wool shirt, and loafers that he had received with his civilian clothes issue; he slipped a transparent rain jacket over his shoulders and went to the dining hall. That evening they had ham steaks, rice and gravy, boiled corn on the cob, and ice cream. Perry went through the receiving line twice, and then spent an hour in the library working on his reading book.

A movie was scheduled for that night, but the power line hadn't been repaired and the recreation hall had no electricity. The rain began to thin, and Perry walked back to the barracks, where the Corpsmen had lighted candles and melted them to the window sills. The rain looked like beads of crystal on the windows. Several boys were shooting pool, and Perry could hear the dice rattle across the tile floor in the bathroom. No gambling was allowed in the camp, but none of the assistant work leaders or the resident worker ever reported a crap game unless a fight broke out.

Popcorn had his battery-operated phonograph turned on full volume. He danced in the corridor by himself, the candlelight flickering on his dark face. He had on a long, striped housecoat, fur-lined slippers that came above his ankles, pajamas with halfmoons all over them, and a woman's nylon stocking rolled down tight over his scalp. He smoked with a cigarette holder between his teeth and spun around in circles.

'Listen to that sound,' he said. 'It's the hippy dippy from Mississippi. Yes indeed, Mister Jimmy Reed. And next we have that late and great secretary of state, Mister James Brown. He is out of sight and out of mind, and he turns your big daddy on. My head might be nappy, but ain't I beautiful?'

'Where you got the glue hid at?' Perry said.

'No glue, man. None of that scene anymore. I can't take those big snakes crawling around behind my eyes the next day. I groove now only with that good spotioti that my soul brothers bring back from the dentist run. It's mellow and yellow, and it'll peel the paint off your walls.'

'Throw it out behind the barracks before the resident worker gets back,' Perry said.

'Cool, do you think I am going to give my good muscat to these North Carolina stumpjumpers? I didn't pay my hard-earned seventy-five cents to water this southern soil.'

'You're up for your merit raise. Don't do nothing to blow it.'

'Man, I ain't pulled an extra hour since I came to camp. That's because I don't lose my cool in front of the wrong people. In Hough you learn how to look like Sunday school all over when you deal with the Man. That's a good thing to know, Double O. You can blast and get high every day as long as you look good on the street for whitey.'

'It still ain't a-helping you none if the resident worker smells it on you at bed check.'

Popcorn reached inside the pocket of his coat and pulled out a bottle of synthetic wine. He unscrewed the cap and took a drink. 'What's the word, baby? It's thunderbird,' he said. The wine rolled down through the stubble of his beard.

'Put that goddamn bottle in your locker and get under the shower,' Perry said.

'You come on like gangbusters with that moral attitude,' Popcorn said. 'Have a drink of spotioti and stop letting that badge ruin your mind. What's this I hear about you playing on people's heads with the ballpeen hammer?'

'I didn't hit nobody with a hammer.'

'They say Birl looked like he'd crapped his pants when you brought him to Henson.'

'He didn't give me no choice when he come out with the knife.'

'Somebody should have fixed that stud a long time ago.'

Perry looked through the rain-streaked window and saw a man run bent over through the trees towards the front door of the barracks. The mountains looked like iron in the dark.

'The resident worker's back. Get rid of that bottle,' he said.

'Not your high rolling daddy. Popcorn will get under the sheets with sneaky pete and let the rest of you cats worry about the Man. Good night, soul brother.'

The Negro boy went to his bunk, took a flashlight and comic book off his night stand, and climbed under the covers with his bottle. He pulled the army blanket over his head, raised his knees to make a tent for himself, and flicked on the flashlight. Perry could hear him laughing under the blanket.

'This Plastic Man character stretches out like chewing gum,' Popcorn said. 'I bet he's got a dong thirty feet long.'

Perry took a thin hand-rolled Bugler cigarette from the tin on his table and lighted it. He breathed in the smoke and felt the day's exhaustion roll through his body. He took off his shirt and shoes, lay back in bed, and listened to the rain beat against the roof. He would get two hours' extra duty on Saturday if he was caught smoking in bed, but right now he didn't care. The light thunder echoed through the valley and rattled the window glass. Two Corpsmen had taken the boxing gloves out of the resident worker's quarters in the dark, and they boxed each other up and down the corridor, slapping the leather and loose strings into one another's faces. Perry was scheduled to call roll at muster the next morning, and he would have to eat with the K.P.s at four forty-five A.M. He put out his cigarette, pulled the pillow over his head, and tried to fall asleep, but the two boxers kept knocking into the walls, and the pool shooters in the foyer yelled every time someone made a shot.

Perry sat up on the edge of the bed and rubbed his

face. His stomach was hard and lean under his T-shirt. 'You fellers ain't supposed to have them gloves out,' he said.

'We don't have nothing else to do. You want us to lay in the rack all evening?' one of the boxers said.

'You giving us an extra hour, Perry?' the second Corpsman said.

'No, I ain't. Just take them gloves and yourselves down to the next bay, and you can punch on each other all night,' he said.

The boys went into the next section of the barracks, and Perry lay back down on his bunk and rested his arm across his eyes. In a few minutes the boys were back in the corridor slugging into one another, and a third Corpsman was with them, hitting at their heads with a leather chair cushion. Perry got up and walked barefooted into the foyer to watch the pool game until the resident worker would make bed check and force everyone to go to sleep.

The Corpsmen had set lighted candles in empty bottles on the four corners of the pool table. The shadows wavered across their faces as they bent to make a shot. The usual dime and quarter bets lay on top of the green apron. A Pima Indian from southern Arizona had won seven games straight, and he was trying to get someone to play him for a dollar a game.

'We'll make it nine ball, and I'll give you the break and two free shots afterwards,' he said.

'You run the table down to the last ball every time you shoot,' L.J. said.

'I'll shoot left-handed. You can't get better odds than that.'

'You're too good, man. There ain't nobody going to play you here,' a big Negro boy said. His face was so black that it was hard to see it in the dark. He wore the cloth liner from his work helmet over his head. 'Pass the stick and let's get back to a dime a game.'

'I got the stick as long as I win,' the Indian said. He had a large, square head and a flat nose, narrow shoulders, and a stomach that hung over his belt line. He was the best pool player in camp, and he had made his living by hustling games in Flagstaff before he came into Job Corps.

'Pick up a cue, James. Get rich in one night,' he said.

'I ain't no good at playing, and I got better sense than to pay for your weekend,' Perry said. Out of the corner of his eye he saw Birl sitting on a metal chair against the wall, watching him.

'I'll put a dollar to your fifty cents,' the Indian said.

'I don't know nothing about pool. I told you that.'

'Pass the fucking stick,' the Negro with the cloth cap said. 'We got bed check in thirty minutes.'

'Last chance around, pale faces. Who wants to beat the pride of the Pima reservation?' the Indian said. 'Write back to your family that you took on the best eight ball and rotation man in Flagstaff.'

'Let James shoot it. He's the big stud around here,' Birl said from the shadows.

No one spoke for a moment. The Indian chalked his cue and rubbed talcum on his palms, then rolled the cue on the table to see if it was warped.

'Go ahead and play him, kemosabe. The work leader gets extra pay every month for copping out on his crew,' Birl said.

'Cut that shit, man,' the Indian said.

'I got booted tonight because of this cock sucker. Don't tell me to cut it,' Birl said.

'I had my fill of this, Birl. You're starting to piss me off,' Perry said.

'Don't lose your cool, Double O,' the big Negro boy said.

'The director says I lost the fifty bucks a month they been putting in the bank for me because I got expelled,' Birl said.

'That's your doing. It ain't because of Perry,' L.J. said.

'You shut up, Missi'sip. I'm getting to Macon as broke as I come here and this fucker is the reason.'

'Go get the resident worker,' the Indian said to another Corpsman.

'We ain't going to need him,' Perry said. 'All right, Birl, any way you want it. You pushed me too much in one day, and I'm a-taking your goddamn head off.'

'Don't give up your badge for him,' L.J. said.

'He drew a knife on me and I didn't do nothing. He lied about me to Mr Henson and I didn't do nothing, either. By God, trash like this ain't going to spit on me again and walk away from it. You hear me, Birl? We can do it with fists and feet, or you can find us a couple of Coke bottles.'

'He's trying to get you kicked out with him,' L.J. said.

'He ain't going to be in enough pieces to see it. Get up, you sonofabitch,' Perry said.

'You guys quit that shouting and let us sleep,' somebody yelled from one of the bays.

'Cool it, Perry. That dude ain't worth it,' the Negro said, and took hold of Perry's arm. He was on the camp boxing team, and the knuckles in his hand stood out like quarters against the skin.

'Turn loose or I'll go over you to get to him,' Perry said.

'Hey man, what's all this shit out here? You cats are

disturbing my high,' Popcorn said from the doorway. He had the wine bottle in his housecoat pocket

'Go tell the resident worker to get his ass down here,' the Indian boy said.

'Why not give Double O his hammer and let him strum on the dude's head awhile?' Popcorn said.

'Let go. I ain't asking you again,' Perry said.

'You're pulling a bad news scene, soul,' the big Negro boy said, and released Perry's arm.

As Perry started around the pool table Birl stood up quickly in the shadows and lifted a cue stick with both arms high above his head. Perry tried to check himself and duck to one side, but the stick whipped down with a suck of air and hit him with the heavyweighted end right between the eyes. Flashes of color exploded in his brain, and he felt as though all the bone and cartilage in his nose had been crushed into his skull. He crashed into the wall and fell over the metal folding chairs, then he rose to his feet with his hands pressed over his face. The blood roared through his fingers over his shirt front. The room whirled about him and blurred, and he thought he was going to swallow his tongue. It was as though someone had fired a shotgun into the middle of his face. He collapsed across the pool table, with his arms spread out beside him, and watched the green velvet turn purple in front of him.

His eyes were wide and staring, and he wanted to close them to make the flashes of light go away, but he felt that his eye lids were stitched to his forehead. Then he began to gag, and a dark yellow cloud slid over him. He rolled back onto the floor and thought he heard the ocean beating in his ears.

chapter five

Perry awoke the next morning in the county hospital. The tape and bandages, spread across his face in an X-pattern, felt like a pair of goggles around his eyes. The bridge of his nose was swollen tight against the gauze. The light outside the window reflected brightly off the patches of melting snow on the front lawn. He raised himself up on his elbows, and a pain as sharp as ice raced through his head. There were small, dried flecks of blood on his upper lip. The sunlight inside the room gave everything a hard, unnatural brightness that hurt his eyes. He tried to recall what had happened the night before; then he remembered the pool stick swinging out of the dark and Birl's murderous eyes behind it. He got out of bed in his nightgown and started towards the bath; but the room seemed to lift up sharply at an angle, and he pitched backwards onto the bed. The radiator hissed quietly. He wanted to pull the tape from his face, and he picked at the edge of the bandage until his eyes watered; then he felt himself go limp inside, and he drifted back into the cool brilliance of the sunlight through the window.

He dreamed of the man on the coal tipple, but this time he felt no guilt. The man looked like Birl, and the rage welled up inside Perry again. *They taken our jobs and credit away, and then they come at me with a knife.* He breathed heavily in his sleep. *There wouldn't be no trouble if they let us alone. We didn't ask for nothing more than that. We ought to take a turpentine can to all of them. They wipe their feet on us like we was a doormat and then they try to cut on us and work us over. He deserved what he got up there on tbe tipple He'd a-done it to us unless we got him first.*

Perry awoke again in the mid-afternoon, his face sweating, and a shaft of sunlight pierced his eyes. He untangled the covers from around his legs and sat on the edge of the bed, his head spinning. After the sleep had cleared from his mind, he saw a fat nurse in a white starched dress watching him. She held a stainless steel container in her hands. The fat on her neck pressed out over her collar, and she wore her hair in tight curls against her head.

'My, but you must have bad dreams,' she said. 'I've had to come down here three times because of the noise you made.'

'How long I been here?'

'They brought you in last night and put thirteen stitches in your forehead and nose. Don't you remember?'

'I don't remember nothing.'

'You fought the doctor and broke a tray of syringes. That should cost the government a few dollars,' she said.

'Where's my clothes at?'

'You can't leave until you're checked out. Do you want to use the bedpan?'

'Get that thing out of here and find my clothes.'

'I'm sorry, but you have to wait for the doctor.'

'I ain't waiting on nobody. Does that highway out there go back to camp?

'Sit down before you start bleeding again,' she said.

He stumbled across the room and pulled open the closet door. His trousers, undershirt, shoes, Popcorn's army jacket, and one cotton sock, all of them splattered with blood, lay in a pile on the floor. Perry took off his nightgown and sat on the floor in his shorts and began to pull on his trousers. He felt that something was dislocated in his head. He had no sense of balance, and he fell on his back several times before he could button his fly.

'You're not going to act like that in this hospital,' she said. 'Get off that floor right now.'

'I didn't ask to come here, and I sure ain't a-staying longer than I want to.'

'I'll put you back to bed with a shot if I have to.'

'No you ain't, because in five minutes I'm going to be down that road.'

He left his shoes untied, put on his shirt unbuttoned, and zipped up the army jacket over it. He stuffed the cotton sock in his pocket and got to his feet.

'You come back here,' the nurse said.

'I'm already gone, lady. Keep them bedpans for somebody else.'

The door swung open and a young intern in white clothes glared at Perry. His face was pale and antiseptic, and he wore large, blackframed glasses on his thin nose. He reminded Perry of the clerk at the company store.

'Was that you making all that noise?' the intern said. He'd had to leave another patient down the hall to come to Perry's room.

'He refused to get back in bed,' the nurse said.

'Where do you think you are?' the intern said. 'When you're in this hospital, you do what you're told.'

'I got the right to leave when I want, ain't I?' Perry held onto the door knob to keep his balance.

'You don't go anywhere until you're checked out. You're not on the street where you can push over people,' the intern said.

'I don't push over nobody, and them white clothes don't let you tell me what to do.'

'Should I call the orderlies, Doctor?' the nurse said.

'No, a forest ranger is waiting for him now. Just get him out of here.'

'That makes a lot of sense, don't it?' Perry said. 'We go through all this, and you was fixing to turn me loose anyway.'

'Get out,' the intern said. 'And go to another hospital to have those stitches removed.'

Perry walked down the corridor to the waiting room. He couldn't shake the dizzy feeling from his head, and the yellow ceiling lamps reflecting off the cracked plaster made him blink his eyes. Mr Henson signed at the desk for Perry's medical bill, and they walked out into the cold, early spring day. The mountains were green and blue in the bright sun, and they seemed to stretch endlessly into the distance. Perry had to shade his eyes to look at the snowcaps on the ridges.

They drove back down the blacktop in a Navy carryall that jarred and rattled with each bump in the road. The melting snow had given the pines and spruce a deeper green, and the creeks that ran under the bridges were wide and sandy yellow. Perry saw a groundhog raise up in the grass by the side of the blacktop. It was a big, fat one, with a puffed tail like a rabbit's, and Perry remembered when he used to catch them with dried corn under an apple crate propped on a stick. In eastern Kentucky groundhogs were called 'whistle-pigs' because of the high-pitched scream they made whenever they were trapped in their holes, and Perry had once kept four of them in a cage in his room for Irvin to play with until his father made him turn them out.

'The director wants to see you in his office,' Mr Henson said. His wind-chafed hands were brick red on the steering wheel.

'I reckon they're a-sending me home this time. I wouldn't have gone after Birl, but a feller can't keep taking it all day. Pulling a knife on me didn't get to me as bad as when he said I was to blame for him losing all his savings money.'

'It don't have anything to do with the fight,' Mr Henson said. 'Popcorn and the others told the director what happened, and he had Birl put in the county jail overnight and shipped him home this morning.'

'They ain't calling a board of review on me?'

'No.'

'What's he want me for, then?'

Mr Henson drove the carryall into the parking lot and cut the engine. His weathered, grey Stetson was pulled low over his sunburned forehead. He stuck a cigarette in his mouth and popped a match on his thumbnail.

'Did you eat lunch at the hospital?' he said.

'No, sir.'

'Go change clothes and wash the blood off your face, then tell the cooks that I said to fix you a meal. Report to the director when you get finished.'

'Something's wrong, ain't it?'

'Get down to your barracks.'

'You don't have to hold back on me. I rather hear it from you than the director.'

'That ain't my job, Perry. But you listen to me and

remember what I say. You're a good heavy equipment man, and if you get yourself a couple more months' experience and training, they'll give you that union book. In time, you'll be as good an operator as I ever was. Just don't let anything make you quit, no matter how hard things seem to get.'

'It's somebody in my family. Something's happened that's going to pull me out of Job Corps, ain't it?'

'Just keep in mind what I said. Don't give up your trade because you take a hard punch now.'

'Was it Irvin again? Goddamn it, tell me.'

'I told you to go get changed, son.'

Perry walked through the trees to the barracks and put on a clean set of fatigues. The work crew had not returned yet, and his bay was empty. He washed the dried flecks of blood from his face in the basin and peeled part of the bandage off his nose. The stitches looked like raised black welts in his skin, and the bridge of his nose had two crooked, discolored knots in it. He touched his fingertips lightly between his eyes and felt a sickening pain rip through his head. He held onto the washbasin until it passed, and then spread the bandage back across his face and pressed the tape flat against his skin.

He had no appetite, and he went directly to the administration building to see the director. A sudden gust of cold wind rippled the water standing in pools in the parking lot. The shale was a sharp white in the sun. It was all going too good, he thought. There ain't nothing that goes along this good for so long without something happening. Things just don't stay straight like that. At least not for us. There's always something that's going to shove a stick between your feet when you think you're almost there. It's like winning the wage election at the mine. You think you got something, and then they raise the charge at the store, and you know you didn't win nothing at all.

He waited on a chair in the administration building and listened to the static from the two-way radio until the director called him into the office.

'How do you feel?' the director said.

'I had worse happen to me.'

'Did you get the cooks to fix you something to eat?'

'I ain't hungry. What's wrong at home?'

'I have a letter from your mother. I guess she thought you still have some troubles with your reading.' He handed Perry a soiled envelope with the address scrawled and misspelled across the front. 'You can use our phone to call home if you want.'

'We ain't got electricity in our house.' Perry unfolded the single page of lined notebook paper and read the penciled words slowly:

to the camp Directer. Can you let Perry come home cause his daddy wants to see him. They blowed up the UMW meetin and hurt him real bad. He is old now and the Doctor dont no if he can make it. I didnt want Perry taken away from his trade but may be he will not be abel to see his daddy agin. we dont have money for his bus ride so can you send him for us. God bless you. Mrs Woodson James.

Perry felt something tighten across his lungs, and the pain behind his eyes began to ache again. I told him they wasn't going to let us alone, he thought. We got one of theirs, and they was going to pay us back. Except they got him and he don't even belong to the union anymore. Why'd he have to be there? Just to set around and talk about what they done to the operator thirty years ago. An old man that couldn't do nothing but happy-pappy for the government.

'How soon can I get home?' Perry said.

'We'll put you on a plane tonight, and you'll have a round-trip ticket.'

'I can't come back.'

'We'll give you two weeks' emergency leave. If that's not enough, we'll let you have more. I don't like to lose a good man.'

'I got to go back to work. We ain't going to have no income at all now.'

'Do you think you can help your family by going back to the same dollar-twenty-five job you had before? They'll never know anything better than what they have now.'

'Who's going to feed the kids and pay for Daddy's doctor while I'm going to school? It won't stop with what they done to Daddy, neither. They'll do everything they can to run us out of the holler. Once the company men shot into the cabins on the next ridge to us. It don't matter to them if they hit kids or old men. It ain't that I don't want to stay here. I told you before this is the best chance I ever had at anything, but I got no choice.'

'You know you have a place here if you decide to come back.'

'I owe you a lot for all the help you give me since I been here, and I thank you for it. Where do I check my gear in?'

'You've got your mind set on quitting the program?'

'Yes sir.'

'I'll send the clerk down in an hour. So long, Perry. When this thing passes, give yourself a break and get out of those coal fields.'

Before supper Perry cleaned out his foot locker and folded his fatigues, dress khakis, work uniforms, rain slicker, socks, and underwear neatly on his bunk, then laid out his shoes and work boots in a row on the floor. He changed into his slacks, sport shirt, and loafers, and put the rest of his clothes into a cardboard suitcase that he had bought from another Corpsman for three dollars. The tip of the fading red sun showed above the rim of the mountain, and long blue shadows began to fall across the valley. The swallows dipped in circles out of the sky and spun over the tops of the buildings. In the distance a solitary star burned coldly in the twilight.

Later, after the clerk had checked off all his clothing, Perry sat on the edge of his mattress, smoked a hand-rolled cigarette, and watched the darkness gather in the pine trees outside. Most of the Corpsmen had returned from supper, and radios and record players blared, the showers roared against the tile walls in the bathroom, and someone at the far end of the corridor kept banging a locker door. The company must have brought in strikebreakers, Perry thought. There ain't none of them scabs brave enough to blow a union hall. The last time the coal field struck, they hired them wrestlers from Detroit to take the scabs through the picket. They caught Merle Flatt in the saloon and stomped on him till they broke all his ribs.

'What's this bad news about you splitting the scene?' Popcorn said.

'I got to go back to Kentucky.'

'Man, what you doing? Henson says they'll graduate you to a job in a few more months.'

'My daddy's dying. The company thugs blew up the U.M.W. meeting,' Perry said.

'Maybe it's not as bad as you think.'

'He ain't going to live.'

'Double O, I hear those gears turning in your brain.

You're going back to get the studs that did it, aren't you? You didn't get enough of that shit before.'

'It ain't your business.'

'Man, I know that. But I don't like to see you eating grits in some hillbilly jail. You got too much soul for that. Forget about all those Little Abners back there. Finish up at Job Corps and you can really roll.'

'I don't feel like talking, especially about things you don't understand,' Perry said.

'Listen, I've been on this scene long enough to know the way you southern dudes think. I am hip to your mind, baby. A Confederate flag starts waving in your brain, and you set out to scramble some guy and you don't care if you get your ass shot off doing it. Tell me if I'm right or wrong.'

'My daddy didn't have nothing to do with the strike. He ain't been down in the hole in ten years. He couldn't hardly do the work for the Forest Service.'

'What can you do for him after you build a big rap in the pen?'

'I ain't worrying about that now.'

'No, you'll catch the cat at night with a shotgun, and then you'll wonder what you're doing out on one of those crazy road gangs. Those southern pens must be a great scene.'

'I got to get started. They're a-taking me to Asheville in a half hour.'

'You're really blowing your cool.'

Perry folded his blankets, placed them on top of his foot locker, and rolled up his mattress on the bedsprings. He put on his jacket and picked up his suitcase.

'So long, Popcorn. Don't go blind on that muscat.'

'Wait a minute. I got something for you to pour in the airplane tank in case you run out of gas. It's out of my best stock.' Popcorn went to his foot locker and pulled loose the plywood bottom on the inside. He had four bottles of wine and a pint of bourbon wrapped in pieces of newspaper. He took out his pocketknife and cut the seal from the whiskey bottle. 'I've been saving this for a special high. Here you are, Cool.'

Perry took a drink and let the whiskey roll back into his throat. His stomach was empty, and he felt a warmth go through his body as the whiskey ran down inside him. He started to pass the bottle back to the Negro.

'Put it in your pocket, Double O. I can't drink sneaky pete later after good stuff. Get that heavy equipment job in Cincinnati, and I'll meet you at the ball game one Sunday and we'll crawl home on our elbows.'

'Take it easy, buddy,' Perry said.

'Don't go back to that mine bit, either. Leave all that shit for the groundhogs.'

Perry went into the recreation hall and shook hands with several other Corpsmen, and then walked through the purple dusk to the parking lot, where a carryall was waiting to take him to the airport in Asheville. There was a rain ring around the moon, and a black sparrow hawk floating motionlessly in the sky on the wind currents. The air was heavy with the smell of the spruce and fir and the new sap in the pines. The last afterglow of the sun darkened over the mountain, and in the distance Perry thought he heard the thin roll of thunder.

chapter six

Perry's father had been taken to the town's private clinic in the back seat of a deputy sheriff's car. The union meeting had been held in the wood-frame school building constructed by the W.P.A. during the Depression. A Negro farm worker, who had been plowing in the field across the road at dusk, said later that he had seen three men carry a cardboard box and an army jerry can around behind the building, but he had paid little attention to them at the time. At nine o'clock, when the building was filled, the explosion blew splintered boards through the roof, and the flame roared upwards as if pure oxygen had been touched with a lighted match. The gunny sack stretched across the windows burned in the heat like a cobweb, and glass was imbedded in the tree trunks close to the building. Three miners were killed outright, and twelve more were drenched with burning gasoline. A woman holding a child in the back of the room was hit by part of a school desk and knocked unconscious. Men climbed through the windows, jammed the front door closed with the weight of their bodies, and some broke through one charred wall by wrapping their coats around their heads and throwing themselves against it. One man, a part time Church of God preacher, began to scream incoherently about the apocalypse. In minutes the building burned to the ground. The men who had been killed had been sitting right on top of the charge, and the sheriff and his two deputies put what remained of them in a canvas tarpaulin. A sickening odor, like that of burnt pork, arose from the canvas, and the sheriff had his deputies drag it into the trees. One man stumbled through the smoke, his hands over his ears, his mouth working without sound. His sleeves had been seared off to the elbows, and his forearms were covered with yellow and red blisters. Another miner, blackened from the fire, went back into the ruins and began lifting up charred timbers with his hands. The embers scorched his palms, and the frayed bottoms of his overalls sparked and then curled in flame. Three men dragged him to an automobile.

Woodson James lost all his fingers on one hand except the thumb, his face was badly burned, and a sliver of board was driven through his back into the lung. He lay pinned under a section of roofing and held the stump of his hand against his chest to stop the bleeding. The hot cinders burned into his face and scalp, and his chest felt as though someone had poured acid inside it. People were yelling, and feet trampled over the debris on top of his body. He tried to shout louder than the noise, but he coughed on the ashes and dust, and his eyes watered and filmed from the heat. The side of his head was pressed flat against the floor, and he could feel a nail penetrating into the small of his back each time someone stepped across him. He choked and almost vomited when he touched the place where his fingers had been. The blood on his hand had coagulated and turned black around the pieces of bone. After a few minutes he heard no sound except the pine boards bursting like firecrackers in the flame.

You ain't got the right to do this to me twice, God, he thought. You buried me once, and you ought to taken me then if you was going to do it. There ain't no sin I ever done that could let you put me through this again. I been a Christian man as best I could, and I already paid three times over for anything I done against you. If you're set on doing this to me, bring the whole roof down and finish it quick.

He could smell his hair burning, and then he passed out. Two of his cousins couldn't find him in the crowd outside, and they went back into the fire and pried the debris off him with an iron bar. They carried him out just as a large section of roofing collapsed in a roar of sparks and flaming boards. The cousins put out the fire on Woodson's clothes with their hands, and took a handful of cobweb from an outbuilding and rubbed the wound in his back to stop the bleeding.

He almost died during his first night in the clinic because no one could find a doctor closer than Lexington who could treat anything more serious than colds and poison ivy. Woodson lay face down on the emergency table for eight hours and spit blood on a pillow, while the plasma ticked slowly into his arm. The next morning the union flew in a surgeon from Huntington, West Virginia. By mid-afternoon he had removed a nine-inch-long shaft of wood that was wedged in Woodson's back as though it had been hammered there. The doctor knew that the burns on Woodson's face would eventually require skin grafts, but he said nothing to Mrs James because he did not expect the old man to live more than a few days at the outside, since Woodson had already lost one lung and the other was left with a ragged wound inside. The following day the only ambulance in the county, a stationwagon with the back seats taken out, took him to the hospital in Richmond, where there were at least two doctors who had experience with respiratory cases.

The school was not the first building to be blown up in the last four months. Two operators' homes in Sterns and Pikeville had been dynamited, and the union agent's office in Letcher County had been soaked with kerosene one night and set aflame. Strikes had shut down half of the truck mines in the state, and in Harlan and Perry counties the operators brought in out-of-state scabs rather than sign new union contracts. The U.M.W. demanded a dollar-a-day wage increase in mines under contract, and miners put up picket lines around almost every coal tipple and C & O loading platform in eastern Kentucky and West Virginia. Four men died in a gun battle outside of an auger mine in Floyd County after a truckload of scabs had tried to crash through a picket, and the sheriff and two of his deputies in 'Bloody' Breathitt resigned their jobs because they had been threatened by people from both the union and the operators' association.

Woodson James lay in a semi-coma for a week. Every time he became conscious he began screaming and the doctors had to give him heavy dosages of morphine. One eye and half of his face were covered with bandages. A nurse had shaved the hair from the burned places in his scalp, and a thin film of blood and spittle collected on his chin when he breathed. His feet were yellow and calloused, sticking out under the bed sheet. Once, the doctor had inserted a tube in Woodson's nose, but the old man pulled it out and fell off the bed.

In his morphine dreams he saw himself as a young man back in the hollow, when he had built his cabin for his new wife. He had hauled the white oak logs from the forest with mules and chains, working in the hot sun, with the leather reins wrapped tightly around his hands and the sweat bees swarming around his head. He split the logs with his axe and wedges, beveled them, notched the corners, and shaped them level with a carpenter's plane. The wood shaved off evenly under the steady pressure of his arms, and he knew that he would not need much chinking when he set the logs across one another. He was as good a carpenter as he was a shaft miner, and he had a feeling for wood when he ran his rough hand across a board plank or put his axe with all his weight into the base of a tree trunk. Wood always had a good smell, like pine sap in the spring. It was something that belonged to the earth above the ground, where a man could see sky every day and breathe air that wasn't filled with coal dust, where men didn't work six or seven at a time in a small pocket two miles back in the mountain, their picks striking into the limestone, to get at the seam while the carbide lamps on their helmets sent up dirty streams of smoke.

He had brought his wife into the cabin, after the wedding at the Church of God chapel in Jackson. Her skin was soft and smooth, the color of a pink rose petal, and the blood flushed to her temples when he showed her their bedroom that he had covered with green wallpaper from Montgomery Ward's and furnished with a double bed – not a mattress stuffed with corn shucks, which most people in the hollow used. During the late 1920s, before the strip mines had ruined the soil with the yellow sulphuric drainage from the exposed coal seams, he grew tobacco on shares in the meadowland along the creek bottom. Even after he paid off the owner, he always cleared several hundred dollars in a season. The first year he was married he added another room onto the cabin for his first child and bought his wife a foot-operated sewing machine that had to be shipped all the way from Memphis.

During those first years of his marriage he worked in the mines only in the winter, after the tobacco had been cut, strung on sticks, and hung to dry in the barn for the dealers' auction in Winchester. In November he would go back in the hole again and make two to three dollars a day loading coal by the ton. At that time no miner was paid any type of fixed wage, and if a man had the bad luck to work in a pocket where he couldn't reach the seam in his twelve hours underground, he received no money at the end of the day. Sometimes a miner would spend two shifts in the hole, tearing limestone and slag away from the coal, before he could start loading for pay.

But Woodson did well with his tobacco farming in the spring and summer, and his five months in the mine during the winter. He had no money in the bank, but his wife had two machine-made dresses to wear to church on Sunday, he bought a black suit and white shirt for himself, and he was one of the few people in the rural section of the county to own an iron stove with four lids on top. He planned to save his money and buy two acres of land in the next hollow near the south fork of the Kentucky River so he would no longer need to farm on shares; then the Depression cut back production in every shaft mine on the Cumberland plateau, and the tobacco buyers from Raleigh showed up in fewer numbers at the auction in Winchester and eventually stopped coming altogether. Many of the independent coal operators went broke and closed their mines; others tried to stay open by paying miners eighty cents a day for their maximum load, and the big corporations in the East began to make up their stockmarket losses by raising the rent in company-owned towns in Kentucky, West Virginia, eastern Tennessee, and Virginia. Then John L. Lewis came to Harlan County and organized the first local in Kentucky of the United Mine Workers of America. Thousands of the rank and file began to carry union cards, and the worst gun battles, bombings, and burnings since the Civil War broke out throughout the eastern part of the state. In 1939 the governor called up the National Guard to protect scabs crossing picket lines, and many striking miners were shot down in the streets of Harlan.

It was at this time that Woodson James killed two soldiers in a battle outside a shaft on the Virginia line. On an early spring morning the Guardsmen had been given orders to clear away the pickets from the mine entrance. A miner was knocked to the ground with a rifle butt after he refused to move, and he slashed a soldier across the face with his knife. Other striking miners pulled their pistols, and in the battle three union men were killed. Later that day Woodson James, his brother-in-law Bee Hatfield, and ten other men crawled up on the mountain overlooking the mine with Winchester rifles that had been passed out by the union. Two soldiers were carrying a body to the back of a government stake truck. They wore World War I issue campaign hats, canvas cartridge belts, and leggings; their sleeves were rolled, and their shirts were damp with sweat. Somebody below saw a miner raise up over a ledge, a shot was fired, although no one ever knew by whom, and the explosions from the .30-30s and the Springfield .03s crashed through the hollow. The two soldiers dropped the body and ran for the cover of the truck. Woodson brought the V-sight of his

Winchester down on the neck of one soldier, led him slightly, and squeezed off the trigger. The man struck the ground on his face as though he had been hit by a block of concrete. As Woodson worked the lever action and pumped another shell into the chamber, he could see the dark area spread from the base of the soldier's head into the coal dust on the ground. The second soldier was pinned down before he could make the truck. He crawled behind a small pile of rocks and huddled against them as bullets splintered the slag around his boots.

Woodson had never believed that he wanted to kill any man, but once the shooting started, he felt as cool inside as if he had been firing at a bear or a deer. He had no time to think about the fact that he had just killed a man. The rifle felt natural and easy in his hands, and the lever action seemed to work by itself. He fired shot after shot down on the man behind the rocks while bullets ricocheted off the ledge in front of him in a spray of limestone powder. His gun snapped empty, and he pulled back from the crest of the mountain and reloaded his magazine from the shells in his pocket. The brass shells had a good feel in his hand as he slipped them into the slot below the chamber. The blood beat in his temples and he felt a strange exhilaration that he'd never had before.

Kill union men because they want a decent wage, will you, he thought. Come in here from outside and shoot us down because we want more money than eighty cents a day. You get government clothes and government pay for keeping us down in the hole twelve hours a day without enough money to show for it to buy groceries at the store. By God, you scab-loving sonofabitch, get up on your feet and catch it like a man.

Woodson slammed the lever on his rifle back into place and rested the end of the barrel across a rock. He aimed the top bead of his sight just above the exposed boot of the soldier to allow for the drop in the bullet's trajectory. This ought to bring you out, you company bastard, Woodson thought. He let out his breath slowly and squeezed the trigger. The bullet tore into the soldier's legging above the ankle. He jerked backwards, his foot in his hands, and exposed his body completely. His face was grey with pain, and his mouth was open wide, as though a silent scream were coming from it. Woodson raised up quickly on one knee and drilled a shot into the center of the left pocket over the man's heart. Then they saw a truckload of more soldiers, armed with Springfields, grinding its way up the road to the mine, and Woodson ran with other men back down the mountain to the cover of the pine trees.

His heart beat as though it were going to burst inside him, and he felt the sweat rolling off his face. The sun was white over the timber line, and the colors of the forest and the cliff walls in the hollow seemed more brilliant than he had ever seen them before. Then he started laughing, although he didn't know why. He put his hand over his mouth to make it stop, but he laughed harder, choking on his own breath as he ran through the rust-colored tree trunks in the woods, until he fell on his knees and had to hold his sides. He saw that the other men were laughing too, and he wondered if his face looked as horrible as theirs.

During the next few years Woodson felt a greater sense of guilt over his laughter than about killing the two soldiers, although after the shooting he kept no guns in his cabin and refused to have any part in the tipple bombings that were common throughout the forties. Sometimes in town he would see one of them who had been with him during the gun battle, and he would sense a secret smile, a bright flicker of private knowledge in the eyes and a feeling of shame would go through him. We didn't have no choice about what we done, he told himself. They gunned our men down on the picket and we give it back to them. We just ask to get treated fair, and they brought in outsiders to murder us. Maybe them soldiers didn't know what they was doing, but they was shooting down our men, anyway. But a man don't laugh over taking a life. It was something we had to do, and we fought them fair and it ain't something we got to walk around a-smiling about inside like we was ashamed of it. Because then we ain't no better than them hired gun thugs that get drunk in the jenny-barn and talk about the miners they worked over on the picket.

As Woodson grew older he began to form in his own mind a type of fierce personal relationship between himself and God, about the nature of sin and atonement. He had an Old Testament vision of God as a wrathful person who was for the most part stern yet fair in His punishment; but nevertheless Woodson believed that God had to be corrected and defied sometimes because He had too much power on His side and often He forgot that He had made a deal and as a result He didn't honor it. Woodson had been raised in the Church of God, but he hadn't been to the Wednesday night or Sunday meetings since he was fifteen except for the day he was married. Right after the World War II snake cults became common throughout the Cumberland Mountains. In clapboard schoolhouses and in big tents set up in fields, people listened for hours while preachers yelled incoherently about salvation through the test of faith. During the sermon women became hysterical, children cried out in fear, and some miners would light the carbide lamps on their tin hats, remove the glass cover, and hold the flame under their throats. On a table at the head of the congregation the preacher would set a cardboard box full of copperheads and rattlesnakes that had been caught in the woods during the day. Before midnight, when the congregation had lost all sense of reasoning, the preacher would call for the test of faith, and people would come down the aisle between the rows of folding chairs and plunge their arms into the cardboard box.

The state government passed a law against the snake cults, but their popularity spread. Several people died after their test of faith; however, the preacher usually explained later that the dead person had not truly believed in God's protection, and the congregation would pray to God that the deceased's lack of faith would not cause him to be punished in the afterlife.

Woodson had attended snake cult meetings six months before he went forward to give testimony and accept his salvation. He sat on a wooden chair in the back of the tent, his huge hands folded between his legs, and looked at the sawdust floor while the preacher spoke. He had just finished the four o'clock Sunday shift at the mine, and his face was black with coal dust except for the white area around his eyes where his goggles had been. His wife was next to him, wearing one of her machine-made dresses that she had laundered in boiling water and corn starch until the colored design was almost completely faded from it. Her face had a fearful, serious expression, and she bit her lip as she listened to the preacher's words. She had always believed that the Church of God, or possibly even the Baptists, offered the only salvation, and she was fearful of Woodson's involvement with the snake cult, because she had the same distrust towards it as she did towards the Catholics and Hebrews.

The preacher, Father Clock, was a tall man, well over six feet, who wore a seersucker suit, a candy-striped necktie, and a large gold cross on his watch chain. He had a lean, ascetic face, black eyes that looked like chipped obsidian, and his thin, black hair was combed straight back to cover the bald spots in his head. His sweat-filmed face glistened in the light from the kerosene lamps. He was the most popular of the snake cult preachers because he'd had a faith-healing radio show several years in Nashville on the same station as the Grand Old Opry. He was as well known in eastern Kentucky as Roy Acuff and Mother May-belle Carter.

'How many of you out there have been saved?' he said. 'Which one of you is ready to say that you have taken God into your hearts and don't fear His punishment because you have renounced your sins and you have faith in His mercy? Is it enough to set there and say you have been forgiven without coming forth to make your testimony and prove to yourself and the Lord that you have been cleansed? You answer me that one, brother.'

His voice began to rant, and he jabbed his finger in the air when he spoke. His face looked flushed with fever. His sermon would build to a point where he was screaming, and the congregation would shrink in their chairs and look at the floor with guilt-ridden eyes; and then suddenly he would lower his voice, push back his coat and place his hands on his hips, and speak softly as though to children.

'Yes, you are repentant, or you wouldn't be here. You've taken Jesus as your Saviour, and you've been baptized in the blood. You've put aside the lust of your youth, the ways of men that follow Mammon; you've stopped listening to the false prophets who deny the way of the cross. I know all of this, brothers and sisters, because I have gone through the same temptations, the same traps and snares that Satan lays before us. In the schools they tell us there is no God because science has proved it. Yes, they tell us God no longer exists. I went to schools where people were taught that science is even better than God. I had my faith tested, and I'm here today to tell you that it has not been shaken!'

His voice began to rise again, and his eyes burned even more brightly. He rested one hand on the box of snakes.

'Now I'm going to ask you to come give living witness to your faith. Not to just set and say that you believe, but to take up snakes and cast them down without fear like it says in the Bible. I want you to show God that right here in Perry County, Kentucky, we have continued his word. Can you do it, brothers? Do you have it in you to show God your love? I want to hear and see a testimony that will make God know that we haven't followed after the false prophets. That's right, get up from your chairs and come down the aisle. Yes ma'am, you go right ahead and weep in joy of your redemption. And the rest of you cry tears of happiness, too, because we're breaking through as witnesses to salvation tonight.'

Woodson rose, his face rigid and his eyes glowing hotly. He moved mechanically, as though he were walking in a dream. His wife held onto his sleeve.

'Don't do it, Woodson. Please. It's the devil he's preaching,' she said.

He walked up the aisle with the others as she pulled

after him. People began singing and clapping their hands, and one woman sank to the floor in front of the box of snakes and moaned and cried because of some dark sin in her youth.

'Lannie Dotson got killed doing it,' Mrs James said, her voice climbing higher now. 'We can't do without you at the house. You want me to raise the children by myself?'

'Get your hand off me, woman. I heered the calling,' Woodson said, and flung his wife's arm away from him.

He walked through the crowd and stood before the box. Brother Clock pulled off his seersucker coat, rolled up his sleeves over his elbows, and picked up a rattlesnake in each hand. The snakes coiled their bodies in the air and shook their rattles, their mouths and fangs yawning open at the congregation. Brother Clock's face looked as though he had been drugged.

'There it is, brothers and sisters,' he said. 'The proof that we have prayed through and the Holy Ghost has descended right down into this tent. We have given witness to the word.'

The people shouted and clapped their hands louder, and a miner stood up on a chair, lighted his carbide lamp, and let the flame lick over his arm. Woodson reached into the box and picked up a copperhead by the middle of its body. He looked up at the top of the tent and felt an ecstasy surge through him like a sexual orgasm. 'Great God, I been saved,' he yelled. 'I been to the river and I been baptized, and now I got redemption in the word.'

Then the snake coiled back in a loop, arched its neck, and its smooth metallic head struck through the air into Woodson's shoulder. He felt a burning sensation hit him, and he threw the snake high into the air above his head. He tore his overalls strap and shirt loose and saw the two small punctures in his skin to one side of the collarbone. 'It got me, boys! I ain't got no chance now. It's a-pumping into my heart.'

He ran through the crowd, knocking people down in the aisle, and pushed through the tent flap into the night. He thought he could feel the green venom working its way through his veins. Two men chased after him and held him to the ground. Someone brought out a kerosene lamp, and in the flickering orange light a man cut an X with his pocketknife on each one of the fang wounds, then kneaded the flesh with his fingers and sucked out the poison with his mouth. Another miner took a handful of string-cut tobacco, wet it in a pool of water, and pressed it down tightly on the wound.

Woodson lay in bed at home for three days in a sick coma until his system worked out the remaining poison in his body. He would have probably recovered sooner, except that Bee Hatfield brought him a gallon of corn whiskey, and they both got drunk every time Woodson became conscious again.

But what Woodson called his redemption never really came until he was trapped for two days under a pile of rock in a Virginia coal mine. In the first hours of darkness, with the great pieces of slag and limestone across his body, he listened for the sound of men moving about or for the distant shutter of air hammers cutting through the shaft wall. He knew that other miners had been working farther up the corridor, and some of them must have gotten out to tell the people above ground that he was still somewhere under the debris. He had seen other cave-ins, and he knew that miners didn't leave a man underground, even if they had to dig for weeks just to bring out his body.

Eventually they would get to him. If they couldn't clear the corridor or get down through the shaft, they would sink an auger from the surface and break through the roof so that they could lower a team down on cables.

As the hours went by, his lung filled with blood and he passed out. When he awoke he didn't know if he had been unconscious for a few minutes or a day. He had relieved himself in his pants, and the air was much harder to breathe. The inside of his mouth and throat were filmed with coal dust, and he was so thirsty that his spittle was like string. Once he thought he heard picks and shovels scraping in the distance, and he listened for the sound to grow louder until his ears began to hum. Later, the silence made his head reel, and he realized that there was probably nobody alive within a mile of him. He remembered how the explosion had filled the corridor with an electric yellow flash and how some miners were blown along the floor like piles of rags. He had seen the pinning break loose in the ceiling, and the three men in the pocket next to him had been covered with tons of earth. He would have been killed outright, too, but he was under an overhang when the shaft caved in, and he was protected from the great pieces of rock that came down with the force of freight cars.

He was alone. The weight of all God's earth was resting on his back, and the people above ground had probably counted him off as dead. They would get to him sometime, but right now the rescue teams would be working their way to areas where they believed some men might still be alive. Then Woodson knew the way he was going to die. He would either suffocate slowly or starve. He remembered once in Pike County when a hot mine exploded and everyone in it was considered dead because the heat from the blast had melted the steel cables on the elevator cage. The rescue teams couldn't open up the shaft because of the fumes, and they had to put ventilator fans in the hole for a day before they could begin digging. Two weeks later they found a miner pinned upright in a wall crevasse; he had died from thirst and dehydration.

On the second day Woodson began to pray for death. The pain in his chest caused him to pass out periodically, and his bones ached in the damp cold. Each time he slipped into unconsciousness he felt a sense of relief and hoped that he wouldn't awaken again. Then suddenly his mind would come clear with more pain, and he knew that his death would take very long. The darkness seemed to seep into his eyesockets and fill his brain, and he felt the terror that a blind man feels when his sight is first snuffed out. He had always had a fear that after death a man was conscious of lying in the grave while people shoveled dirt over him, and many times at night he had awakened, sweating, after a dream in which he saw himself locked under the earth while people walked about overhead, deaf to his cries.

Towards the end of the second day he began to see different patterns of color float before his eyes. You're finally coming for me, ain't you, Lord, he thought. I reckon things is set straight now for them men I killed and everything else I ever done. I don't hold it against you for this if you think it's right, but it can't go on no longer. I can't take it no more. If I ain't paid enough for what I done in the past, strike me dead now and send me straight to hell, because I don't want nothing more to do with you if I got to stay alive down here anymore. I ain't defying you. I figure I made a bargain for punishment when I dropped them two soldiers, and now the bargain's complete, and you got to let me walk out of here or let the rest of the shaft come down on me.

Then the color patterns before his eyes began to change, and he saw a brilliant square of yellow light open up in the corridor wall. He thought that the sun itself had exploded into the room. A light, warm feeling went through his body, and he felt that someone was pulling the great weight of rock off him. The cold ache left his bones, the fresh air went cool and deep into his lungs, and he was no longer thirsty. He knew that he could get up and walk now. The square of light was a stairway up to the surface. He just had to raise himself and walk up to the top of the earth, where his wife and children would be waiting for him. The dogwood was in full bloom on the mountainside, the sky was filled with summer rain clouds, and the wind was blowing across the meadows with the smell of horses and new tobacco. Tomorrow he and his wife would go to the county fair in Jackson, and he might spend an extra fifty cents to buy a pint of whiskey.

His skin seemed to glow with the radiance of ivory in the light. The coal itself was a luminous blue in the aura from his body. You done it, God, he thought. You put me through my punishment, but you played fair and you're a-letting me go back up. I ain't giving you call to punish me again, and I'll keep my end of the bargain as long as you keep yours.

Then Woodson passed out. Six hours later a rescue team in gas masks cut a small hole through a wall of debris blocking the shaft, and one man saw Woodson's boot sticking out from under the pile of rock.

He saw figures silhouetted above him in a haze. There was a taste of ether in the back of his mouth, and a dull drumming sound beat inside his head. The eye that wasn't covered by the bandage hurt him as he tried to open it wide. There was a film of dried mucus over his eyelashes and lid. He expected to see the square of light in the wall shaft again, and he wanted the cool wind that smelled of the land above to blow over his body and take away the pain in his hand and lung. A bottle of white fluid, like clear syrup, hung from a metal rack over his head, and he could see the liquid run in bubbles through a tube into his arm. He didn't know where he was, nor could he remember what had happened to him. His mind was still back in the shaft, deep under ground.

Someone held a glass with a plastic straw in it to his mouth, and the water washed that sickening ether taste down into his stomach. The dream about the light in the mine began to fade, and the figures around him became more clear. A doctor was writing on a chart at the foot of the bed. There were cracks like spiderwebs in the plaster ceiling, and a nurse had just opened the blinds to let light into the room. He tried to stir under the sheets, and then he saw that his arm was lying in traction and the tape wrapped around his chest. One side of the room remained dark to him, and he didn't know why his other eye wouldn't open. He heard a woman crying quietly, and he turned his head slowly to one side.

He saw his wife, her face drawn and lined from lack of sleep; the children were beside her, dressed in ragged overalls or in dresses made from Purina feed sacks. They stood in a row like stairsteps, and all of them had the classical features of the James family face – the high, pale forehead, the wide-set eyes, and the hard jawbone that came from the Indian blood in the family. He started to ask why they were not waiting for him outside the cabin to go to the county fair in Jackson, and then the memory of the explosion and fire at the union meeting came back to him, and he felt like a man who had painfully awakened from a long alcoholic binge. He saw the yellow belch of flame tearing through the floor and the boards shattering down on people's heads. He heard the screams and the men trying to kick down the wall, like horses trapped in a burning barn. Fear shot through him again, and he wanted to roll back under the cover of sleep. His chest convulsed and he coughed blood on his chin.

'It's us, Woodson. You're safe now. You ain't got to be afraid no more,' his wife said.

'Why can't Daddy come home?' Irvin said.

'They left me under the boards. It was burning on my back.'

'That was two weeks ago. Put all that out of your mind,' she said. She twisted her handkerchief in her hands. 'The doctor don't want you to think about nothing except getting home.'

'I seen Ike Phelps and his brother blowed all to pieces. They just come apart right there in their chairs.' His voice was weak, as though somebody were talking outside himself.

'Don't talk no more about it or the doctor will give you another of them shots,' she said.

'I made a bargain with God. He shouldn't have done it to me twice.'

'Please, Woodson, don't talk that way. I been a-praying since they brought you in here.'

'He didn't have no right. I paid.'

'Daddy, do what mama tells you,' Perry said.

Woodson leaned his head sideways on the pillow and saw Perry sitting in a chair, dressed in slacks and a sport shirt, something which he had never been able to buy his son, and with a haircut and a good suntan on his face. He could not visualize Perry in anything but his wash-faded overalls, denim shirt, cloth cap, scuffed brogans, and the suitcoat that Mrs James had mended for him year after year.

'Why, it's you, boy,' Woodson said. The phlegm rattled in his throat. 'You're looking just fine. I ain't ever seen you look so fine. But why ain't you in school?'

'I come home when mama wrote the camp.'

'What they done to your face, son?'

Perry touched his fingers to the red S-shaped scar on the bridge of his nose.

'It ain't nothing. I got hurt out on the job.'

'You're going to be real proud of him when you get home and he tells you about all of what he done at that camp,' Mrs James said. 'He learned how to read and write, and they made him some kind of government leader. His teacher told him that he can get a job running a machine if he gets a couple of more months' schooling.'

'I knowed you could do it,' Woodson said. 'There ain't a James yet that couldn't do a job better than the next man if he had the chance to. I want you to go on back to that camp and finish your schooling. Then you won't be a-running off to work in no hot mine in Virginia. You can operate a shovel at the strip mine and stay on top of the ground like God intended men to be.'

'I'm staying around here awhile till you get well,' Perry said. 'They give me leave at the camp and I can go back any time I want.'

'I ain't asking you to do it, son. I'm telling you to go back there to North Carolina so you ain't got to make your living the way I had to.' The effort of talking made him feel weak inside, and his head began to spin. Small grey dots appeared before his eyes. He breathed deeply and let his head sink back into the pillow. He felt that his skin was sagging against the bone. His body and mind were tired, as though a lifetime's energy had been sucked out of him.

'He ain't going against you, Woodson,' his wife said. 'The boy just wants to be around and help out till you're home again.'

'My daddy fought against them, and I did too, and it didn't do neither one of us any good. They ruined the land, they taken our homes, and they made good men take up guns to get back just part of what was theirs to begin with. I don't want no more of it for my children. One of our boys has got a chance now to be something better than a whistle-pig scratching up and down a shaft for barely enough to eat. By God, he ain't a-throwing that chance away to look after me.'

Woodson gagged and had to turn his face into the pillow to let the saliva drain out of his throat. He felt as if a big clot of blood was caught in his windpipe.

'We got to go. The doctor don't want you to talk long,' Mrs James said.

'I'm dying, woman. You know that. All the doctors in Kentucky can't change a man's time when it comes. I seen the sign in my sleep.'

'Why's Daddy talking like that?' Irvin said.

'Hush up, child,' Mrs James said, her eyes beginning to water again. 'You others get outside and wait on me, and don't give me no cause to get a strap to you when we get home.'

'I should have died back in that shaft in Virginia. I know God was set on taking me then, and for some reason He must have changed his mind at the last minute. Maybe He thought I ought to be punished some more later. But He give me the sign last night, and I ain't going to be able to walk away from it this time.'

'I'm going to call the doctor back. It ain't good for you to talk so long,' Mrs James said.

'You ain't going to see me again after you leave this room, and I got something to say to this boy.'

'We got to go, Daddy,' Perry said. 'They said we wasn't supposed to stay more than a few minutes.'

'Set still. I know what you come back for. I seen it in your eyes when I first looked at you. I know you too good. You come back to get even for what they done to me. It's Devil Anse Hatfield's blood running in your veins. You're set on revenge, and you won't rest till you kill a man. Hatfields was always that way. From the time they tied them McCoy boys to paw-paw trees and shot them down, they've paid everybody back in blood for anything that was ever done to them. You ain't going to grow up like that. I ain't going to have a boy for a murderer because of my death. Do you understand that?'

'I ain't killing nobody.'

'You're a-lying to your daddy on his deathbed.' Woodson reached his hand over and caught Perry by the wrist. His body had wasted until his fingers were like bone. The movement made his chest swell with pain. 'I can feel that Hatfield blood beating inside you. You got murder in your heart, son. I ain't going to be here to stop you from what you want to do, but I want you to remember that you're part James, too. We never gunned down no man unless they pushed it on us, and we never shot no man out of revenge. There's been people shot all over these coal fields, and there ain't anybody that was ever better off for it. We're just as

114

poor as we always was, and a lot of our people and theirs got put in the ground for nothing.'

'You didn't do nothing to them. Maybe the J.W.s or the others got something coming, but you ain't been on a picket in ten years.'

'I done my share when I was younger, and I'm still a-paying. You get back in that school.'

Mrs James called the doctor, who filled a syringe to give Woodson another shot of morphine. As the doctor rubbed an alcohol-soaked pad on the skin, Woodson held up his hand weakly to push away the needle. Then the light began to grow fixed in his one uncovered eye, the muscles relaxed in his face, and his breathing became more shallow and even. He rested his head back on the pillow and looked up at the ceiling. A grey strand of hair stuck out from the bandage on his forehead. He felt a longing inside him for sleep and an end to the fury that had burned in him for a lifetime. A warm feeling, like a mild fever, began to glow inside his body, and a pink mist, the color of blood diluted in water, seemed to circulate in the room. 'You ain't going to need it this time, Doc,' he said.

The doctor drew the blinds, and everyone left the room. The stillness made the distant drumming grow louder in Woodson's head. The mist was so thick that he could feel it in his hand. It changed color, to crimson and then to purple, and he knew that he was back in the mine shaft for the last time. He didn't have to worry about the clot of blood in his windpipe any longer. He could breathe the cool air through the pores in his skin. The burned wounds in his scalp had healed, his mutilated hand could grasp an axe handle with the strength of a man in his twenties, and he felt his darkened eye burn through the gauze until it could see the broken timbers hanging from the limestone in the top of the shaft. I'm going under ground to stay this time, ain't I, God, he thought. I ain't got to fight with you or make no bargains anymore. We're a-going home.

For the first time in his life he rested quietly, without heat or anger or struggling against that fierce, unknown enemy that had always tried to strike him down. A square ripple of fire broke through the rock wall, burning a great doorway in the shaft. The flame showered out in sparks like a welder's torch, and the room was again flooded with yellow light, but it was brighter this time. Then he felt himself being absorbed into the light and carried to its source. He seemed to rise from the floor without willing his body to move. As he went up through the earth towards the sky, he could smell the wind blowing in the white oaks and poplars, the new pine sap in freshly cut logs, and the sweat glistening on the horses. He rose faster to the surface now, closer to the light, and he saw that the sun had descended from the sky and spangled everything with a radiance that made him shield his eyes. He floated higher, feeling himself dissolve and become a part of all things, and he could see to the far reaches of the earth on both horizons. The oceans were blue and green, and the mountains rose up jagged against the sky behind them. He had never known the world was so immense. He felt the light enter his mind and consume him, and the radiance became so bright that he was conscious of nothing else.

chapter seven

The day after his father died, Perry walked the seven miles from the cabin to town. The mountains were green from the spring rains and melting snow, and the leaves on the trees in the hollow glistened wetly in the morning light. The dogwood had broken out in a spray of white flowers, and new green vines had begun to crawl up the cliff walls. The rain had cleared the air of the smell from the burning slag heaps, and the creeks were flooded and rushing brown over big limestone boulders. From the shale road on top of the ridge Perry could see the Cumberland range stretch away in a long blue haze towards the West Virginia line. Hawks hovered high above the hollows, dipping occasionally out of the sky when they saw a ground-hog or fieldmouse below. The winter leaves were still on the forest floor, piled around the tree trunks, and the first red and white flowers had begun to grow near the creek beds. High up on the next ridge a man was cutting wood in front of a poplar log cabin, and smoke curled from the stone chimney into the wind.

Perry was little aware of the spring changes around him. In his mind he continued to see his father's wasted form on the bed, the wounds in his scalp, the stubs of his fingers wrapped in gauze, the sunken chest, and he still heard the rattling sound of his dying voice.

Perry's mind was pointed at revenge the way a man points a rifle at a target, and no other thought could enter his consciousness for very long. He knew that he would find the three men who had blown up the schoolhouse and kill them in any way he could. If he didn't find them today, he would catch them next week or next month or however long it would take him to make them pay. They ain't going to walk away from it this time, he thought. Them three thugs killed their last old man. We ain't a-taking it no more. I'll send them three men to hell or, by God, I'll go there myself. They can put me in the electric chair for it if they want to, but at least there ain't going to be as many men wanting to hire out to the operator to blow us up.

Perry took thirty dollars of his Job Corps discharge money to pay part of the credit at the company store down the road so they could continue to charge through the rest of the month. He still had seventy dollars left, and the government owed him another one hundred and fifty from his back savings. But the camp director had told him that his money wouldn't be sent to him for a couple of months, and Perry had to find a job soon. The rent on the cabin was thirty-five dollars a month, Irvin had to go back to the doctor in Richmond, and the children needed new clothes. The family had not been able to buy shoes for the last two years, and the youngest three children had one pair of shoes among them. Also, the woman at the health unit said that Irvin needed a better diet than the powdered milk, peanut butter, and canned meat given out by the federal surplus food center could provide.

A half mile outside town Perry caught a ride with a family in an old Buick. The inside was crowded with women and children, and he had to stand on the running board and hold onto the window jamb. They bounced over the ruts in the county road as they rolled down off the mountain slope into the town limits. Perry looked at the clapboard shacks with lumps of bulk coal piled outside, the junker cars parked in the yards, the farm equipment that had been left to rust, the barefoot children playing in the dirt, and the few cracked sidewalks that were overgrown with weeds. The Buick pulled into the center of town by the courthouse, and Perry dropped off the running board onto the street.

Although it was the middle of the week, men stood around on street corners and in front of poolrooms. Most of the mines in the county were closed because the operators' association would not sign new contracts until the industrial referee from the National Labor Relations Board in Washington held a hearing. Some miners walked the picket line a few hours a day outside the shafts and then returned to town and got drunk on seventy-five-cent bottles of synthetic wine or moonshine whiskey that sold for two dollars in a Mason jar. Five years ago the mines had shut down throughout the state because of strikes, and the entire labor force had been laid off; but the strike had fallen in late summer, when the tobacco was ripe over in the bluegrass region, and many miners went to Winchester to pick tobacco for a half cent a stick. Now, there was almost no work to be had on the Cumberland plateau. Some men left for Cincinnati and Columbus to look for work as laborers on construction jobs, others caught two or three days a week cutting trees and cleaning picnic areas for the Forest Service. Most men sat on the curb, spit tobacco juice on the hot cement, and put their change together for another bottle of white port. The sheriff arrested at least two dozen men a day on drunk charges or for fighting, and by the time the pool halls and taverns closed at two in the morning, there was usually one shooting or knifing. The one-room sandstone jail next to the courthouse was crowded with drunks. The sheriff brought charges against no one because he didn't have space for all the men he arrested during the day, and he kept a man in jail only four hours to give him time to get sober, and then put him out on the street again.

Perry walked down the tobacco-stained sidewalk past the hardware store. Groups of men in slug caps and tin helmets stopped their conversation and nodded to him as he passed. They shifted the toothpicks in their mouths in silence, with a knowing expression in their eyes. An elderly, fat woman with sagging breasts and varicose veins in her legs touched him on the arm as he stepped off the curb. She wore a faded print dress and her teeth were rotted and stained with snuff.

'We was real sorry to hear about Woodson,' she said.

'Thank you.'

'My old man was there the night they blowed the building. I'll be out to see your mother and bring some soup this week.'

'That's mighty kind of you. She'll be grateful.' He started across the street towards the pawnshop. The sun was bright on the dirty store fronts.

'You keep your chin up, boy, and don't let this thing get you,' she called after him. 'Your mama's going to need you now.'

The window of the pawnshop was filled with rifles, pistols, brass knuckles, banjos, guitars, blackjacks, one dobro, fiddles, mandolins, switchblade knives, watches, and sets of dice. Perry looked at the German Lugers, the .38 specials, the army .45 automatics, and the cheap nickel-plated mail-order revolvers that usually exploded after they had been fired a few times. He counted the money in his wallet and went inside. The interior was dark and smelled bad from lack of ventilation. The owner was a consumptive old man whose white shirt always looked soiled. For thirty years he had run his pawnshop in the same location, and almost every man in the county had borrowed money from him at one time or another, because few miners could get loans at the bank. He could have probably become rich in the pawn business, but his interest rates were lower than the finance company's, and he often gave out more money for a pawned item than it was worth. He slipped a tray of guns into the glass case and looked up at Perry over his rimless spectacles. His skin had a yellow tint to it.

'Well, lookie there. I thought you was off in the Job Corps somewhere,' he said.

'How do, Mr MacIntosh. I come to buy a pistol from you.'

'I saw Mrs James on the street the other day, and she said you was doing real good in your schooling.'

'I ain't in Job Corps no more. How much are those kind you got in the window?'

'She said they was awful proud of you. One of my nephews went off to the Job Corps last week. They flew him way out to California.'

'I got thirty dollars to spend on a pistol. I don't want to go no higher than that.'

'I rather see you come in here to borrow money from me, Perry. Your family could probably use it now, and I wouldn't push you about paying me back till you all get on your feet again. I knowed your daddy all my life, and I'll go out of my way to help you if I can.'

'That ain't why I'm here. How much you want for them Lugers?'

'Those are all in pawn. They ain't for sale.'

'What about these here in the case?'

'Your family ain't got the money for you to spend on guns. You take that thirty dollars and buy those kids some decent food. Get them some eggs and vegetables and whole milk.'

'I'm the one that's got to worry about what my family lacks. Let me see that Buntline revolver.'

'I know what you want it for, and I can't say that I blame you. Maybe if one of my kin was killed in that schoolhouse I'd go after somebody myself. But that won't do your daddy no good, and your people won't have anybody to look after them if you get yourself in jail. I know Woodson didn't keep guns in his house, and he wouldn't want you to do what you got in mind.'

'Every man that comes in here to buy a pistol ain't got but one thing in mind,' Perry said.

'Maybe that's right, but that don't mean you got to be like them. You give yourself a week to think about it, and you'll feel different. The sheriff's going to catch them men sometime, and they'll get punished the way they deserve. The trouble in the coal field's going to pass, and you'll be glad you didn't do nothing without thinking about it first. I seen it get a lot worse around here, but one day the mines always open up again and the shooting and the bombings stop. In a month or so men will be coming in here to get their banjos and fiddles out of pawn, and they'll want to sell me back every gun they bought.'

'I got to go see some people,' Perry said. 'The tag on that Buntline says thirty-five dollars, and here it is. Give me a box of magnum shells to go with it.'

'I hate to sell it to you, Perry.'

'My money ain't no different in color than anybody else's, is it?' Perry laid a row of five-dollar bills out on the counter top. He felt a sense of guilt in spending money that his family needed, but he was intent upon carrying out what he had resolved to do when his father died.

'It's secondhand and I won't put no guarantee on it.' Mr MacIntosh set the blue Colt revolver down on the glass. It was a .22 magnum with a ten-inch barrel mounted on a heavy steel frame for balance, and it was accurate at fifty yards and could hit with the impact of a .38. The front sight had a gold bead on it, and the single-action and hair trigger worked as smoothly as a fine watch.

Perry cocked the hammer and snapped it twice on the empty cylinder. He felt the pistol had been made for his hand. The wood grips fitted into the curve of his palm, and the weight of the gun was balanced so perfectly that he could swing the sight onto a target in a second.

'I want you to keep it for me until this evening. I'll be back for it,' he said.

'I ain't ringing up the money on the register. You can pick up your thirty-five dollars any time you want it, and I'll keep the gun.'

'That's money you can take to the bank now, because I'll be here for my pistol before dark.'

Perry went out on the street again and into the bright sunlight. The cool spring air felt good to his face after the smell of the pawnshop. Parts of the mountains were shaded by clouds, and the treetops were dark blue in the distance. A battered pickup truck loaded with miners and picket signs pulled to the curb in front of the men standing outside the pool hall. The truck was covered with U.M.W. stickers and hand-painted inscriptions that read:

KEEP KENTUCKY UNION
VOTE AGAINST RITE TO WORK
SOLIDARITY FOREVER WITH UNITED MINERS
HOLD OUT FOR A FAIR WAGE
WE WANT SCALE

The men in the back of the truck piled out and went inside the poolroom, and others took their place for the ride back to the picket lines outside the mine shafts. Most of the miners were drunk to some degree, unshaved, their clothes covered with dirt because they hadn't been home in several days; some of them didn't know if they were going on the picket or leaving it. A thin woman with skin the color of old newspaper, holding a crying child in her arms, tried to get her husband out of the truck. She smiled weakly when she spoke, because in that part of Kentucky women didn't go against their husband's will in front of other men. She wore tennis shoes without socks, her legs were covered with hair, and her fingernails were broken to the quick. Her husband, tall and gaunt, with a wet, hand-rolled cigarette in his mouth, stood against the cab of the truck, holding a cardboard union placard in his hand. He sipped out of a whiskey bottle filled with corn liquor.

'We got to go to the food surplus, and I can't mind all the kids,' she said.

'Get on back to the house and stay there till I come home,' he said.

'Wilfred, I just can't–'

'Goddamn, you heard me, woman. I got to do my time on the picket.'

Perry went up the street to the tavern where he knew

the J.W.s would sometimes be during the day. There was broken glass on the sidewalk in front of the door, and someone had knocked out a large triangular section from one of the windows with a pool ball. A barmaid in bluejean shorts and a sweater, with tattoos on her arms, leaned against the doorway and picked her teeth with her little finger. The rank smell of flat beer, cheap wine, cigarette smoke, sweat, bathroom disinfectant, and chili breathed through the ventilating fan above the door.

'Where's the J.W.s at?' Perry said to the girl.

'How should I know? They don't punch no time card with me.'

'Have they been in here today?'

'No, they ain't. And if I had my way they wouldn't get back in here at all.' Her face looked as hard as plaster of Paris.

'What time do they come in off the picket?'

'You talk to the bartender about them two. I got no time for their kind.'

Perry went inside and stood at the end of the long, wooden bar. There were dirty spittoons by the brass foot rail, the mirror behind the bar was cracked and had turned the green of stagnant water from age, and empty beer cases and broken bottles were stacked against one wall. Clouds of smoke floated in the air, and several men were passed out on the tables. The U.M.W. business agent had been buying beers since early morning for miners just off the picket. One man sat on a table with his feet on a rick chair and strummed a guitar with three steel banjo picks. Like every other man in the bar, his face was filmed with soot and covered with three days' growth of beard.

A miner's life is like a sailor's
Aboard a ship to cross the waves,

Every day his life's in danger,
Yet he ventures forth being brave.

Union miners stand together,
Heed no operator's tale,
Keep your hand upon the dollar,
And your eye upon the scale.

The tune was to an old religious ballad called 'Life is Like a Mountain Railroad,' and Perry had heard it sung on every union picket he'd ever been around. He waited an hour for the J.W.s to come in, then ordered a beer and ate a plate of pig's feet when he became hungry. Men who had known his father shook hands with him, and in their faces he could see the look of expectation. In the dried sweat he could smell their desire to see violence against the operator – but a violence that wouldn't involve themselves. The palms of their hands were moist, and their eyes shone dully with the same knowing expression he had seen in the faces of the other men on the street.

'Every man here is with you,' they said.

'There ain't a man in the county that wouldn't take a gun to them three.'

'Even that's too good for them. They ought to get found in a burnt-up car.'

'There wasn't a scab on the street for a week after they blowed the school.'

'You want another beer, boy? The agent's a-buying.'

'The explosion knocked out my window glass. I run out on the porch and seen a car take off down the road. If I'd knowed what happened, I could have pumped holes all over them.'

'By God, we'll catch up to them one day, if we have to go through every town in Kentucky and West Virginia to do it.'

Perry drank two more fifteen-cent draught beers and spoke little to the men around him, because none of them knew anything except that they might eventually get to see another shooting. By mid-afternoon Perry had drunk too much, and the pig's feet had made his stomach vaguely sick. He started to leave when he saw the J.W.s come through the door, each of them framed in the sunlight outside, as though they were cut out of wood. Big J.W. had a hand-rolled cigarette in an empty space between his yellow, horse teeth, and he had a torn sign in his hand that read: THIS MINE SUPPORTS RIGHT TO WORK. Little J.W.'s hard, round stomach pushed against his suspenders, and he wore a crushed felt hat and a pair of overalls that had been cut away around the hips. His deceptive, quiet brown eyes looked straight at Perry without blinking. He pulled a piece of chewing tobacco off his lip and flicked it on the floor with his thumbnail. Perry had always had a sense of fear about the J.W.s since he had last seen them outside the sheriff's office before he went to North Carolina, but now he had no feeling at all towards them other than that they might be useful to him.

'Look what I had to tear off the tipple,' Big J.W. said, and waved the torn cardboard sign in his hand. 'I'd hate to have to feed this to that operator. Somebody put it out by the honey hole in case we run out of toilet paper.'

Everyone in the room laughed, and Little J.W. held up two fingers to the bartender. He and his brother looked like a comic Mutt and Jeff team in their worn, soot-stained trousers, bleached denim shirts, and frayed suitcoats. Little J.W. took a bottle of corn whiskey from his pocket and poured it into an unwashed glass on the bar. He cleared his mouth of tobacco, spat it on the floor next to the spittoon, and drank the whiskey down in one swallow and then chased it with a draught beer. He looked at Perry with a flat expression, as though he had seen him only yesterday rather than five months ago.

'Well, just look who's there, baby brother,' Big J.W. said.

'I thought you was off in school with the colored boys,' Little J.W. said.

'He wouldn't be around no colored people with that Confederate flag on his arm.'

'Who done it?' Perry said.

'Scabs don't come talk to us,' Little J.W. said. 'You don't see none in here, do you? And you won't find none anyplace we're at.'

'We been a-looking for them. Three men nobody ever seen before bought dynamite over in Letcher the day before the bombing and some people saw an old Chevrolet come tearing down the mountain like it was burning alcohol right after the explosion,' Big J.W. said.

'That don't tell me nothing. Who were they?'

'If we knew that, they'd be down in the bottom of an old shaft now,' Little J.W. said. Perry could smell the odor of corn liquor and tobacco juice on his breath. 'Your daddy wasn't the only man killed in that building. My wife's cousin got a board drove through his head.'

'Which operator's a-paying for outside people?'

'Maybe the big one down the street, or maybe everybody in the association is putting in,' Big J.W. said. 'They got men with guns around every hole in the county. They call them special deputies, and every one of them is an ex-convict from Dayton or Detroit.'

'You run off before the real shooting started,' Little

J.W. said. 'They was taking shots at union men like ground squirrels down in Harlan while you was riding airplanes.'

'They would have burned our agent out, but our boys caught them behind the building with the kerosene first.' Big J.W.'s wan, narrow face took on a greenish cast in the dim light of the bar.

'You ain't got to worry about it, anyway,' Little J.W. said. 'When it comes time we'll take care of them men for you.'

'You ain't going to do nothing for me,' Perry said. 'I don't want nobody else mixing in it.'

Little J.W. poured another glass of whiskey and sucked his teeth. 'The last time I seen you go up against something I believe I had to carry you to the car because you was too afraid to move.'

'I didn't wait here all afternoon to hear what you got to say about me,' Perry said. 'It don't interest me. If you find out where they're at, you tell me. And I ain't fooling when I say I don't want no help from either one of you all.'

Perry finished his beer and ordered another one. The glass was beaded with moisture, and under the foam the beer looked like amber light.

'You must have had your head in the jug too long today,' Little J.W. said.

'I just give you warning. Don't mix in it. It wasn't none of your blood kin that got killed in there.'

'I reckon you better pick every word you say pretty careful,' Little J.W. said. His eyes lost their quiet, doelike quality and became as sharp and bright as agate. His lips were a tight line across his face.

'You got no call to get in something that ain't your business.'

'A man don't talk to me like that more than once.'

129

'I ain't saying no more to you. Find out the ones that done it, and I'll be in your debt. But don't take up what's mine to do.'

'Baby brother's just telling you that one man can't do it by himself,' Big J.W. said. 'You got three of them up against you and maybe more. It don't hurt to have a couple more men with you.'

'You never done me no favors before, and I ain't asking you for one now.' Perry drank his beer glass to the bottom. He knew he was getting drunk, but he was already past the point of caring or remembering the long, sick weekend he had spent after the night he was tattooed in Asheville.

'Like Little J.W. said, there's more people than you that had somebody hurt in that schoolhouse. If my car hadn't broke down I might have been a-setting on top of that charge with them other fellers. So I figure that gives us the right to do what we want with them men.'

'What you got made up in your mind is one thing, but you heered what I said.' Perry clicked his glass on the bar for another beer.

'How long you figure you can keep talking like that, boy?' Little J.W. said. He had his bottle of whiskey half raised to his mouth. His face had grown ashen, and his jaws worked with each breath, as though he were chewing. His eyes seemed to shrink and recede into his forehead.

Perry paid the bartender and wiped the foam off the beer with the side of his hand. He said nothing and upended the glass. He could see the red, twisted scar on his nose in the mirror behind the bar.

'You ain't looking at me. Turn around,' Little J.W. said.

'Let it go, honey. The sheriff's set on putting us in jail now,' Big J.W. said.

'Look at me! Then open that mouth again. You set in a government camp and come back here and tell us what we're going to do and what we ain't. The man don't walk that tells me what to do.' His voice wasn't loud, but the heated intensity of it made other people in the bar stop talking.

'This ain't the place,' Big J.W. said. He rested his long, narrow hand over his brother's arm.

'Goddamn you boy, are you going to look at me or am I going to have to lay hold of you?'

The bartender moved down the counter and placed his hand on something under the bar; his face never changed expression and he looked straight ahead.

'I didn't come for trouble with you, but I ain't afraid of you no more, either,' Perry said. He turned and looked at the hatred in Little J.W.'s eyes and remembered the story about how Little J.W. had almost beaten his uncle to death with a fire poker and left him to die in the front yard.

'You ain't going to have the chance to be afraid.'

Perry couldn't see a sag in either one of Little J.W.'s pockets from the weight of a pistol, but he knew that Little J.W. always carried a short bowie hunting knife, filed sharp on an emory wheel, in a leather scabbard inside his overalls. Perry kept his hand on the handle of his beer mug in case he had to swing.

'We're a-going down the street, baby brother. Finish it another time,' Big J.W. said.

'It's getting done right now.'

'I done told you I don't want trouble,' Perry said. 'But do what you're a-thinking and your hand won't clear your pocket.'

'You young sonofabitch, you bought it now,' Little J.W. said.

'My place ain't getting tore up on account of you all

again,' the bartender said. He was a big man with a granite head, a large pock-marked nose, and a thick ear. His scalp was shaved bald, and there was a deep blue scar that ran across his cranium. He had been a wrestler in Nashville until someone had hit him in the head with a metal chair. 'Take it outside or I'll pick up what I got in my hand.'

'Go ahead and draw it, you bastard,' Little J.W. said.

'Leave it where it's at, we're going,' Big J.W. said. He pulled his brother away from the bar.

'You're letting them wipe their feet on us,' Little J.W. said.

'I ain't giving the sheriff no excuse to put us in jail.'

'Just get the hell out,' the bartender said.

'You made a mistake sticking your face in this,' Little J.W. said. 'I hope you paid up your fire insurance.'

'I ain't waiting on you much longer,' the bartender said.

Big J.W. pulled his brother out the door onto the street. They argued for a moment in the square of light before the doorway, then climbed up on the union pickup truck that was headed back to the mines. Perry felt a drop of perspiration form on the corner of his eyebrow and run down the side of his face. He cleared his throat and spit dryly on the floor, and then drank down the rest of his beer. It felt like ice in his stomach. He wondered if truly he had not been afraid, or if the nervous twitch in his leg muscles and stomach was just a symptom of the anxiety that men felt when they were very near sudden violence. He knew that it had been close. If the bartender had not intervened, or if Big J.W. had not been there, the knife would have been out and it would not have been just a threat followed by more words; it would have flashed at Perry's stomach as quickly as a snake's head. He realized that his shirt was wet with sweat and his hand had left a damp print on the bar. The bartender drew another draught and set it before him.

People began talking again, and the guitar player rang the steel picks on the strings and sang:

Watch the rocks, they're a-falling daily,
Careless miners always fail.
Keep your hand upon the dollar,
And your eye upon the scale.

Perry sipped the beer until the hard, tense feeling inside him began to fade. The barmaid came back from the front doorway and leaned against the counter in front of him. Her face had an unnatural shine in the light. She took a cigarette from a pack tucked inside her shorts and waited for him to light it.

'Ain't you got a match?' she said.

He handed her a book of matches from his shirt pocket. Her eyes were black in the flame.

'You're the first I seen to put one of them two in his place,' she said. 'I'd like to see them both laid out behind here some night.'

'I didn't put nobody in his place.'

'There ain't many men around here that's gone up against Little J.W.,' the man next to Perry said. He wore a dirty straw hat and there was a streak of chili on the side of his mouth. 'I seen him beat up on a feller with a chair leg once, just for looking at him the wrong way. Woodson would be proud of what you done.'

'I didn't do nothing,' Perry said. 'I don't want no more trouble with him. He'd a-cut me open if the bartender didn't stop him.'

'You wasn't backing off from him none, and we all seen it,' the man said.

'I didn't say nothing against him, and I ain't a-doing it now. If he's got it in him for trouble, that's his business. But I ain't the cause of it.'

'I've put up with that little sonofabitch since I come to work here, and I ain't seen another man talk back in his face yet,' the girl said.

Perry knew the stories that would spread about the barroom incident with Little J.W. By that night people would say that he had backed down both the J.W.s, and they would remember little of what actually happened. In telling the story to other miners who came off the picket, they would say nothing of the sweated areas on his shirt, his moist palms, or that rigid, naked feeling in his stomach when he waited for Little J.W. to bring his knife out of his scabbard. The next day the story would be even more distorted, and then someone would stop Little J.W. on the street and casually mention that he'd heard something about a seventeen-year-old ex-Job Corps boy backing him down before a room full of people. Later Perry would have to face the J.W.s somewhere again. He would have to tell them that he had nothing to do with the rumor and then be accused of lying and cowardice, or fight both of them with any weapon he could get his hands on – neither of which he wanted to do. He was determined not to take any more abuse or threats from them; but even if he fought one or both of them and won, they would eventually catch him alone on a road at night, and the next day someone would find him lying in the weeds or thrown down the hollow.

'I got to find a job, and I ain't got time to worry about that pair,' he said.

'What did Little J.W. mean about carrying you to a car?' the man said.

'Go ask him. I don't know what goes on in his head.' He drank off his beer and had another. His head was starting to reel, and when he raised his glass he spilled part of the beer over his chin.

'You shut the little bastard's face up,' the girl said.

'Is there any strip work a-going on?' Perry said to the man in the straw hat.

'Buddy, there ain't no work anywhere around here,' another man said. He wore a tin hat, with a pair of colored goggles pulled up on its elastic strap above the brim. There was a heavy, brown mole in the corner of his eye that made him blink constantly, and his mouth was discolored from chewing snuff.

'A working man can't find no job except driving whiskey up to Ohio and Michigan, and the A.B.C.s cotched half of the runners before they got to Lexington,' the man in the straw hat said. 'They give a man a year at Frankfort if they catch him with just a couple of drops in a bottle that ain't got a tax stamp on it. The federal people is even worse. Last January they got my uncle going over the Ohio bridge, and they sent him down to Atlanta for three years.'

'Ain't the Forest Service got any jobs?' Perry said.

'They won't hire no fire crews till it gets dry, and the happy-pappies is doing all the work on the trails.'

'It might pay a feller to string a couple of fires,' the man with the mole in the corner of his eye said. 'I reckon they'd be handing out some work if we burned up a couple hundred acres of their timber.'

'What they paying a runner now?' Perry said. There was another full glass of beer on the counter before him, and he couldn't remember if he had ordered it or if the union business agent was setting up the bar again.

'I heered fifty dollars, if you ain't got to go across the state line. I guess the fellers a-carrying it all the way to Detroit in their own car are splitting with the still. But the money ain't worth no three years in the pen.'

'It ain't like it used to be,' the man in the straw hat said. 'I never knowed them to give a feller more than thirty days on the honor farm his first time around. Now they fine you for every dime you got and lock you up for a big stretch, too.'

Perry was unsteady on his feet, and he held onto the bar with one hand when he drank from his glass. He couldn't remember how long he had been in the bar. Outside, the sun cast long shadows over the blue tops of the mountains, and the air had begun to chill. The pickup truck returned from the picket line, and more miners came into the bar. Their eyes were red with alcohol.

'What time is it? I got to pick up something at the pawnshop,' Perry said.

'Take some of this. Mr MacIntosh ain't going nowhere. I don't think he ever gets out of that place except to drop his britches out back.'

'I better not drink no whiskey.'

'It's good corn. It was kept buried in a charcoal barrel for five months. You can't tell no difference from it and red whiskey except for the color.'

Perry took the bottle and drank. He could see small threadlike flecks of charcoal inside, and the taste was like turpentine and corn meal. He chased the whiskey down with a beer and had another swallow from the bottle. He shivered slightly when he felt the raw heat of the alcohol hit his stomach.

'Drink some more of that and you might try a little

bit of that jenny-barner,' the man in the straw hat said. The girl in the shorts had moved farther down the bar.

'Where's the head at?' Perry said.

'Right in back. Don't fall in that honey hole. We couldn't find the last feller that dropped down in it.' Both men roared, but their laughter had a dry, phlegmy quality to it.

Perry walked unsteadily towards the back of the bar. He could feel his heart beating faster from the whiskey, and drops of sweat formed on his forehead. He pushed open the plank door that was held in place with a metal spring, and the odor that arose from the hole in the board seat made his eyes water. The small room had been built onto the back of the bar over a ten-foot drop to the slope below. An open pit, filled with creosote, had been dug in the ground, and the overflowing drainage ran into a creek down in the gulley. Through the cracks in the boards Perry could see piles of broken bottles in the creek bed, bags of garbage, a rusted bedframe, part of a car, and hundreds of beer cans. He buttoned his trousers and went back into the bar towards the front door. His face was flushed, and a noise like an electrical short kept humming in his head. It took all his effort to walk in a straight line onto the street.

The light was fading beyond the rim of the mountains, and dusk had settled into the hollow. The ridges had turned from dark green to purple, and in the east the sun's reflection was scarlet on the clouds. There was a sulfurous smell in the air, and Perry knew there would be an electric storm by nightfall. One of his uncles had been killed by lightning while leading a pair of mules along the mountain crest above his cabin. The force of the shock had blown off both his shoes. Perry thought about walking the half mile to the first hollow from town where Bee Hatfield lived; then he remembered that he had to go to the pawnshop before it closed, and he forgot about the storm. He felt the sidewalk tipping under his feet as he moved down the street through the groups of men putting change together for another bottle of white port.

Across the street Perry saw the office of the Lockwood Mining Company, one of the few in the area that had never signed a union contract. Two expensive new cars were parked outside, and a company deputy, with a badge and a revolver on his hip, stood by the front door. A leather-covered blackjack hung out of his back pocket. Two miners in raincoats with picket signs in their hands walked back and forth on the sidewalk. A man in a blue business suit, tie, and white shirt walked out the door and through the pickets as though they were not there. As he got into his automobile, Perry saw the light gleam on his silver cuff links and polished black shoes. Perry didn't know his name, but he knew that he was a lawyer from somewhere up North who came to town and stayed at the association president's house whenever a big strike threatened the coal field. Once, when the union thought it had won a contract and a wage increase, this man had the case transferred for a later hearing before the Labor Relations Board in Washington, and nothing more was heard of the matter for nine months. Most of the miners couldn't hold out, and they went back to work at their old scale. Perry felt a sudden intense hatred of this Northern lawyer, his new car, the company deputy by the front door of the office, and the men inside who were devising ways to break the strike before their stock fell too far and their investors in New York pulled out on them. His father had been wrong when he said that fighting the operator had never helped the miner. Violence in kind was the only thing the association understood. They owned the courts, the special deputies, the tax assessors, and maybe even some of the industrial referees, and when a politician came to the plateau to campaign for Congress he always stayed at the association president's house on the hill. They had money that could reach all the way to the governor's mansion in Frankfort, or National Guard troops would never have been sent into Harlan to protect scabs and to break strikes. A company deputy never went to the penitentiary for shooting a miner, but union men were jailed for trespassing when they walked the picket in front of a shaft.

The rain began to fall evenly on the street. In the north lightning struck into the hollows, and a black thundercloud rolled over the top of the mountains. A white bolt split the sky apart and exploded in a ball of fire on the ridge above town. A few moments later flames were burning around several trees and spreading into the undergrowth with the wind. Perry pulled the bill of his cloth cap down over his eyes and walked under the eaves of the buildings to protect himself from the rain. In the west he could see the last afterglow of the sun fade beyond the mountains; then the storm seemed to spread from one horizon to another, and dark clouds swirled overhead like pieces of torn, black cotton.

The corn whiskey had made his mouth dry and he wanted another drink. He went into the first poolroom he passed and drank two draughts in five minutes. He felt he could pour down every bottle of beer in the bar and still drink more. It seemed as though the energy in his body burned up the alcohol as soon as it hit his stomach. Before he left, two men asked him if the story was true that one of the J.W.s had backed off from him that afternoon.

'The man that told you it was a liar,' Perry said. 'You go get somebody else cut up.'

On the way to the pawnshop, he had another beer and two shots of wine at a bar farther up the street; his clothes were soaked through, and his shoes were full of water. He couldn't open the front door of the pawnshop; then he realized that he was pulling it shut against the jamb. His eyes were glazed and his body had no sensation in it. The wind crashed the door back against the wall when he entered, and the rain swept across the floor.

'I want my gun,' he said.

'Shut that door,' Mr MacIntosh said. His shoulders were bent with the weight of two heavy ledgers in his arms.

'I got to get to Bee Hatfield's before the electricity starts.' Perry swayed back and forth on his feet.

Mr MacIntosh set the books down, came around the counter, and closed the door. The front of his dirty white shirt was splattered with rain drops.

'You must have drank up every dollar in your pocket,' he said.

'Wrap up the shells in a paper bag so they don't get wet.'

'You won't ever make it to Bee's. You'll get hit by lightning or fall down on the road somewhere and get run over.'

'That's my lookout. Where's the gun at?'

'I can't let you have it when you're drunk. You can sleep on the cot in back tonight, or you can go home and come for it tomorrow,' Mr MacIntosh said.

'I paid for it. It ain't yours no more, and you ain't got the right to say when I can take it.'

'It will still be here in the morning. There ain't a lot going to change between now and then.'

'Goddamn it, you give me that pistol.'

'Who you got to shoot tonight? You want to blow holes in the Lockwood office? Them three men that killed your daddy will like that. They won't have to worry about you for the next six months while you're in the county jail.'

Perry saw the long blue barrel of the Buntline revolver and the box of shells inside the glass case. He walked forward off balance, reached over the counter, and tried to slide back the glass door.

'You ain't going to do this in my shop, Perry. I'll call the sheriff on you,' Mr MacIntosh said.

'You do what you goddamn like.'

'Woodson was too good a friend of mine for me to have his boy put in jail. Don't push me into it.'

'I ain't made you do nothing. You wouldn't give me what's mine.' Perry wrapped his cloth cap over his fist and shattered the glass counter top. He felt a sharp pain slide across the inside of his palm, and he rolled his cap up in his hand and clenched it tightly to stop the blood. He reached inside the broken case with his left hand and picked up the pistol from among the splinters of glass.

'You don't know when a man's trying to help you,' Mr MacIntosh said.

'I'll be back tomorrow and pay for the case.' Perry slipped the box of magnum cartridges into his back pocket.

He walked out the door into the black rain while Mr MacIntosh dialed the telephone. Perry could hardly see to the other side of the street. He held the pistol loosely in one hand at his side and stumbled along the sidewalk. He was drunker than he had been in

Asheville. The yellow light from inside the mining office reflected off the wet street. The deputy still stood by the front door with his raincoat pulled up over his head. Perry had little awareness of what he was doing as he sat down on the curb and took six cartridges from the box in his pocket. He dropped his cap into the gutter and slipped the shells one by one into the cylinder. The blood from his cut palm diffused in the rain and ran in streams along the inside of his forearm. He fell back on the curb when he tried to get up. Finally, he got to his feet and walked down the middle of the street towards the mining office. He could see the shadows of several men against the window glass, and he put the gun on half cock under his thumb.

'What in the hell are you doing, Perry?' somebody called at him from the front door of a poolroom.

'Mind your goddamn business.'

The deputy looked up from under his raincoat, and his hand went to the revolver on his hip. Farther up the street a car pulled away from the curb in front of the courthouse and roared towards Perry. In the headlights the rain looked like spun glass. As the car neared him he thought he was going to be run down, but his legs wouldn't move under him. He pulled back the hammer of the pistol to full cock and raised it level with the windshield. Then he saw the red spotlight on the driver's door and the tall radio aerial whipping back and forth on the rear fender. The car slammed to a stop at an angle between him and the mining office, and the sheriff opened the door and lifted his huge weight out of the driver's seat.

'Lower the gun and let that hammer down slow,' he said.

'I didn't know it was you. I thought one of them scabs was trying to get me.' Perry used both thumbs to ease the hammer back into its place. He held the revolver sideways in his palm, with his fingers over the cylinder.

'Set it on the car.'

'I got no reason to go against you. You ain't got to worry about trouble from me.' He placed the pistol on the car fender. The sheriff picked it up, shucked out each cartridge on the street, and stuck the barrel down inside his belt.

'Mr Mac don't ever call me unless somebody gives him a real bad time, and you must have done just that. Get in the car.'

In the distance Perry saw the fire from the ball of lightning burning in the trees. He wiped the blood from his hand on the front of his shirt. The rain beat on his bare head and ran down into his shirt collar.

'You putting me in jail?'

'That's right.'

'I ain't broke no law on the street. I told him at the pawnshop I'd pay for his glass.'

'If I hadn't stopped you before you got to the mining office, I'd be arresting you for something else or picking you up off the street. Don't make me put you in the car, son.' The sheriff's khaki uniform was streaked from the rain.

'I can't spend no time in jail.'

'You'll get out in the morning, and maybe you'll have a little more sense then.'

Perry pulled open the car door and sat back in the seat. His wet clothes were like ice against his body. The sheriff backed the car around in the street and headed towards the courthouse. His stomach reached almost to the steering wheel. His great legs and buttocks spread over half the seat, and his breath expelled with a dry rasp while he drove.

'You had warning from me before Perry, and I don't reckon I have to tell you what I'll do if I catch you trying to carry out what you got in mind. I can't hold you for the gun because you didn't have it concealed, but I'll send you to Frankfort if I even hear you're in on blowing a tipple or burning out the operator. I ain't going to stand for no more of it in my county.'

'I ain't done nothing but get drunk. My daddy didn't do nothing, either, but they killed him, and they're still out there somewhere.'

'I had a lot of respect for Woodson, and if you give me time I promise you I'll get them three that did it.'

'I ain't seen a company man go to the pen yet for killing a miner.'

'You'll see it this time, even if I got to walk over everybody in the association to do it. But you try to do my job for me, and I'll put you away with them.'

The sheriff parked the car in front of the courthouse and cut the headlights. Thunder rolled through the hollows, and the poplars and white oaks shook in the wind. The courthouse lawn was already flooded, and wine bottles and beer cans floated in the gutters. Perry got out of the car and started toward the one-story sandstone jail.

'Go into my office,' the sheriff said.

'You said you was putting me in jail.'

'You'll get there in due time. Don't worry about that. I just don't want you bleeding on my mattresses.'

Inside the office Perry soaked his hand in the washbasin. The cut on his palm was ragged and blue, like a wound from a rusted nail. The blood began to coagulate on the edges of the torn skin. The sheriff took Perry's Colt revolver from his belt and tucked it in his desk drawer.

'Do I get my gun back tomorrow?' Perry said.

'You're set on making me come after you again, ain't you?'

'Any trouble we got was pushed on us. There wouldn't none of this started if they'd let us alone and treated us decent.'

'The best thing that could happen to you would be to get on the first bus back to that Job Corps center. I already heered that you was almost in it with Little J.W., and that's the best way I know to get down in the back some night. He ain't a man to forget anything. He could kill you and drink a beer while he was doing it.'

'Are you going to give me my pistol back?'

'I'd be doing you a favor if I throwed it in the creek. But you'd probably spend the money your family needs on another one, because you're stubborn and you get your mind set on something till you can't think no other way, just like every one of the Hatfields. Stop dripping blood on my floor and wrap your hand in that towel.'

The sheriff put a piece of cotton over Perry's cut, and wound his palm with tape; then he took him through a side door to the jail. The rain drove at an angle to the ground, and the water on the lawn came over the tops of Perry's shoes. There was no window glass in the jail, and the men inside had propped pieces of cardboard behind the bars. A fire of newspaper and twigs, broken off the trees outside, burned on the concrete floor. The sheriff unlocked the chain on the barred front door.

'Out in the morning,' Perry said.

'I told you that, didn't I?' the sheriff said. 'And I keep my word. I ain't got enough room to keep anybody for more than a night, anyhow.' He closed the door behind Perry and fastened the lock back on the chain.

The inside of the jail was filled with smoke from the fire. Some men slept on dirty tick mattresses and others were still drinking from bottles in the firelight. A sickening smell came from a large bucket in one corner that was used for a bathroom. One man was going through the D.T.s, and he moaned loudly and rolled about on his mattress. He pulled his knees up to his chin and shook all over. Someone tried to give him a drink of wine, but his eyes stared wildly, and he struck at the man with his fist. Perry sat back against one wall as far away as he could get from the bucket in the corner. It must not have been emptied in days. The stone was hard and cold against his back, and he tried to stretch out on the floor and sleep; but his head spun from the beer and whiskey, a man stepped on his stomach, and one of the drinkers at the fire took some newspaper and went to the corner to relieve himself. Perry pulled a piece of cardboard off the window to let in the air, and the rain swept across the man sleeping on the concrete. Perry pressed his face against the bars and breathed the sweet smell of the spring storm and the new grass on the lawn.

'Close up that goddamn window,' somebody yelled.

Perry fitted the cardboard back in place and sat down again, with his arms folded across his legs. He felt the thick nausea of a hangover beginning to grow in his body. There wasn't enough heat in the room to dry his clothes, and his skin was pale from the cold. After an hour of the drunken voices and the rancid odor of unwashed bodies and tobacco spittle, he lost consciousness of time and kept expecting the sun's first light to break over the rim of the mountain and flood through the jail window. Then his head sagged on his chest, and he could not tell if the voices he heard were from inside himself or the men around him. During the night bottles were thrown at the windows, men fist fought, and someone overturned the bucket in the corner, but Perry lay on the floor in a sick stupor and dreamed nightmares about the schoolhouse exploding in flames and three men, with hideous, laughing faces, roaring down the mountain in an automobile through the moonless dark.

chapter eight

The brown leaves were deep on the forest floor, wet with dew, and the long white trunks of the beech trees rose high above Perry's head. In the light of the false dawn he could see the edges of the limestone cliffs on the far side of the hollow, silhouetted against the purple sky. There was little undergrowth because of the lack of sunlight and rainfall through the tall green canopy of trees overhead; and the great outcroppings of rock glistened faintly in the mist. The floor of the hollow dipped away from him to a creek that ran over a waterfall into the Kentucky River, and he could hear the water rushing from the springs farther up the mountain through the drainages into the creek bed. The rocks and cliffs seemed to change shape as the red strip of light on the horizon began to swell into the sky, and the vapor in the bottom of the hollow flattened and settled low over the stream. He smelled the oak logs burning under the still in the rock house and the coffee grounds boiling in the tin pot over the fire. As the first sunlight glowed through the trees he saw a whitetail deer and several groundhogs and rabbits drinking from the stream. The water was dark blue in the twisting current; then it changed to green, and he could see the pebbles washed smooth in the sandy bed.

The smoke from the fire in the rock house curled up around the fifty-gallon cooker, collected briefly on the ceiling, and strained off from under the ledge into the wind. One man fed logs into the flames, and another stirred the mash with a five-foot tapered branch from a poplar tree, shaved clean with a knife and wrapped with barbed wire at the fork to turn the corn meal, water, and sugar. The two mash barrels were pinned rectangularly with oak logs and shored with dead leaves to contain the heat and to hurry the fermentation. A metal extension ran from the cooker to the thumping keg, a small barrel that collected water from the vapor and allowed the alcohol to rise and condense in the coil. There was a hand-beveled wooden plug in the bottom of the thumping keg for bleeding off the excess water. The steam coughed and pumped through the metal arm and dripped off the coil onto a strip of peeled birch bark, which had been rolled into a funnel inside the neck of a gallon milk bottle to cut the taste of corn in the whiskey.

During the eighteenth and nineteenth centuries this particular area had been used by whiskey makers because there was a spring in almost every rock house in the hollow. The entrance through the cliff walls was right by the Kentucky River, down which they used to float their whiskey in kegs on big flatboats onto the Ohio and eventually down the Mississippi to New Orleans, where people had acquired a taste for Kentucky bourbon. At that time the mountaineer could take all the game and fish he needed from the forests and streams, the land was so rich that it grew almost any kind of crop, and he made whiskey so he could have a few hard dollars to buy shot and powder, and occasionally something from a traveling drummer. Then when most of the game was gone, the streams polluted, and the land ruined by the mines, whiskey making became his sole income. The hollow was still the best place in a three-county area to set up a still because there was no access to it except over a mountain that even mules had difficulty climbing. One rutted dirt road led to the base of the mountain; and a man on top of the ridge could see for miles in every direction. If someone from the A.B.C. or a federal tax agent started up the steep incline towards the gap in the cliff wall, the still would be torn down in minutes and hidden, the mash barrels emptied into the creek, and the fifty-dollar copper coil buried in a rock house.

Perry knew every cave, rock formation, ledge, and drainage in the hollow. The Warriors' Trail, which Daniel Boone had followed into the Ohio Valley after he opened Cumberland Gap, ran right by the hollow, and Perry had dug up handfuls of arrowheads and stone knives in the silt floors of rock houses where Indian braves had buried them. Since the time he was a small boy he had also searched here for the lost silver mine of John Swift, an English sailor who came to Kentucky through Pound Gap in 1761 and worked a vein of ore in a cave for eight years. Swift took his smelted silver back into Virginia each winter, but several times he was attacked by Shawnee Indians, who stole his horses, and he had to bury seventy thousand dollars' worth of silver on the trail. In 1769 he murdered his partners as they slept outside the mine, and he sealed the entrance with a rock the size of a salt keg, covered it with earth and locust branches, and left over two hundred thousand dollars in smelted ore inside the shaft. Later, he was imprisoned as a revolutionist by the British and during the years in jail he lost his eyesight and was never able to find the mine again, although he searched for it until his death in

1800. However, a map and part of his diary had been passed down through the generations, and Perry's aunt had read a copy of it to him so many times when he was a boy that he knew it by heart. He had found some of the Shawnee turkey tracks and crows' feet cut in rock that Swift described, and once he found part of an old smelter half buried in a cave. Swift had written of a window in the mountain close to the mine, and at the head of the hollow was a natural bridge that let in light through the cliff wall. Perry was sure that the mine was somewhere along one of the ledges, but the land had changed over the years, snow slides had brought avalanches of rock and earth down over the base of the mountains, and the wind had eroded away many of the Indian carvings.

The sun rose above the ridge, and the grey light thinned through the trees, and blue shadows from the trunks fell on the forest floor. Sitting on the damp leaves Perry felt a chill, and he went inside the rock house and sat by the fire under the still. The oak logs scorched up yellow and red over the rusted cooker. He picked up the tin pot from the fire, poured some coffee out over the rim to cool the metal, and drank. There were eight army jerry cans of whiskey, each containing five gallons, lined up against the back wall. They had loaded eight more on the mule in the dark hours before dawn and had taken them down the mountain to the 1953 Chevrolet, with the GMC truck engine, hidden in the trees by the river. A tall, old man with white hair bobbed on his neck, a hat with the brim pulled down all around his head, emptied the full milk bottle into one of the cans. His long underwear showed at his neck under the three shirts he wore, and his overalls were held on by one torn strap across his shoulder. His stubble of white whiskers was as coarse as wire, and the big knuckles on his hands almost stuck through his wrinkled skin. He was Lemuel McGoffin, and he had been making whiskey in this hollow as long as anyone could remember. He had been sent to the federal honor farm four times, fined for five hundred dollars twice, and once he had been sentenced to Atlanta for three years, but was released early because of his age. Most of the federal tax agents knew him well enough to stop and talk with him on the street in Richmond or Winchester, and the Forest Service had offered him a permanent job as crew leader on the trails if he would stop moonshining. But he had never done any other type of work; his Scottish ancestors had made whiskey with Daniel Boone when Kentucky was first settled, and he believed that he violated no moral law in continuing what his father and grandfather had done.

'That's the last of it,' he said as he pulled the copper coil loose from the thumping keg. The coil was the most valuable piece of equipment on the still, and he couldn't afford to have it chopped into bits if an agent happened to find the rock house while he was gone and there was no lookout up on the ridge. 'Go catch up the mule and we'll move the rest of it down to the car.'

Noah Combs, bent and crippled from the bullet wounds he had received in front of a mine when he tried to dynamite the loading platform, shuffled off towards the bottom of the hollow, where the mule was tied by the creek. One of his arms stuck out stiffly in a crook at an angle to his side, there was a scar the size of a quarter in his cheek where a bullet had knocked out all his teeth in one side of his mouth, and a splinter of lead still lay imbedded in his spine, which caused him to walk as though he had a great block of concrete on his shoulders. He caught the mule by the reins and led him back up towards the rock house. Noah couldn't hold his head erect, and his eyes bulged from under his brow as he worked his way to the top of the incline. Half of his facial muscles were paralyzed, and the skin along one jaw had deadened to a grey color and had begun to peel in dry scales.

They heard the sound of an airplane in the distance; then the droning of the engine came closer, and through the tops of the trees they saw the plane bank out of the sun and begin a low sweep over the hollow. The pilot cut back his speed and glided on the wind currents above the ragged cliffs. Perry could see the silver haze of the propeller spinning in the light and the black silhouette of the pilot in the cockpit. The plane arched up high in the sky like a crop duster, turned, and headed back for another pass over the hollow.

'It's the A.B.C.!' McGoffin yelled. 'Get that mule in the rock house! Don't look up at the sky, neither. They can see the light on your face.'

He and Perry pulled back inside the limestone overhang and threw dirt on the fire under the cooker, while Combs labored uphill with the mule. The animal was spooked from the noise of the airplane and was jerking sideways. The dirt, moist from the spring in the back of the rock house, spit and hissed on the flames, and steam fanned out in the breeze.

'Hit that mule between the eyes and get him in here!' the old man said.

'I can't hold him,' Combs said. His crooked arm looked grotesque as he pulled at the reins.

'I ain't a-taking another stretch in Atlanta for no ten-dollar shithog of a mule.' McGoffin picked up a short, thin oak log from the pile of wood near the cooker and moved fast down the incline. His move-ments were stiff and awkward because of his age, but his body was still strong from years of toiling up and down the mountains. He jerked the reins out of Combs' hands and slashed the log down between the mule's ears. The mule's mouth convulsed and pulled back from his yellow teeth, and he tried to bolt to the bottom of the hollow. McGoffin struck him hard twice more in the same place, and Perry could hear the wood 'thunk' against the bone. The mule's eyes were wide with pain and fear. 'Now move, you sonofabitch, or I'll beat your goddamn skull in.' The mule thudded his hooves into the earth and struggled after McGoffin while Combs whipped his flanks with a switch.

'They'll see the smoke. The breeze ain't carrying it off,' Perry said.

'They ain't ever spotted me from the air yet,' McGoffin said as he pulled the mule into the rock house, the log still in one hand. 'They got me before because they found a trail or they'd paid somebody to tell them where the still was at. But that ain't going to happen again because I don't come up through the hollow the same way twice and I don't stay set up in the same rock house more than a week. Put them branches across the opening.'

Perry picked up the green poplar limbs they had cut the night before and propped them against the roof of the rock house at the entrance. The old man and Combs kicked more dirt over the remaining embers in the fire, and ground the cinders under their feet. The plane dipped down over the ridge above their heads, the engine gunning in the updrafts, and roared through the hollow just a few feet higher than the canopy of trees. The leaves shook in the backwash from the propeller, and the mule reared sideways and kicked his hooves into the wall of the rock house. The plane was so low that Perry could see the metallic shine of the guy wires on the wings.

'You think he seen us? The smoke's still a-hanging in the trees,' he said.

'We ain't going to be here to find out. Get that mule loaded,' McGoffin said. 'They raid this time and they ain't going to get nothing for their trouble except a rusted-out cooker and two empty mash barrels.'

'They might get us going out,' Combs said. 'Maybe we ought to hide the load and pick it up later.'

'I don't dump five-hundred-dollars' worth of whiskey for some loggers to find. My boy's hid out on the ridge, and there ain't nobody getting into the holler without him seeing them first.'

The smoke from the dead fire collected behind the poplar branches over the entrance and hung in the air.

'I don't want to be around no more shooting,' Combs said. His body was twisted like a dwarf's in the shadows.

'Put the brace on the mule.'

'I ain't getting shot up again for all the whiskey in Kentucky.'

'You been paid for a full day's work and I expect to get it,' McGoffin said. 'I taken corn out of this hollow for thirty-five years and I ain't got shot yet. I reckon they know better than to draw a gun on a McGoffin. They do it once and I'll string fires all over their goddamn forest.'

Before the plane reached the end of the hollow it rolled upwards and slipped sideways in the wind stream over the next ridge. The yellow wings flashed in the sun and then dipped out of sight beyond the timberline.

'Them federal men got scopes on their rifles. They could knock us down from a half mile,' Combs said.

'I'd say that would be a real mistake on their part.'
McGoffin picked up a rifle leaning against the wall and
slung it over his shoulder by the strap. It was an old
bolt-action .30-.40 Kraig, with the box magazine on
the right-hand side of the chamber.

'I still say dump the load. It ain't worth it,' Combs
said.

'I put you on at the still because you couldn't get no
work any place else. Now if you ain't going to do what
I say, you can get off this mountain and forget what
you seen in here,' McGoffin said. 'I ain't got time to
mess with you.'

'A man don't like to get shot up.'

'I can't hear the plane no more,' Perry said.

'Maybe he just let us think he didn't see us,' Combs
said.

'That's right, or maybe he was taking a piss up there
in a tin can and he wasn't looking down here at all.
Get that goddamn jackass loaded. Perry, hide the
thumping keg in them rocks across the creek.'

Perry pulled the beveled wooden peg out of the
bottom of the keg and drained the scalding water on
the rock house floor; then he disconnected the arm
from the cooker and lifted the keg up on his shoulder.
The smell of distilled corn meal was strong in the air.
He walked over the dead leaves, through the trees, to
the creek bed. The light through the beeches and
poplars was green on the forest floor, and the water
was brown over the rocks in the stream. He put the
keg between two limestone boulders, covered the
crevice with branches and leaves, and then returned to
the rock house.

Combs had laid two gunny sacks across the mule's
back, and he set the pack brace over the sacks and
pulled the cinch tight around the mule's belly. The

mule drew air into his lungs to expand his body against the cinch, and McGoffin kicked him hard in the ribs. 'I ought to boil you down for glue you sonofabitch,' he said.

'You don't want to move the cooker?' Perry said.

'Let them have it. It ain't worth a shit, no how. Pour the mash out and bury it with the sugar sacks. It won't look like nobody's made whiskey in here for months.'

Perry pulled the oak pinning loose from around the two mash barrels and kicked them over with his foot. The corn splattered out in a wet pile on the dirt and drained over the lip of the rock house floor into the hollow. His eyes burned from the smell. He took an army entrenching tool and threw most of the corn out into the undergrowth and covered the rest with earth. Then he folded up the shovel into the position of a hoe and chopped a hole in the ground to bury the sugar sacks. In the back of the cave was a squared poplar trunk, which loggers had hollowed out years ago to use as a trough for their animals. McGoffin had propped it under the flow from the limestone spring to collect water for the still. Perry flipped it over backwards with one hand and dragged it outside into some brush.

'I hear that plane again,' Combs said.

'You don't hear nothing,' McGoffin said. 'Grab up them cans and get them on the mule. We're a-running late now.'

Perry looked towards the top of the ridge near the entrance to the hollow for any sign from the old man's son.

'Boy, don't you think I got my eye on the same place?' McGoffin said. 'I'll be the first to tell you if there's anyone a-coming up from the river.'

They loaded the jerry cans of whiskey on the X-shaped wooden racks on the mule. The animal's legs splayed outward from the weight. They cleared the entrance of the branches and moved down the incline through the green shadows. Combs couldn't walk as fast as the others, and he held onto the mule's cinch.

'You can't see your boy now if he tries to warn us,' he said.

'He's got a shotgun pistol with him you can hear in the next county,' the old man said.

'We should have moved it out during the night,' Combs said.

'Go on back to the rock house and set there. The boy and me will take it out,' McGoffin said.

'I ain't said nothing about going back.'

'I know you ain't. But I'll leave you here if I hear any more from you.'

'It don't make sense moving it in full light.'

'Noah, I told you once already. I didn't go a-looking for you on this job. You knowed what you was hiring on for when you come to me.' The Kraig rifle was pressed flat on its sling against the old man's back.

They reached the creek bed and followed it down-hill. In the heavy areas of shade there was moss on the rocks and lichen grew on the tree trunks. The breeze was cool through the shadows, and Perry could smell the dark, moist earth under the leaves. The mule tried to drink from the stream, and McGoffin jerked his head savagely with the reins. The incline became more steep and the hollow narrowed as they neared the entrance in the cliff wall. In the distance Perry saw the natural bridge in the mountain and the glow of the sun beyond it. On the top of the bridge was a Shawnee horse track, cut into rock, that pointed in the direction of John Swift's mine. The sunken marking, carved with flint tools, was as big as Perry's hand and three inches deep. Many times he had climbed to the top of the ridge, laid flat on the limestone ledge, and aimed a stick across the track towards every conceivable place on the opposite side of the hollow where the mine might have been. He knew that somewhere in the mountain a rock the size of a salt keg still lay plugged in the shaft opening, and beyond it were the remains of the men Swift had murdered.

'It ain't there. I'd have found it if it was,' McGoffin said. 'There ain't a place in this holler I don't know.'

'What are you talking about?' Perry said.

'Nothing, boy.'

'I got something better to do than chase after a mine nobody ever seen.'

'I reckon you do. It wouldn't hardly be worth a man's time to look for two hundred thousand dollars in silver.'

Perry's face reddened with embarrassment. 'Why ain't your son driving the load?' he said.

'Because every highway police between here and Michigan knows him. He got arrested once when he was driving his family to the ball game in Cincinnati.'

'I got to rest,' Combs said. His face was white, beaded with sweat, and his breath was labored. He hung onto the side of the mule and wiped his forehead on his sleeve.

'We can't wait on you long,' McGoffin said. 'If you can't make it, you can set down here and walk out later.'

'I don't want to stay here. Give me a minute.'

'They can't put nothing on you for just being in the holler.'

'I wasn't expecting nothing when they caught me on that road in my car, neither. They opened up without giving no warning.' His wrist hung limply from his crooked arm. 'I was just at the top of the grade when I seen their rifles go off. Then the windshield broke and I felt the whole side of my face come half off.'

McGoffin's eyes strained through the trees towards the entrance to the hollow. His eyes were as grey and hard as shale under his white eyebrows.

'You ought to have let the union done its own dynamiting,' he said. 'What they done for you since you got shot up?'

'I don't hold that against them. They can't put a cripple man in the hole.'

'By God, they'd owe me something if I got my ass blowed off for them,' McGoffin said. 'Them union people up North cheats you out of as much money as the association does. They ain't in here because they like the way a miner smells. They make more money in a year than you do in a lifetime, without ever getting in the hole. I wouldn't give you a big mouthful of spit for the bunch of them.'

'We never got no wage till they organized the coal field,' Perry said. 'We wouldn't get fifty cents an hour if it wasn't for the union.'

'What you got now?' McGoffin said. 'You can't work nowhere in Kentucky except scabbing. You're running whiskey and taking a chance on going to the pen for fifty dollars. Your daddy got his lungs crushed in over there in Virginia, and they never give him five cents for it. And I bet there ain't been no union people out to your mother's to see about taking care of them kids.'

'You ain't ever worked in the hole,' Combs said. 'You don't know nothing about the old days before the union, when we worked in gas without no fans.'

'I figure I got better sense than to get under the ground before my time, and I don't need nobody from

160

up North to look after me.' He shifted the weight of the rifle on his back and stared out from under the down-turned brim of his hat towards the far end of the hollow. The dappled light through the trees caught in his stiff, white whiskers. 'We ain't got much time. Let's get it moving.'

'I ain't caught my breath,' Combs said.

'We can't hold up no longer. The plane might make another run on the holler, and we'll be setting here with our peckers hanging out.'

He slapped the mule against the flank and they moved off down the incline, the cans of whiskey banging against each other on the mule's sides. The blood had gone out of Combs' face from exertion. He hooked his hand inside the cinch again for support; then he let go and stumbled along behind them. Finally, he had to stop and prop himself against a tree trunk. There was a line of sweat down the front of his shirt.

'Maybe we ought to give him more time to rest,' Perry said.

'He ain't going to be in no trouble staying where he's at. Worry about yourself. If they catch us they'll put me back in Atlanta again, and they'll send you to the honor farm for a year.'

'They ain't ever getting me in no pen.'

'Keep dragging your ass because of Combs and you'll be a-working on them Forest Service trails with the happy-pappies, except you won't get no money for it and you won't go home at night.'

They reached the bottom of the hollow and started up a steep rise towards the entrance in the cliff walls. The opening was narrow and crooked above the mountain, and the rock sides rose up high above to the top of the ridge. The ground was worn bare and imprinted with mule and horse tracks. The sun never reached the bottom of the opening, and there was still a film of ice on the limousine. As they neared the top of the incline Perry looked back at the vastness of the hollow, the tall trunks of the trees, the hard line of cliffs against the sky, and the spray of mist over the waterfall at the base of the stream.

'Goddamn that sonofabitch! Here he comes again,' McGoffin said. 'Get that mule inside the cliff!'

Perry couldn't see the plane this time, but he heard the roar of the engine echo through the hollow. He picked up a knotted poplar branch from the ground and whipped it across the mule's scrotum.

'Someday when I ain't got nothing better to do I'm going to shoot one of them bastards down,' McGoffin said, yanking at the reins. The mule's hooves kicked dirt and leaves into the air.

Perry dug his boots into the soft earth and lunged uphill towards the crack in the mountain. He slipped on his face and grabbed onto some small bushes to pull himself erect.

'Hurry up! He's a-coming over the trees,' McGoffin said.

'He'll see Combs.'

'Shit on Combs. That pilot don't care about him. He's looking for somebody loaded down with whiskey.'

They led the mule back deep into the shadows between the cliff walls. The stone smelled cool and damp, and water dripped slowly down from the melting ice onto the ground. High above them they could see a long stretch of blue sky through the opening in the mountain. McGoffin turned one ear into the wind to listen for the plane while he filled the side of his mouth with loose-string Red Man chewing tobacco. He cleared his throat and spat.

'I don't know about you, but I got to drain the old pecker,' he said.

'Let's get on down to the car.'

'There ain't a better place to be than right here till that plane heads back to Winchester.' The old man urinated against a rock.

'Goddamn, he's flying right over the ridge. Where's your son at?'

'He's got a hole dug under a ledge. You ain't got to worry about him.'

'How did he get them three stretches in the pen?'

'He never done more than fifteen months, and that ain't bad for a man that run whiskey to Detroit over twenty years. Buddy, I tell you there ain't nothing better than a good piss.'

'Look back down the holler. Combs is still coming,' Perry said.

'I don't know which has caused me more trouble, him or this worthless shithog mule. I deserve to go back to Atlanta for hiring him. Get down, you dumb sonofabitch, before you bring them in on top of us!' he yelled at Combs.

'He can't hear you,' Perry said. Combs worked his way slowly up the incline and stared upwards at the plane.

'I have half a notion to shoot him and bury him right where he's at.'

'He's scared and he don't want to get left alone. His hands was shaking when we cleaned out the rock house. You can't hold it against him for being afraid after he got shot up like he did.'

'You goddamn right I can. I ain't got many years left, and I sure ain't a-spending them in jail because of somebody else screwing me up. They ain't going to do nothing to Combs because he's a cripple. He can walk out of court without even a fine, but by God they'll lay it on me and you. You hear me, Combs! Lay down on your face!'

'Here comes the plane,' Perry said.

'Get close against the wall. Look at the ground and don't move.' McGoffin pushed the mule flat against the cliff with his weight and held the rein close by the bit. The mule shuffled in the dirt and reared his head. The old man hit him in the head with his fist. 'Stay, you shithead, or I'll cut your balls out.'

They remained motionless in the blue shadows as the airplane curved back out of the sky and flew low above the entrance. The noise from the engine was like the roar of a train between the cliff walls and Perry thought he could feel the backwash of the propeller. After the sound decreased, he looked upwards and saw the plane bank at an angle against the clouds.

'I know he seen us then,' Perry said. 'He was flying sideways when he come over.'

'It don't matter if he did or not. In ten minutes that whiskey's going to be in the car with you on the way to Newport, and I'll be a-setting on the river with a cane pole in case anybody from the A.B.C. wants to know how the fish are biting. Get it moving.'

'Maybe he'll make another run.'

'Piss on him. We been in this holler too long already. If we stay around any longer, that goddamn Combs will do something else, like set the woods on fire or climb up on the mountain so everybody from here to Virginia can see him.'

They led the mule through the narrow entrance towards the sunlight near the river. The breeze was cool from the river, and Perry could see the green of the treetops on the slope that led down to the water. Heavy vines grew along the high portions of the cliff wall where the sun struck. On a flat outcropping above his head there was a deep crow's foot carved in the rock, weathered smooth at the edges, pointing back into the hollow. Perry rubbed his hand over it as he passed.

'It don't point to no mine, boy,' McGoffin said. 'I think them Shawnees had a jenny-barn back in a rock house somewhere, and they was just putting out their road signs.'

They came out of the gap between the cliffs and started towards the river through the trees. The canopy overhead was much thinner than in the hollow, and the sunlight spangled on the cans of whiskey. Perry wished that he had taken sides with Combs and had argued for hiding the load until night. The tree trunks were spaced far apart, the ground was bare of undergrowth, and he knew they could be seen by anyone from a hundred yards. Their footsteps on the dead leaves were loud in the stillness of the forest.

'I hope your boy covered up the car good,' Perry said.

'You don't think he knows his business?'

'I didn't say that.'

'You see a car anywhere?'

'It's where we left it at, ain't it?'

'Look right straight in front of you about seventy-five yards and you'll see some beech branches laid over them two big boulders. If you can't see a car inside, you ain't got to worry about nobody else finding it.'

'You ain't told me yet where I drop the load at,' Perry said.

'You get off the interstate on the last street before the Ohio bridge and turn into the first filling station.

There's a street map of Newport marked under the seat. When you get there you ain't got to say nothing to them. They know the car, and they'll take care of everything after that.'

'How much you pay a feller to drive it all the way to Detroit?'

'I don't have no one man ever make the whole run for me anymore. If a driver gets arrested after he leaves Newport, he don't have no idea what part of Kentucky that whiskey come from.'

'The police will trace the car right back to your son.'

'No, they won't, because it ain't got a number any place on the engine, and them plates come off a lot of different cars. Next week the boy will pick up his car and drive it back home empty with the right tags on it. We don't get as much money this way like we used to, but we don't run a big chance of going to the pen, neither.'

The incline became more steep, and the weight on the mule's back almost toppled him forward. Perry slid part way down the embankment to where the Chevrolet was hidden. The moisture on the great limestone boulders steamed faintly in the sun. The car had been backed between the two rocks and covered with branches and a large piece of army canvas camouflage. A federal agent would have had to walk right up on it to see the outline of the body under the leaves. Back through the trees Perry could see tire tracks on the ground; they ended where McGoffin's son had spread dead twigs and leaves over them.

'Clean it off and bring it out to load,' McGoffin said. He tied the mule to a tree and began lifting the heavy cans off the pack. The blood veins in his throat swelled as he worked.

Perry caught the canvas tarpaulin by one corner and

pulled it off the car, then climbed up on one boulder and threw the branches off the roof. The sun reflected off the windshield, and he looked up at the sky, waiting for the plane to reappear again over the crest of the mountain.

'Come on and get it out here!' McGoffin said. 'We ain't got time to screw around here. If they catch us, this is where they will do it. I ain't ever got busted in the holler before. I always got caught taking it out.'

Perry started the engine and drove the Chevrolet out from between the boulders. The twin exhausts roared when he touched the gas pedal just lightly. The car had a four-speed floor stick transmission, a new GMC motor with two carburetors, a modified cam, over-sized pistons, and a hot electric system. He had to keep the clutch depressed to stop the car from bolting forward.

The top portion of the back seat swung upwards on two metal springs, and the separating wall to the trunk had been cut away. The lock on the trunk had been deliberately smashed so that it couldn't be opened from the outside. Perry loaded the cans one by one into the car, distributed the weight evenly over the axle so the back end wouldn't sag noticeably, and replaced the seat. The day had grown warmer, and he began to perspire.

'You still reckon you can handle it?' McGoffin said.

'I'll tell you after you give me my fifty dollars.'

The old man took a wallet from inside the bib of his overalls and counted out the money with his thumbs.

'It ain't much for the risk a man runs, but I don't get that much out of it myself after I cut with everybody between here and Detroit,' he said. 'I'd make it more if I could.'

'I ain't asking for no more than anybody else is a-getting.'

'There's a set of Ohio and Michigan plates stuck up under the dashboard. Tell them boys at the filling station I want them Kentucky tags off before they cross the river.'

'Does anybody at the toll station know this car?'

'You don't need to go through no toll station. Stay on the county road along the river and go up to Winchester through Boonesborough. I ain't got much else to tell you, except I seen you put that pistol under the seat this morning.'

'What's that got to do with anything?'

'My boy's got twenty-five hundred dollars in that car, and he don't want no holes in it. I don't want to see no holes in you, neither. If the A.B.C. starts chasing you, pull over and let them take the load. Don't get shot for no corn whiskey that we can run off any time we got a mind to.'

'I ain't got that gun to shoot at the A.B.C.'

'I reckon I know what you got it for. I heered about the sheriff picking you up in front of the operator's office. That's your business and it don't concern me, even though I figure you got the right to get back at them men that killed Woodson. But I don't want you pulling no gun on a man while you're working for me.'

'The sun's over the mountain. Them log crews will be in here soon,' Perry said. 'I got to get moving.'

'All right, boy. Just make sure that pistol stays where it's at.'

Perry drove the Chevrolet out through the trees, avoiding the rocks and dead logs, and shifted into second gear as he started down the last part of the incline that led to the dirt road running along the river. The weight in the trunk caused the car to hit high-center several times. The trees began to thin, and he could see the river flowing green along its banks. Next to him on the seat was his canvas Job Corps overnight bag, packed with a change of clothes, two fried pork chops with bread, and a box of .22-magnum shells. The car bounced over the last of the incline onto the smooth, bare area by the river, and he floored the accelerator and headed down the dirt lane, with the exhaust pipes roaring.

Once on the blacktop, he shifted into fourth gear and passed every car he met. The sun was bright on the green meadows and mountaintops, and he let the wind rush through the window full into his face. The new tobacco in the fields had grown several inches high, and the farmers had strung cheesecloth across it on wooden stakes, to protect the plants from rain and occasional sleet. The air was sweet with the smell of spring, and in the distance he could see the mountains roll away and gradually become smaller near the edge of the Cumberland plateau. The light from the east cast dark shadows in the valleys, and the trees looked blue when the clouds passed overhead. His ears began to pop from the change in altitude, and he shifted down to third gear as the road sloped off towards the level country below the mountains.

He crossed the Kentucky River at Boonesborough. He looked through the spars of the great metal bridge and saw motor boats churning white wakes in the current far below; and people in wet bathing suits lay on the stretch of sandy beach by the water. Somewhere on the mountain high above were the rotted remains of Daniel Boone's fort, which he had built to protect the first white settlers from the terrible attacks of the Shawnee. Ahead was the even, rolling land of the bluegrass country. The road was lined with stone

fences that had been built without mortar by slaves
when they cleared the fields before the Civil War. The
earth was rich here, and the grass was tall with a blue-
green tint to it. Perry had never seen this area of
Kentucky before. The streams were clear, there was no
garbage on the hillsides, the stands of timber were
untouched by the strip and auger mines, and the
farmhouses were painted, the barns filled with hay, the
yards planted with mimosa trees and rose bushes, and
in the fields there were fine race horses and rows of
white bee hives. He wondered how any man could
have enough money to buy land like this, where
tobacco paid two thousand dollars an acre and corn
grew to seven feet within half the season.

A feller could work and save his money all his life
and not be able to buy nothing like that, he thought.
You don't get things like that for your sweat. They got
it by stealing it from the Indians, and they held onto it
by cheating other people out of their money and
paying a man hardly nothing for planting and cutting
their tobacco. A feller don't ever get anything worth
keeping for the work he does. You don't have the
chance to even get ahead of the charge at the store.
You get this kind of land when you're smart enough to
make other people work for you so they can pay their
wage right back into your pocket. Them Northern
mining companies knowed what they was doing when
they come into the Cumberland.

Perry followed the narrow blacktop through the low
green hills into Winchester. It was Saturday, and the
streets were crowded with cars and people. Winchester
was the only wet town on the edge of the plateau
besides Mount Sterling and Richmond, and the bars
and poolrooms were filled with men from the mountains, in overalls and tattered bluejeans, who had

driven their junker automobiles over the twisting roads to drink, fight over three-dollar whores, and eventually pass out in a drunken stupor behind a tavern Sunday morning. There were several uniformed policemen directing traffic through the center of town, and Perry felt drops of perspiration begin to form on his forehead and upper lip as he moved slowly through the line of cars. The engine idled too fast, and the Chevrolet's twin exhausts sounded like straight pipes off a diesel truck. He had no driver's license, and if a policeman stopped him to check for a defective muffler, he knew he would be taken to jail and the car would be recognized as a transporter's and searched. He wiped the moisture off his brow into his hair with his palm. The traffic began to lessen after he had passed through the downtown area, and as he went by the last policeman on the stretch of road leading to the highway he depressed the clutch and let off the accelerator to deaden the roar through the exhaust pipes. He coasted as far as he could until he was sure he was out of the policeman's earshot, then he shoved the floor stick into second gear and pushed the gas pedal to the floor. The Chevrolet rocked back against its springs, the tires burning rubber, the front end uplifted, the two four-barreled carburetors sucking air, and tore down the highway with the fence posts and telephone poles racing by like an accelerated film strip.

He got back onto the four-lane interstate and rolled towards Lexington. The engine hummed under the hood, the cool wind streamed through the window, and he rested one hand lightly on top of the steering wheel as the road signs flashed by. He'd had nothing for breakfast except coffee before dawn in the rock house, and he ate one of the fried pork chops and a piece of bread. Ahead, there was a car parked under the underpass, with the trunk up and a spare tire resting against the back bumper. He braked the Chevrolet slowly until he was under the speed limit, and as he went through the underpass he saw the police officer behind the wheel of the highway patrol car and the red light on top that was concealed by the open trunk.

Perry reached the outskirts of Lexington by noon, and he turned north towards Cincinnati. On both sides of the road, racehorse farms stretched back over the blue meadows into the hills. The fences were white, the barns made of stone, and the stables were as big as two-story houses. Shiny black horses that took up to twenty thousand dollars for a stud fee stood in the fields, and huge ante-bellum homes were set back in groves of oak trees. Negroes were grooming and shoeing thoroughbreds outside the stables, and Perry saw a woman in strange riding clothes and a peaked cap posting on a mare around a training track. He didn't know names like 'Spendthrift' or 'Calumet Farm' or 'Keeneland,' and he had never seen anything that approached this type of wealth. The breeding barns were better than any house on the Cumberland plateau, and the money from the whiskey in his car couldn't even buy the paint on one of those big, columned plantation homes.

He entered the southern tip of the Ohio Valley, and gradually the land began to flatten on each side of the highway. The horse farms became small in the distance behind him, and now there were neat farms planted with corn, man-made brown lakes dug for irrigation, small clumps of locust trees on the rises, and grey outcroppings of limestone where the highway cut through the low hills. The wind was strong here, and it rippled the lakes in heavy gusts and buffeted his automobile. The sky was cloudless, and the young green leaves on the corn bent back against the wind. The grass in the fields still had a blue tint to it, and it waved back and forth as far as the eye could see.

The smell of spring and the soft haze of the sun on the meadows made Perry sleepy; then in the rearview mirror he noticed that a new Plymouth had stayed behind him for the last several miles. Slowly, he accelerated and increased his speed by ten miles an hour; the Plymouth did the same. He let off the gas, the mufflers rumbling with the back exhaust, and watched the other car slow, also. In the mirror he could see two men in hats behind the Plymouth's windshield. It ain't only the fellers at the filling station that know this car, he thought. The A.B.C.s probably seen it through here so many times they don't even need to stop it to know what it's carrying.

He stayed at the same speed for the next fifteen miles, and the Plymouth kept at a distance behind him. The highway was being repaired near Cincinnati, and a flagman stopped the line of cars while a bulldozer moved a load of earth over the embankment. The traffic forced the Plymouth to pull almost abreast of Perry, and he turned and looked at the two men inside. They kept their faces forward, unconcerned, and one of them lighted a cigarette casually; but Perry saw the small pin aerial for the mobile radio on the back fender. They're a-following me in till I make the drop, he thought. They figure to hit me at the filling station and get the other transporter and the still, too. Well, buddy, I hope you got a hot engine in that thing, because I ain't playing your kind of baseball game. While he waited for the flagman to release the line of cars he spread the road map out with one hand on the seat beside him and looked for the next exit before Newport.

Ten miles before the Ohio River he began to pass cars and put as many as possible between him and the Plymouth; then he saw the Erlanger exit sign and floored the gas pedal. In his mirror he could see the Plymouth weaving through the traffic that was bunching up for the one-lane crossing over the Ohio bridge. The Chevrolet's tires screamed as Perry went into the exit at seventy miles an hour. He shifted down, popped the clutch out, and hit the brakes momentarily just before he reached the stop sign, skidding sideways; then he double-clutched into second and burned across the intersection. An old truck stopped suddenly to let him pass, and a car slammed into its rear end, and for an instant Perry saw several pedestrians leap back to the curb, their mouths open and their eyes wide. The rows of brick homes, trees, and yards whipped by him, and people watering their grass and working in flower beds looked up quickly at him as his exhaust pipes echoed off the house fronts. He braked at the end of the street, cut a sharp right turn, the back end fishtailing with the weight of the whiskey, and shoved the gear stick into third.

He drove fifty miles an hour down the side street, running three stop signs, and he almost tore the door off a parked car. They'll weld that jailhouse shut on me if they catch me now, he thought. But by God they're going to earn their money before they get me there. He let the engine wind down against the transmission and cut into a narrow alley between two rows of houses. One fender hit a garbage can and smashed it flat against the garage. An old Negro ragpicker, rooting through some cardboard boxes, jumped out of the way of the car as it passed. Perry bounced out of the alley and turned up another street, reducing his speed slowly. He knew that somebody had probably already called the city police after he had roared through this quiet neighborhood section of town, and every patrol car in the area probably had his license number and a description of the Chevrolet. He cut around several corners in a row, staying under the speed limit, and drove back towards the feeder lanes near the interstate highway.

Before he reached the entrance to the four-lane, he turned into a filling station and pulled his car into the empty grease rack. Now they can look up and down the road for me till their eyes cross, he thought. A fat attendant in a stained blue uniform with a lacquered-brim cap on his head and dirty rags in his pockets came out of the office.

'There's another car ahead of you. I was just going to bring it in,' he said.

'I don't want nothing but a grease job. It ain't going to take you ten minutes,' Perry said. Before the attendant could answer, Perry got under the Chevrolet and set the iron braces on the rack into place.

'That engine smells like it's burning,' the attendant said.

'The fan belt's slipping. You got a screwdriver? I ain't put on my new Ohio plates yet.'

'I think we have a fan belt that will fit it.'

'I ain't got time for that. Run it up on the rack,' Perry said. He reached under the dashboard and pulled out the Ohio license tags.

'I'd put a new belt on it if I was you. There's steam whistling out of your radiator now.'

'Just give me the screwdriver.' Perry looked out through the gas pumps at the flow of traffic in the street. He saw the two men from the A.B.C. cruise slowly past in the Plymouth. The driver was speaking into the microphone of his radio. Perry pulled his cap down over his eyes and turned his back. The attendant pushed down the hydraulic lever and raised the Chevrolet on the rack while the air compressor in the back of the station labored from the pressure.

'You got them new kind of sliding doors. We don't see many of them back home,' Perry said. He pulled down the door part way, until it covered the back of the car from view.

'Open that door. It's too hot in here as it is.'

'It's stuck. Maybe you better do it.' Perry watched the Plymouth turn onto the entrance ramp of the highway and head back south towards Lexington.

He put the Ohio tags on his car and threw his Kentucky plate into a trash can; then he rolled cigarettes, and smoked while he waited for the attendant to finish. In the next half hour two city police cars passed, but the men inside seemed unconcerned about anything, their arms resting easily in the open windows, and Perry knew they had probably stopped looking for him.

'You must have a big load in that trunk the way it's sagging,' the attendant said.

'I'm hauling a load of bricks for a feller. You done with it yet?'

'Yeah, but you better watch that engine. I could feel the heat coming right through the oil pan.'

'I got to worry about that for only ten more miles, then it can catch fire and burn on down to the ground,' Perry said.

After he paid the attendant, he backed his car off the grease rack, shifted into first gear, and drove onto the interstate towards Newport. Great silver planes approaching the airfield came in slowly at a downward angle over the highway, the sun white on their wings, and fine hotels and restaurants sat up high on the hillsides. Billboard signs advertising German beer and Kentucky whiskey stood along the road, and cars were strung out in a long line before the Ohio bridge. He could see small, suburban towns with neat houses and green lawns and chestnut trees, and there were no clapboard shacks, log outbuildings, or wrecked cars piled one on top of another in dirty vacant lots.

The traffic began to slow as he went over a rise, and then through a cut in the hill he saw the wide sweep of the Ohio bridge, the long stretch of blue river winding through the green slopes, and the broken skyline of Cincinnati high above the valley. Along the riverbank, in the old section of town, narrow, brick German buildings, with chimneys on each side, stood in rows, pressed tightly together, almost like squeezed cardboard structures, and trees grew along every city block. On the hills above town there were more nineteenth-century European-style brick homes, with wood verandahs, set back in the oaks and poplars. Below the bridge a huge, white paddle-wheel boat churned down the river, the decks covered with people in canvas chairs, and the two scrolled metal smoke stacks trailed off dark clouds in the wind. In the distance Perry saw the grandstands at Crosley Field, where the Reds were playing the Dodgers that weekend, and the white concrete ramps and overpasses were loaded with cars going into the ball game. The girders and spars of the bridge were like etched gray lines against the blue above the skyline, and wisps of torn clouds hung on the far horizon in the opulent green haze of the Ohio Valley.

Someday he would live here, after he had taken care of everything back home, he thought. He would get out of the coal fields, find a job that paid a living wage, and he would walk down those wide, tree-lined boulevards after work in the spring evening in a fresh pair of ironed khakis and a denim shirt and with a paycheck in his back pocket. It would just take time. Then he'd meet Popcorn at the ball game and they would crawl home on their elbows.

Just before the bridge he turned off the interstate into Newport, a dirty, run-down working class area on the Kentucky side of the river. The old German buildings had turned into slum tenements, the streets were often littered with newspaper and beer cans, and there were rows of dingy bars and pool halls in which gambling, narcotics, and prostitution were not recognized by the local police. There was supposed to be no liquor sold on Sundays or after two in the morning in that area of Kentucky, but the law hadn't been enforced in so long that it was considered a joke. Men, who looked much like people in the hills, stood on street corners, and there were dour women with dyed hair and big handbags in front of the bars. Most of the cars parked along the curb had license plates from counties back on the plateau, and the town itself was as grimed and depressed-looking as Harlan or Hazard.

Perry found the filling station where McGoffin had described it. He pulled around the side of the building and saw the attendant look up at the car over his newspaper through the window in the office. Perry took the pistol from under the seat and zippered it up inside his overnight bag. The attendant came out the side door, with a thin cigar stub in a gap between his teeth. His hair was long and covered with grease, and the skin on one side of his lower jaw was drawn and puckered where part of the bone was gone. His pinstriped uniform was frayed at the cuffs and sleeves, and his T-shirt was covered with dirt under his throat. His eyes were expressionless, but Perry could feel them examining him.

'What do you need?' he said, taking the cigar out of his mouth to spit.

'I thought I'd leave it with you.'

'Come back tomorrow if you want it serviced. I can't get to it today.'

'I was told to drop it here. I reckon you know what I'm talking about.'

'No, I don't, mister.'

'Listen, I ain't got time for this. The other plates is under the dash.'

'You must be looking for somebody else.'

'I'm working for old man McGoffin. Does that name mean something to you?'

'What's he do?'

Perry picked up his canvas bag and got out of the car.

'I don't know who you was expecting to see, but I ain't waiting around here no more,' he said. 'I had people after me most of the way from Lexington, and I reckon it's somebody else's turn to play games with them. I done my part of the bargain, and I don't give a goddamn if you roll that car into the river.'

'Take it easy and come inside.' Perry followed him into the office, which was stacked with tires and cases of empty pop bottles. 'What's this McGoffin look like?'

'I told you I didn't have time to waste here.'

'You don't have a private airplane or something waiting on you, do you?' The attendant's mouth spread back over his bad teeth.

'He's got two heads and a hump on his back. What the hell do you think he looks like?'

'Okay. Don't get pissed off. We just got to be careful. The A.B.C. busted a transporter a few weeks ago and put one of their own men in the car. They arrested five guys over in Covington. Where did they spot you?'

'They followed me to Erlanger, and then I outrun them.'

'You sure you don't have a tail on you?'

'They never seen me after I cut off the highway, but I wouldn't move that stuff for a few days.'

Outside, another man from the station drove the Chevrolet into a tin garage in back.

'We'll handle all that. Just forget you ever been in this filling station.'

'Buddy, I already forgot what you look like,' Perry said, and went out the door with his bag in his hand.

He walked down the street past the rows of honky-tonks and dollar-a-night flophouses. He felt good leaving the automobile, the jerry cans of rank-smelling whiskey, and the worries about the A.B.C. behind him. He hadn't slept at all the night before, and the events of the last two days wouldn't stay straight in his head. His mind was tired, and it seemed like weeks ago that he had moved the whiskey downhill with McGoffin while the plane swept by overhead and Noah Combs toiled along behind them with his stiff, crippled movements. On the corner there was a barbecue stand and draught beer parlor, and his empty stomach ached when he smelled the hot sauce on the smoked pork and saw a waitress drawing cold mugs of beer for working men, with plates of ribs and links before them. He wanted to go inside and eat the buttered pieces of garlic bread and rare beef and wash it down with glass after glass of beer; but he had risked too many things for the money in his pocket to spend it on himself, and he still had feelings of guilt for getting drunk on part of his Job Corps savings after he bought the pistol.

The bridge across the river was high above his head, and he started up the steep, cobbled street that led to the walkway along the interstate. The day was warm now, and he took off his army field jacket with the big pockets and slung it over his shoulder. He could still smell the cooking in the barbecue stand, and he wanted to stop and eat the remaining pork chop and slice of bread in his overnight bag, but he would have nothing left for the trip back home. Cars going to the ball game were jammed along the entrance to the four-lane highway, and a Negro police officer stood in the middle of the intersection directing traffic. Perry walked out into the center of the street and stood beside him.

'Where's a feller get a bus back to Richmond?' he said.

The policeman had a whistle clenched in his mouth, and his eyes were intent upon the cars.

'I want to get back home. Where do I catch a bus at?'

'Richmond where?' the Negro said, his face still turned towards the traffic and his hands gesturing rapidly in the air.

'Kentucky. There ain't no other except over in Virginia.'

'I never heard of it. Get out of the street before you get hit. Go ask somebody at the depot in Cincinnati.'

Perry started across the bridge, and his head swam when he looked down at the water far below him. He could hear the wind sing in the girders and cables above him, and the long stretch of the bridge seemed to sway under his feet. He wondered how men could ever build something this wonderful and big across such a great span of water. Green and white eddies boiled around the concrete foundations below, and he could feel the force of the river vibrate through the handrail along the walkway. The skyline of Cincinnati loomed up even higher than before. The buildings looked as tall against the clouds as the top ridge of the Cumberland mountains, and there were restaurants that served food from all over the world, arbors of chestnut trees around newsstands, a big recreation park with Ferris wheels and roller coasters on the beach by the river, and the breeze through the valley had the smell of new grass and the first spring flowers.

For a moment he thought of forgetting the bus depot. He had almost fifty dollars in his wallet, and that would be enough until he could find some type of job. He could rent a room and find a job parking cars, working in a service station, or doing common labor out of the sweatshops. There was no work at all now back on the plateau, and his family would be better off if he stayed in the city and sent them part of his paycheck. There would be no J.W.s to worry about, no long evenings in the cabin while his mother stared blankly at the fire, and no more quiet hatred or that anticipation of sudden violence when he stood next to a scab or a company man on a street corner.

chapter nine

The bus trip back home that night took seven hours, and Perry was not able to go to sleep until just before daylight, when the sun broke above the mountains and shined directly into his face through the window. His body felt thick with fatigue and his face was lined and pale. In the Richmond depot he put his head under the tap and let the cold water splash over him.

The morning was cool as he walked out to the highway, and the air smelled clean after the seven hours in the bus. He caught a ride on the back of a flatbed truck into the next county, where he lived, and he lay back on the metal floor, put his canvas bag under his head, and watched the strips of cloud stream by overhead. He felt the hard outline of the pistol through the canvas, and he sat upright when he remembered that all six chambers in the cylinder were loaded. The truck climbed higher into the mountains, and the sun began to grow warm on the limestone cliffs. The narrow road wound through the hollows, crossed streams on one-lane wooden bridges, and eventually reached the crest of the plateau. As the truck pulled into the county seat, Perry banged on the cab with his fist and dropped off the back.

It was Sunday, the pool halls and taverns were closed, and the streets were almost deserted except for a few families dressed in their best clothes walking towards the clapboard Church of God building on the hill. The sound of singing and organ music was faint in the distance. The sheriff was opening the door to the sandstone jail, and the drunks who had been arrested the night before were crowded around the steel bars. They stumbled out into the bright sunlight, their faces drawn from hangovers. One man still couldn't walk straight, and the sheriff turned him around by one arm and walked him back into the jail.

Perry started across the street, then he heard the sheriff's voice behind him; 'Hold on a minute. I want to talk with you.'

He waited while the sheriff crossed the lawn towards him. He felt uneasy about the revolver in his bag, and he set it down by his foot and rolled a cigarette. The sheriff's great weight made him walk with his legs spread apart slightly, and although the day was still cool, his face was flushed as though he had been working under the summer sun.

'I got to get back to the house,' Perry said.

'A minute of your time ain't going to hurt you none. Noah Combs got drunk in town last night and I had to drive him home.'

Perry folded the cigarette paper around the tobacco and licked the glue on the edge.

'He was talking about a lot of things that he probably don't remember this morning,' the sheriff said.

'That ain't got nothing to do with me.'

'It does if you're a-working for old man McGoffin.'

'I ain't working for nobody.'

'Combs said some whiskey got moved yesterday and you was the transporter.'

'You don't see me driving no car, do you? I ain't even got a driver's license.'

'You reckon fifty dollars is worth going to jail for?'

'I can't tell you nothing about what Combs told you. I been looking for a job in Lexington.'

'And you didn't happen to drop off a load of whiskey while you was at it?'

'If you're sure I been working with Combs and old man McGoffin, why ain't they in jail?'

'I know McGoffin's got a still somewhere in that holler, and I know that half the moonshine in this county comes out of it. If I was set on arresting him, I could do it without much trouble. But I figure the A.B.C. gets paid for that sort of thing, and I got enough to do without having to sleep all night in a rock house to put an old man and a cripple in jail.'

'I got to go now. There's a feller up the street I can get a ride home with.'

'You wait till I'm finished. The A.B.C. or them federal people ain't going to just talk with you. They don't care what happens to your family if you get put away in Atlanta. It don't mean five cents different to their paycheck. Or if they got to put a couple of holes in you, they'll do it faster than you can spit, because enough of their people have got shot down around here to make them a little nervous when they walk up on a still.'

'Tell me where you expect a man to get any money today? The association's got us locked out of all their mines, and there's a picket in front of all the independents. The tobacco won't be ready to cut till the end of summer, and the Forest Service ain't a-hiring because the happy-pappies is doing all the trail work.'

'You can get on the welfare. There's plenty of people drawing it now.'

'My family ain't. You ever knowed my daddy to line up at that welfare office?'

'Sometimes you ain't got a choice about things, Perry.'

'By God, I still do. We can take care of ourselves without no help from anybody else.'

'There ain't much use in trying to talk with you, is there?' the sheriff said. 'You can't understand nothing outside of what you've got made up in your own mind. Get in my car and I'll drive you home.'

'Thank you. I feel like walking.'

'All seven miles. Just because you're so damn fond of walking,' the sheriff said.

Perry flicked the stub of his cigarette into the street, picked up his canvas bag, and slung his army field jacket over his shoulder. He didn't think that he had ever been so tired before, not even after working two straight eight-hour shifts in the mine. His back and neck were stiff from trying to sleep on the bus, and his legs felt weak and awkward, as though he had been standing in one position a long time. He walked to the edge of town and started up the rural road that led to his ridge. There had been a shower the night before, and the hardwoods in the forest had taken on a deeper green and blue. Two miles up the road his legs began to ache, and he sat down in a grove of maple trees that overlooked a deep chasm below. The sun had moved into the south, and it shone down through the trees and spangled the ground with areas of light and shadow. He lay down on the cool grass, his jacket under his head, and watched the squirrels racing across the limbs overhead. The light began to diffuse through the leaves, and in moments he was asleep.

In his dreams he saw the man on the coal tipple again. He was framed against the black horizon, his face transfixed in terror and his skin as white as bone, then Big J.W. started the car engine, the spark jumped through the cap wire, and once more the flame and smoke exploded across the face of the mountain. The screaming continued in Perry's mind until he rolled his face down in the grass. Then he was standing on a street corner in town in the violet twilight just before dark. The air was hot and still, and even the sidewalks radiated heat. The billiard balls clicking together in the pool hall sounded metallic in the dry air, then the door crashed open and the three men who had murdered his father walked out onto the street. Each of their faces looked alike, twisted and sallow, the teeth rotted, eyes with the insane glimmer of chipped glass. He felt the heavy weight and even balance of the pistol in his palm. He put his thumb over the hammer, cocked it into place, and aimed at the face of the first man. None of them seemed to pay any attention to him. 'I'm Woodson James' boy and I'm putting you in hell tonight,' he said. Still they took no notice of him. He steadied the revolver, the metal cool in his hand, and fired directly into the first man's face. The explosion of the magnum shell was deafening, and the recoil kicked his forearm upwards. Then he cocked the action again and fired shot after shot into their faces. He smelled the burnt gunpowder, and the blue smoke drifted in a haze before his eyes; and he knew that the hollow-point shells had ripped through the flesh and bone of those awful faces and he would never have to look at them again. But when the smoke cleared, he saw them grinning at him obscenely. He shucked the empty hulls out on the sidewalk with the ejection rod and began pushing in fresh cartridges through the loading gate. The three men started laughing at him, at first slowly, their faces creasing like dry paper, then they roared, tears came down their cheeks, and they had to hold their sides. 'Boy, you don't know when to leave things alone,' one of them said. 'We might have to cut out your balls now.'

Perry awoke suddenly. He was sweating, his hair was matted with grass and twigs, and he saw that his hand was clenched on the revolver through the canvas bag. At first he wasn't sure where he was, and he looked about him for the three men, the sidewalks and dirty buildings, and kept thinking that it should have still been twilight. Slowly things became fixed in his head, and he realized that he was on a ridge overlooking a huge hollow where spring was in full flower and squirrels raced through the new maple leaves.

He walked another mile up the road before he caught a ride the rest of the way home. There was a new car parked at the bottom of the hill below his cabin. At first Perry thought someone from the mining company was on the ridge again to collect back rent or credit bills at the store, but then he saw the official license plate on the back. He walked up the crooked dirt trail through the litter of rusted cans, molded feed sacks and broken glass. The A.B.C. got on to me somehow, he thought. They must have hit the filling station after I left or maybe they got old man McGoffin. But they still can't put nothing on me. They got to catch a feller with the whiskey before they can put him in jail.

Two of his younger brothers, both barefoot and in overalls, ran around the side of the cabin. Their hands and faces were covered with dirt, and their long hair hung over their eyes. Even though they were over a year apart, they looked enough alike to be twins. Their straw-colored hair, the same texture and shade as Perry's, had started to bleach from the sun.

'Why they got to go, Perry?'

'Who?'

'They're a-taking Irvin, Mae, and Collie.'

'What are you talking about?'

'Mama says they got to go somewhere in Richmond.'

'You ain't making no sense. Get in the house,' Perry said.

'Mama won't let us come in till them people leave.'

'What people's in there?'

'I don't know. Let go of my arm.'

'Where do they come from?'

'Richmond, I reckon. Turn loose of me.'

Perry crossed the porch and opened the battered screen door. Inside, he saw Irvin and two of his sisters eating quietly at the table, their faces turned down into their plates. They were dressed in their best clothes, which their mother never put on them except to go to the Church of God meeting once or twice a month. A man and woman whom Perry had never seen before sat uncomfortably in the wooden chairs, shifting their weight occasionally against the stiff boards. Perry felt the instinctive distrust towards these people that he felt for all strangers. Also, their clothes were expensive, they were too out of place in his cabin, and he knew that they were there for some reason that would cause trouble for his family. Few people from outside of the county ever came onto the ridge unless they represented the law, the association, or a finance company. The man was thin, balding across the top of his head, and the clip-on bowtie he wore didn't match his tweed coat. There was a business satchel by his foot. The woman was in her fifties, with a blue tint to her grey hair, and her chest swelled out like a robin's against her blue suit.

Mrs James took a pot from the wood stove and ladled spoonfuls of grits onto the children's plates. Her face was tired, and there was a lackluster quality in her eyes.

'This is Mrs Lester and Mr Call, son,' she said. Her eyes didn't meet Perry's. 'They come up from Richmond.'

The man rose to shake hands and the woman smiled pleasantly, but Perry did not look in their direction.

'What's this about somebody a-taking Irvin and the girls away?' he said.

'Set down at the table and I'll get your dinner.'

'I ain't hungry.'

'You didn't have nothing to take with you except them two pork chops.'

'Why ain't Irvin and the girls outside playing with the rest of them?' he said.

'These people come from the welfare, and they got a home where the children will get taken care of like they should.' She looked at the table and bit her lower lip.

'The program can be a pretty good deal for kids,' Mr Call said.

'I ain't talking to you.'

'It's a good home, Perry,' Mrs James said. 'The children get the food they need, and they got doctors to take care of them.'

'We don't need no welfare people.'

'I don't think you'd feel so badly about this if you saw our home,' Mrs Lester said.

'I got no plans about seeing it, and my brother and sisters ain't going to see it, either. So you all can get in your car and head right back to Richmond.'

'It ain't right to talk like that to people in our house,' Mrs James said.

'They ain't got to stay.'

'We don't treat people that way in this house.'

'You can't support all these children without a job,' Mrs Lester said.

'I got fifty dollars, and the Job Corps still owes me money.'

'Would you like to go back to the Job Corps?' the man asked.

'You ain't got to do nothing for me. If I want to go back, all I got to do is call the camp collect and my ticket will be in the next mail.'

'What are you going to do when your money is gone?' the man said.

Perry sat down in a chair by the table and rolled a cigarette between his fingers. He felt the fatigue rush through his body. 'I can't see how that's any of your business, mister.'

'We'd like to help your family, if you'll let us,' Mrs Lester said. 'Our program can make things a little better for your mother as well as the children.'

'I don't reckon you been a-listening to anything I said. This family's staying together, and you burned up a few gallons of gasoline for nothing.'

'We're not trying to break up your family,' the woman said. 'You can visit the children whenever you want, and it won't be long before you'll be able to take them back.'

'You think your money lets you come in here and tell us we got to change our lives. You all don't like setting in a cabin like this for even ten minutes. You ain't ever lived in a house that didn't cost less than ten thousand dollars, but you figure you got the right to make us live like you want.'

'I won't let you talk like that no more, Perry,' his mother said.

'I ain't going to have to, because they're a-leaving.' He popped a kitchen match on his thumbnail and lighted his cigarette.

'Do you know Irvin needs to be in a hospital? He might have active tuberculosis, and every one of you has been exposed to it,' Mr Call said.

'If you people are so goddamn charity minded, why ain't you ever done anything for him before?'

'Because we don't always have the facilities we need, but I guarantee you that boy will receive treatment,' the man said.

'There ain't a hospital on the plateau where he can get taken care of,' Perry said.

'We have places in Lexington,' Mrs Lester said.

'I'll be the one to take him if he needs it. Now, I'm through talking with you.'

'I'm afraid you're not,' Mr Call said. The blue veins in his temples pulsed as he pulled some papers from his business satchel. 'I don't like to use this, but we have your mother's signed permission to take the children to our home, and she's the only legal adult in this house.'

Mrs James lowered her eyes to the floor and clenched her hands until the fingernails made white marks against her palms. Perry stared at her.

'You done this?' he said.

'I don't reckon we got much choice, son. There ain't enough to eat for all the children, and I don't look for things to get much better.'

'The mines will open up sooner or later, and the union says after we get an election they'll raise our wage,' he said. 'It ain't like I'm always going to be out of work.'

'I've heered the same thing for twenty-five years, and it ain't ever got better. At least when Woodson was alive we had his happy-pappy money, but we ain't even got that now.'

'Bee Hatfield said a man's coming down from Washington in two weeks, and they're going to make the mines open up. There won't be no more strikes and the association can't lock us out. With all them empty coal cars lined up on the spurs, we'll be a-working overtime every evening.'

'Bee don't know nothing but what other people tell him, and he don't hear that right half the time,' she said. 'Even if the mines open, you'll spend more time on the picket than in the hole. I seen it too many years. The union never done nothing for your daddy, and it ain't going to do nothing for us now, except take part of your wage.'

'By God, they still ain't taking the kids,' Perry said. 'Mister, that paper in your hand don't mean nothing to me. Stick it back in your satchel and get on down the road.'

'Perry, I can't set still no more for that kind of talk,' his mother said.

'Look at the kids. You think they want to leave?'

'These things are hard, but your brother and two sisters will be better off for it,' Mr Call said.

'Go on and get out of here. I ain't telling you again.'

'You don't have this right,' Mr Call said.

'Yes sir, I do. Now see how fast you can drive down that ridge.'

'I'm going to leave because Mrs Lester is with me, but I'll be back later.'

'You ain't going to get in this house again, and you can study on that all the way back to Richmond.'

Later, after Perry had watched the two people step gingerly down the steep incline towards their car, he sat on the porch in the sunlight and smoked another cigarette. In the distance the dust from the automobile hung in the air above the ridge. Far off in the hollow the trunks of the birch trees were white against the green hillside. Farther down the road a family from the bottom of the mountain walked towards their home, built of boxes, logs, and tar paper. The man was in the lead, and his wife and five children were in single file behind him. The woman's back was stooped, and the children were dressed in clothes made from feed sacks or cut-down denims. They lived in a settlement called Rachel's Hollow, where no one was sure who held title to the land and the men all made their living by moonshining, bootlegging, or stealing parts off automobiles and farm machinery. People from North Carolina, West Virginia, and Tennessee who were usually wanted by the law moved in and out of the cabins regularly, and because shootings were common in that hollow, the sheriff and the A.B.C. seldom went into it. Them welfare people ought to take their goddamn charity down there, Perry thought. Except they'd get their tires cut to pieces and maybe get throwed in the honey hole, besides.

His mother opened the screen door and set a plate of grits and a piece of ham next to him without speaking.

'I'm sorry for cussing in front of you and the kids,' he said.

She wiped her hands on her dress and started to go back inside.

'It's just I ain't got no use for them kind of people,' he said. 'They look down on us, and they don't have no more real feeling for the kids than they do a dog they feed on their back porch.'

'You reckon it's easy for me to let my own children go?' she said.

'You wouldn't have signed them papers unless they talked you into it.'

'I can't look at them every day and know there ain't enough to feed them. A person don't have the right to keep children when things is like that.'

'It ain't ever going to be so bad that we got to give part of our family away.'

'You can't hold back what's got to happen, son. We just wasn't meant to have things go like we want them to.'

'There ain't nothing going to happen, at least not from the likes of them people.'

But one hour later the deputy sheriff's old sedan sped up the ridge with the shale flying from under the tires, and Mr Call sat next to the driver with his business satchel on his lap. Perry watched them toil their way up the trail in the afternoon sun. The deputy, Bud Winston, worked part time in the sheriff's office, and on Friday and Saturday nights he played banjo and fiddle in a bluegrass band at Mount Sterling. His face was young and lean, red with sunburn, and his tall, narrow frame always looked awkward in his clothes. For a uniform he wore his old army khakis with the corporal insignias torn off the sleeves. The heavy, officer's model double-action .45 revolver hung in a holster on his belt. His blue eyes were intent, but he didn't look straight at Perry when he neared the porch.

'I didn't figure you to come out here with him,' Perry said.

'I do what the sheriff tells me, Perry. This feller's got some papers that says he's supposed to take three of the little ones to a home in Richmond,' Winston said. He looked aside when he talked.

'I already seen them.'

'Then you know he's got the legal right.'

'I reckon I should have torn them papers up before I run him out of the house,' Perry said.

'That wouldn't make no difference. Mrs James give her consent.'

'Would you let him take your brother and sisters?'

'I don't like coming out here this way. In fact, I told the sheriff I didn't want nothing to do with it.'

'Then tell this man he ain't got any business in this county. He don't pay your salary,' Perry said.

'There's not much point in going through this again,' Mr Call said. His face was perspiring from the uphill climb, and the blue veins in his temples were swollen against the skin.

'You ain't even here, mister,' Perry said.

'He's from the state government, and he's got the authority to take the kids,' the deputy said. He spit tobacco juice into the dust.

'Who give it to him? I ain't ever seen him before, and neither have you. He come in from outside with a bunch of paper, and now he can bring the law out to our house.'

'The fifty dollars a week I get for this job ain't hardly worth it, and if I'd knowed I'd have to do this today I might have gone looking for another job,' Winston said. 'But you're going to have to let them kids come out.'

'They'll be out soon as he leaves.'

'That ain't the way it's going to be.' His eyes looked directly at Perry's.

'You got no part of this. It ain't your people he's trying to take away.'

'I got to do what I'm told, even if I don't like it. I reckon you know that by this time.'

'It don't change what I already said.'

'Bring them outside, Perry,' the deputy said. His jaw bone stood out in a stiff line against his cheek.

'That's something I ain't going to do.'

'Buddy, you're putting me between a rock and a hard place. I don't want to have to go inside and take them out myself.'

'You have to make up your mind about that. But I'd say you'd be doing the wrong thing,' Perry said.

'The sheriff told me he took a pistol off you once, and I know you're either carrying it or you got it right close by. If you're a-figuring on stopping me that way, you won't ever get up off that step again.'

Perry heard the screen door slam behind him.

'There ain't going to be nothing like that around this house,' Mrs James said. 'I've lost my husband and one boy already, and I ain't going to see Perry shot down or go to the penitentiary. You take the children.' She pulled Irvin and the two girls through the door onto the porch.

'Get them back in there,' Perry said.

'I don't want no more grief in this family, and I won't let you cause it,' she said. 'Take them, Bud. He won't get in your way.'

'Stay where you're at,' Perry said.

'Years ago I stood at the depot and watched them take your brother's body off the train in a box. Part of my life slipped right out of my soul then, like I could feel it draining away into the air. The same thing happened when I looked down at your daddy in his coffin. I ain't got much more to give now, and if you put me through it again there won't be nobody left to look after none of the children.'

The deputy stepped up on the porch and took the children by their hands. His eyes were bright, and there was a line of sweat down the front of his shirt where it buttoned. Perry started to his feet.

'You set right there,' Mrs James said. 'If you raise your hand to Bud, you'll have to do it to me first.'

'Daddy wouldn't let you do this. He wouldn't care how bad times got.'

'I meant it, son. Stand out of his way.'

'You can't do nothing about it, Perry,' the deputy said. 'Even if you could run me off or shoot me, there would be somebody else out here.'

'He ain't a-shooting nobody,' Mrs James said.

Bud Winston led the children down the steps past Perry. His face was sweating heavily now. He watched Perry out of the corner of his eye. The children's heads were twisted back towards their mother on the porch.

'You people done more harm to us than even them company gun thugs,' Perry said.

'You won't feel that way later,' Mr Call said.

'Mister, I better not ever see you on the same side of the street as me,' Perry said.

'Where they taking us?' Irvin said.

'It's a good place, like I told you,' Mrs James said. Her eyes were wet and she brushed them with the palm of her hand. 'Go with Bud and I'll be down to see you all Sunday. Pretty soon you can come home again, and Perry's going to take you down in the holler to find arrowheads.'

'I don't want to go.'

'Get them in your car and off this mountain, Bud,' Mrs James said. Her grey eyes were filmed, and the thin flesh at the sides of her mouth was pinched in a tight line.

'I won't forget what you people done,' Perry said.

But the deputy and the welfare worker were already part way down the trail and they did not turn around.

Perry looked dumbly at the faces of the children, who continued to stare at him, and he knew that regardless of what he did in reprisal against Bud Winston, Mr Call, or Mrs Lester, they still had the world of paper, legal signatures, and authority on their side, and they could affect his family's life in any way they wished whenever they desired. In his exhaustion, he saw them holding the same power as the mining association, which, on a whim, could suddenly evict his family from the cabin, shut off their supply of food at the store, fire him from his job, blacklist him at every mine on the plateau, kill his father, and finally take his brother and two sisters from home.

He sat on the porch the rest of the afternoon in the still heat and looked out across the great expanse of the hollow below. At twilight he walked down the shale road to Rachel's Hollow and bought a pint of corn whiskey for fifty cents from a bootlegger who lived with his wife and three children in a dirt-floor shack covered with Montgomery Ward brick. There was a yellow sediment in the bottom of the whiskey, and the taste of the corn meal was so raw that it sickened his stomach. The purple dusk began to darken over the ridges, and the swallows spun in the air above the treetops. Later, after the last glow of the sun had diminished in the distance, the full moon rose above the limestone cliffs and reflected off the white road. He walked along in the dark to his cabin, sipping from the bottle and listening to the night birds calling to one another far below. The air was cool, and he could smell the water rushing over the rocks in the stream bed. At the top of the road he finished the bottle and threw it whistling end over end to the bottom of the hollow.

By the time he reached his front porch his heart was

pumping hard, the whiskey spun in his brain, and although he didn't remember it later, he took his revolver from his canvas bag and stumbled down the incline behind the cabin to the creek. The openings to the rock houses were black in the moonlight, and green vines grew along the overhanging ledges. The limbs of the white oaks and beech trees were spread overhead against the sky, and in places the water in the creek flashed like quicksilver over the smooth stones. He cocked the revolver, aimed with both hands unsteadily at a rock house, and pulled the trigger. The flames exploded through the barrel and from the sides of the cylinder, the bullet ricocheted and whined off the walls of the cave, and the noise crashed down the creek bed. He splashed through the water and fell on his face. The cold rushed inside his clothes and work boots, and he rolled over in the wet dirt on the bank. His hair hung in front of his eyes, and the earth, trees, and rocks began to spin around him. He wiped the mud off of the revolver's cylinder, propped his elbows on the ground, and fired the remaining five shots at the rock wall across the creek. The roar of the magnum shells thundered in his ears, and he felt particles of lead shave off the back of the barrel and scald his face. His aim was low and two bullets struck the surface of the creek and blew water to the treetops. He kept cocking the action and squeezing the trigger even after the gun had clicked empty; then he passed out with one arm under his face. He did not awake until the sun came up white in the sky above the ridge.

chapter ten

For three more weeks the picket lines stayed up at the union mines, and the independents continued their lockout rather than sign contracts. There were several shootings, one attempt to dynamite a C & O loading platform near the coal tipple, and the union agent in Hazard was almost beaten to death behind his office by two company deputies. Then the National Labor Relations Board in Washington issued an order for all the mines on the plateau to open again, and industrial referees were sent into every coal-mining county in eastern Kentucky and West Virginia to supervise the union elections. Within hours of the order the Brotherhood of Locomotive Trainmen, who had honored the U.M.W. picket lines, reported back to work, and the first full C & O coal cars to leave the Cumberland in months were on their way north to Dayton and Pittsburgh. The bars and poolrooms in town were suddenly empty, and men stood in long lines outside the company office shacks to sign on for the first eight-hour shift in the hole.

The sun had not risen above the mountain yet, and there was a chill in the grey dawn when Perry arrived, two hours early, at the mine. He took his place in the line that began at the locked door of the company office. He wore his hard hat, army field jacket, and steel-toed boots, and he carried his lunch pail in his hand. The mist glistened on the coal pile by the tipple, and the clouds hung low on the great scarred areas across the face of the mountain. The ground was strewn with pulverized slag and limestone, and the smoke from the slag heap drifted back in the wind over the line of men. During the strike most of the windows in the office shacks had been broken with rocks, and misspelled picket signs were still nailed to some of the doors.

An hour later, after the sun had climbed above the mountain's crest and cast deep shadows into the hollow, no one from either the company or the union had arrived. The miners drank coffee from thermos jugs and passed around pint bottles of corn whiskey in paper sacks, and if a man had to relieve himself, he unbuttoned his trousers and urinated on the ground rather than chance losing his place in the line. Nearly half of the men there were out-of-state scabs and strip-mine workers, and Perry knew that the company would probably try to pack the election with nonunion votes. The scabs stayed grouped together, silent, their faces blank; and their eyes always managed not to meet another man's stare. Perry could hear Big J.W.'s voice at the head of the line and the phlegmy laughter that made him think of something obscene. Little J.W. stood beside his brother, his face hard and impassive, and worked the point of his bowie knife under his fingernails. He had a small lump of tobacco in his cheek, and occasionally he sucked his teeth and spit a drop of brown spittle off the tip of his tongue. There were three scabs from Tennessee behind the J.W.s, and they stayed several feet away from them in the line and looked at the ground or the side of the mountain.

At seven thirty the company foremen, the time-keeper, and the operator drove up the shale road to the shack in three automobiles. Four company deputies, in soiled grey uniforms and with pistols on their hips, followed in a surplus navy carryall. Perry had seen them before when he was on the picket line, and two of them had once beaten three miners with axe handles after the miners had been caught pouring sand into the gas tanks of company trucks. The timekeeper opened the office and brought out a wooden table and chair and a ledger. The cuffs of his white shirt were rolled back over his thin arms, his slacks bagged at the rear, and he smoked one cigarette after another. His face always looked irritated, like the clerk's in the company store by Perry's cabin, and he spoke with the same clipped accent of authority. Two deputies stood behind him like twins, with their heavy leather pistol belts stretched across their stomachs and their big hands on their hips.

'You reckon you got enough fire power there to watch over all these scabs?' Big J.W. said. 'I heered somebody say some of them West Virginia boys might get ground up for dog food.'

'Do you want to work in this mine?' the timekeeper said.

'Buddy, I'll load the first car that comes out of that hole this morning. You just put my name down there,' Big J.W. said.

'You better get something straight, then. There ain't any such thing as a scab in this mine. There's a job open for any man that wants to work.'

'Them three behind me sure look like scabs. I bet they taken jobs away from union men all over the plateau. What do you fellers say about that?'

The three men from Tennessee looked away nervously. One of them had a film of perspiration on his forehead, although the morning was still cool.

'I don't guess they got anything to say,' Big J.W. said. 'They're probably a-thinking about the way they're going to vote this evening – if they come out of the hole.'

'Get out of the line,' the timekeeper said.

'Listen to that, baby brother. That white shirt lets him tell us to get out of line.'

'There's fifty men behind you, and I ain't got the time to waste on you,' the timekeeper said.

'I bet they pay you plenty of money for setting behind a desk with a couple of gun thugs to back you up against union men. You probably get twice as much as us without ever getting that white shirt dirty.'

'Stop talking with these sonsofbitches and get on with it,' Little J.W. said. He pared off the edge of his thumbnail and didn't look up when he spoke.

'You write Big J.W. and Little J.W. Sudduth's name down in that book. After our election I reckon you'll know how to watch that smart company mouth.'

The two J.W.s walked past the table and the two company deputies to the open shaft and climbed into an empty coal car behind the motorman. The sun climbed higher in the sky, and the breeze blew the smoke from the slag heap up the hollow. Perry waited in line until it was his turn to sign the book.

'Can you write your name?' the timekeeper said.

'Yes sir, I sure can. Here's my union card.'

'That don't mean nothing around here.'

'What's the scale?' Perry said.

'That's another word we don't have here. You get a dollar and a quarter like everybody else.'

'They said we would get two dollars.'

'Get your name down there if you want to work.'

'Why ain't we getting what the foreman told us in town?'

'There's ten men for every job in this hole. You can go right back to town, and we won't miss you.'

Perry signed his name on the ledger. The timekeeper looked at it and ran his finger down a list of names on a printed sheet.

'You were working in Blue Belle Number Two when somebody dynamited the tipple, weren't you?' he said.

'Half the fellers in this line has worked in that hole.'

'But I think you were one of them that got pulled in by the sheriff.' The timekeeper tapped his pencil on the desk. He felt his sense of advantage.

'I didn't get arrested for nothing. He just talked to me. That don't mean anything,' Perry said.

'He took you in to pass the time of day. Is that right?'

'Go ask him.'

'I'm talking to you now,' the timekeeper said.

Perry felt his temper begin to rise inside him.

'Them two fellers at the head of the line was taken in with me. You didn't say nothing to them.'

'They ain't on this list.'

An official from the company had come out of the office shack, and stood behind the two deputies. He wore yellow leather gloves, and his bright, print tie was blown over the shoulder of his white shirt.

'Let him go by or he'll run to the industrial referee and charge discrimination,' he said.

'I don't run to nobody,' Perry said.

'You're a real pistol, ain't you?' the timekeeper said. 'In a few days we won't have to take your kind down here anymore. Get on down to the hole.'

'What do you mean my kind?' Perry said.

'Don't worry about that, and just give us a good eight hours,' the man with the yellow gloves said.

'I put out as hard a day's work as any man in this coal field.'

'You're blocking the line,' the timekeeper said.

'What's your name?' Perry said.

'I've seen them come and go like you by the hundreds. You don't bother me, James.'

'You people treat a man like he ain't nothing because he needs a job.'

'Strike his name if he says anything else,' the man with the yellow gloves said.

Perry walked to the coal cars and climbed inside with two other men. His face was hot, and his hands shook when he rolled a cigarette. He glared at the backs of the timekeeper, the deputies, and the company official, and the rage inside him was like a piece of rope twisted across his chest. He smoked one puff after another until he felt the ash close to his lip.

'Take it easy,' the man next to him said. 'We'll catch that shithead in town one night.'

'We ain't got to do that,' the other man in the coal car said. 'After our election we'll get him fired and run him out of the county.'

'I reckon the J.W.s got something even better planned for him,' the first man said. 'Maybe they might catch him in that shack one night and set fire to him and it, both.'

The line of men passed by the timekeeper's table until all the jobs were filled, and fifty men were told that they could report back the next day in case there were more openings. The string of coal cars was filled with miners in hard hats with battery-operated head lamps, picks and loading shovels, and tamping rods for the explosives. The motorman started the engine, and the cars moved down the track into the black opening of the mine. The limestone had been blasted away on the face of the mountain, and great oak timbers shored up the roof around the entrance. Perry felt the cool, dank air of the shaft hit his face as they moved under the limestone ledge, and he could smell the stagnant water that was down at the bottom of the shaft. Under the string of generator-powered light bulbs, the corridors seemed to reach back endlessly into the mountain, and he felt something drop inside him as he looked at the winding course of the tracks between the rock walls. The ceiling was pinned with steel rods set two feet apart; Perry had once seen a square of rock slip out neatly between the pins and break a man's back. In the year and a half he had worked in the mines, he had never grown used to going into the hole; each trip was always like the first. The quiet fear was always there in his stomach, and there was an unnatural feeling inside him that he could never describe. In some ways the mine had the smell of an opened grave, and something primeval in him rebelled against his entering the earth. The weight of the ground above seemed to crush upon his head, and the spiral cut of the corridor made him lose his sense of equilibrium, as though he were rushing straight downwards towards the center of the world. After an hour of loading coal and driving the air hammer into the seam, the fear would begin to disappear; but the next day at the eight o'clock shift that terror would have to be overcome again as he sat quietly against the hard metal side of the coal car.

The fear was in the other men's faces, also, even though many of them had spent half of their lives underground. They chewed tobacco dryly, smoked hand-rolled cigarettes away in a few puffs, rubbed the backs of their wrists against their foreheads, and sometimes talked in loud, strained voices. Someone threw an empty pint bottle out of a car against a wall, and the sound of breaking glass was like an explosion in the corridor. All the miners laughed, and the echo rolled up and down the side tunnels and deserted rooms, where the seam had ceased to pay. The cars clicked over the tracks deeper into the mountain, and Perry felt a drop of sweat form on his temple and run down the side of his face.

'Some of these cars sure do smell bad,' Big J.W. said. His skin was yellow under the lights, and the ingrained coal dust around his eyes and forehead looked purple, like a bruise. 'I bet some of them scabs didn't wash the jenny-barn off themselves last night.'

The three nonunion men from Tennessee sat silently in the car, behind the J.W.s.

'In fact, it smells just like rut off a whore, don't it, baby brother?' Big J.W. said. 'We might have to give some of them boys a bath in that flooded room at the bottom of the hole.'

'I told you not to waste your time on these sonsofbitches,' Little J.W. said. 'They ain't a-working in this mine much longer.'

'Look at these three behind us,' Big J.W. said. 'They come a long way to scab. I reckon they figure on staying a while.'

'They'll stay down here permanent if they try to work scab after our election,' Little J.W. said. He never looked up while he pared his fingernails.

'We ain't done nothing to you people,' one of the men from Tennessee said. He was taller than his two friends, lean, with the same hard mountain features as other men throughout the Cumberland. His arms rested on top of his pick helve. His green and brown flecked eyes looked straight at Big J.W.'s.

'You don't reckon it's nothing to take a man's job?' Big J.W. said.

'We hired on like everybody else. It don't matter to me if this hole is union or not. I just go where the work is at.'

'You been crossing picket lines three months getting strikebreaker wages,' Big J.W. said.

'They never give us more than a dollar and a quarter. And we ain't no strikebreakers. I got people to support back home, and if I don't work they don't get nothing to eat.'

'What do you figure our families eat while we're on the picket?' another man said.

'That ain't my concern,' the man from Tennessee said. 'I got my own family to look out for. It don't have nothing to do with you people.'

'You make money while we go without, and it don't have nothing to do with us?' Big J.W. said. 'You were brought in from outside to take our jobs, and we're going to run your kind off. If that's all that happens to you.'

'I ain't ever been run off a job, and there ain't a man here that can do it. I didn't say nothing to you fellers outside, but you better forget about threatening me anymore. I won't set still for it much longer.'

'There's a lot of dark rooms at the bottom of this hole,' Big J.W. said.

'Buddy, I'll promise you one thing. You'll be the man left down here if you push me.'

'Shut your face, scab,' Little J.W. said. 'You won't do nothing, except maybe get your bus ticket back to where you come from. You're lucky somebody ain't got you already.'

'If you want to ever try it, you better get an apple box to stand on,' the man from Tennessee said.

Little J.W. looked up quickly. His knife rested in his hand, and the callused tip of his thumb lay across the base of the blade. His eyes were dark and hardened, and his round features became rigid.

'You want to walk out of here this afternoon?' he said.

'I don't reckon you'll be the one to stand in my way.'

'I'm real close to laying your face open right now.'

The man from Tennessee set the point of his pick on the edge of the coal car and clenched the butt end with one hand. His blood veins were tight across the bones of his wrist.

'You can try, but they'll carry you out of that car,' he said.

'That ain't going to do you much good with one eye,' Little J.W. said.

'It's up to you, buddy.'

'That's enough of that shit back there,' the motor-man, who was a union foreman, said. 'We got our election tonight, and then we won't need no more of this. These cars got to be loaded and out by ten o'clock, and there ain't going to be no fighting to hold it up.'

'You working to get a white shirt in that company shack?' Little J.W. said.

'When I make a run it comes out on time,' the motorman said. 'At ten o'clock I'm a-making my drop, and the man that makes me late is going to be looking for another job.'

Little J.W. put his knife back in its scabbard and dropped it inside the bib pocket of his overalls. The rest of the way down the corridor he stared rigidly at the man from Tennessee.

They started loading coal one mile back in the

mountain. There was an inch of water along the bottom of the corridor, and the water in some of the side rooms went up to the men's knees. The tunnel was narrow, the ceiling low, and moisture had formed on the outcroppings of limestone. The cold began to soak through Perry's boots, and he wished he had spent three dollars to buy a pair of rubber overshoes. As he shoveled the coal and slag into the empty cars, he felt the fear of the earth's interior begin to grow in him again. There was too much water seepage through the rocks, there were no ventilator fans to draw gas and bad air out of the rooms, pieces of limestone had fallen loose from the overhead pinning, the ceiling seemed to groan above him, and after the men had been working a while he could feel the coal dust down in his lungs. He remembered the stories about the explosions that roared through the corridors and deafened men a half mile from the blast and left them with brain concussions. Once, he had seen a nonunion mine that had collapsed in Letcher County. The miners were paid ten dollars for an eight-hour shift, and they spent most of the time in narrow pockets on their knees, digging low-grade coal out of the seam. The pinning had not been set properly in the roof, and when the mine caved, a long V-shaped sink hole settled on top of it across the mountain's incline. No one was ever able to reach the men inside, and later people believed they either died from lack of air or from starvation.

Perry knew other stories of blow-outs and cave-ins, men drowned in flooded corridors, flash gas explosions that incinerated whole crews; but the worst story he had ever heard was of two men who were buried alive two weeks in a Virginia shaft. Water broke through the side of the tunnel at the end of the first week, and both miners were given up for dead. When the blockage was finally cleared, the rescue team found them sitting against a wall, with water up to their chests. Their skin had faded and wrinkled like wet paper, and their minds were totally insane.

Perry's crew finished loading the slag into the coal cars, and the motorman backed the string up the tracks towards the entrance. Perry picked up the air drill, propped its heavy weight against the coal seam, and thudded the bit into the wall. The hammering vibrations made his tin hat bang against his forehead, and he had to clench his teeth to keep them from chattering against each other. In minutes his palms were sore through his metal-beaded gloves. The dust clouded up around him and stuck to his damp skin. The coal broke away from the wall and fell into the water by his feet. He worked steadily for a half hour, and then he had to stop and wipe the film from his goggles.

'Don't knock down that wall all at one time,' the man from Tennessee said. 'They ain't pinned this ceiling yet.'

'That's because it's a scab mine, and it don't follow safety regulations,' Big J.W. said.

'It don't matter what kind of a mine it is if it comes down on your head.'

'We wouldn't be worried about no ceiling if the union inspection team was down here,' Big J.W. said. 'They ain't ever been in this hole because the company could always bring in outside scabs like you, and a scab don't care where he works.'

'Like I told you before, buddy, I never had no choice about where I worked,' the man from Tennessee said. 'They never asked me to vote in no election, either, and I didn't ask them nothing about it. I figure a dollar and a quarter is better than having nothing.'

Perry filled his fingers with loose, string tobacco and

put it in the side of his mouth. He pulled his goggles down over his eyes, spit into a pool of water by his feet, and set the drill into the wall again.

'Don't knock no more down,' another miner said. 'That drill sounds like a train against this dead end. They ain't a-paying enough to work us that hard or bring one of them walls in on us.'

'The foreman said he wants the seam cleared back to the next room,' Perry said.

'Piss on him,' Big J.W. said. 'He won't be here if this mountain folds in. He's drinking coffee above ground, and all he'll hear is a big crunch down in the hole.'

'I signed on to do a day's work,' Perry said. 'You all can get back around the corner if you figure the wall's a-coming down.' He pushed his weight against the drill handle and triggered the air pressure. He didn't look up at Big J.W. or the other men, although he felt them watching him. He hadn't worked an air drill in a long time, and his hands had grown soft. At one time there was a ridge of thick callus across each of his palms, but now the throbbing cut into his hands as though he had deep stone bruises under his skin. The coal shaled away from the wall until it stood in piles up to his knees. Finally, he couldn't support the drill's weight any longer against the seam, and he cut the air pressure and pulled his hard hat and goggles off his head. His hair was wet with sweat, and water blisters the size of quarters had formed on his palms.

After the motorman had picked up the next load, the men sat on top of the piles of slag and ate their lunch. Their fingers left dark creases in their sandwich bread, and the dust settled out of the air into their thermos cups. There was a damp smell of sweat in the corridor, and most of the miners' clothes were soaked with water. Little J.W. sat across from Perry and neatly pared the skin off an orange. The knife was sharpened on both sides, and there was a thumb guard at the bottom of the blade. Little J.W. had been stringing lights in a flooded room during the morning, and his overalls were dark up to his chest.

'What are you watching me for?' he said.

'I wasn't paying you no mind,' Perry said.

'You was looking at me like you had something to say.'

'I ain't talked to you this morning, and I wasn't figuring on it.'

'I heered you said plenty in town, though. Something about backing the J.W.s down. Is that right?'

Perry dropped his eyes and put a piece of ham and bread in his mouth. He chewed slowly and wiped the grease off his fingers onto his trousers. Don't let it get started now, he thought. He's just talking. He won't pull nothing with this many people around.

'Somebody said you run us out of the barroom,' Little J.W. said.

'I ain't talked about you with nobody. What people say ain't my business.'

'By God, it's mine when somebody can say a Sudduth was run off by a kid.'

'I ain't done nothing to you. What you got against me is in your own head.'

'Who do you reckon told all them people that the J.W.s backed down?'

'Go ask them in town. I didn't have nothing to do with it. You started trouble with me without no call, and I told you once I just wanted you to let me alone.'

'I think you're a goddamn liar that talks behind a man's back and can't face up to it.'

Perry felt something jerk inside him, and involuntarily he set the flat of his hand on top of his pocket

214

where his knife was. He looked at the hatred in Little J.W.'s eyes, the tight mouth, and the lines of sweat through the coal dust on his face.

'A man don't call me that,' he said.

'You got another name for it?'

'I'll walk out of this hole before I'll have trouble with you, but you ain't going to say that to me again.'

'What do you have in that pocket? Take it out and let's see if you're any good with it.'

'I ain't got to prove nothing to you. I ain't bothered you in no way, I didn't start no rumors in town, and if I'd knowed you all was working in this hole I wouldn't be down here. So don't fool with me no more.'

'Your face is sweating,' Little J.W. said.

'It ain't because of you.'

'I don't think you got the balls to back up that big mouth.'

'Leave him be. He didn't start nothing with you,' the man from Tennessee said.

'Keep clear of it, scab,' Little J.W. said.

'I been a-hearing you order people around all morning. You ain't no foreman, and I'm fed up listening to you threaten us.'

'I reckon you might not get to take that bus ride back home after all,' Little J.W. said.

'I'll be working this mine as long as they'll hire me, and when I decide to catch air, it won't have nothing to do with you,' the man from Tennessee said.

'This boy and me got something to settle, and when I get finished with him I'll give you some of it, too,' Little J.W. said.

'I ain't settling nothing with you, because I ain't working around you no more,' Perry said. He put his lunch back in his pail and started down the coal car tracks on the floor of the corridor. His boots splashed in the pools of water.

'He run off quicker than I expected,' Big J.W. said.

'I ain't a-quitting this job or no other on account of you all,' Perry said. 'I'm just getting on another crew where I don't have to be near you.'

'We'll see you again when you come out of the hole. You ain't getting away from us,' Little J.W. said.

Perry followed the winding tunnel up to the next level, where he found the foreman eating lunch with another crew. The coal dust was heavier here because there was less moisture in the air and less seepage through the walls, and the men's faces were completely black except for the area around their eyes, where they wore their goggles.

'I don't want to work in that back pocket no more,' Perry said.

'You work where you get dropped. That pocket ain't no more dangerous than any other.'

'It don't have nothing to do with the pocket. I want on another crew.'

'Is there anything else you want? Maybe a pay raise or a vacation,' the foreman said. The other men sitting against the wall laughed.

'I signed on for a day's wage, not for no trouble. I ain't pulling another shift with the J.W.s.'

'Has that shit started again? By God, I'm going to see a half dozen men fired by this evening if I hear any more of it. Now get on back down where you belong and tell them others to get their ass busy.'

'You better fire me now, then, because I ain't taking no more from the likes of them. I'll run the air drill for you and I'll load as many cars as any man here, but the job don't pay enough to put up with them two all day.'

Normally, the foreman would have fired Perry for

speaking back to him, but the election was that night and he knew the union couldn't afford to lose any votes against all the scabs who went down into the hole that morning.

'All right, you can stay with this crew, but you'll be a-filing your unemployment if there's any more of this crap.'

Perry worked on the upper level the rest of the day. The blisters on his hands broke, and the tender skin peeled back from his palms as he dug his shovel into the piles of slag. The small of his back began to ache from working stooped over, and the coal dust became so bad that he could taste it in his throat. Some of the older men coughed fitfully, with the deep chest rattle of silicosis, and one man set his shovel down and walked back towards the entrance with a handkerchief over his mouth. The day's tedium wore on, and Perry stopped thinking about the weight of the mountain above his head, the cracks in the ceiling around the steel pins, and the possibility of a soft wall suddenly collapsing. He thought only of the pain in his hands and back, the fetid smell of men's bodies and stagnant water in the flooded rooms and the click of the coal cars coming down the track for another load. By the end of the day his blisters were bleeding and he could hardly remove the gloves from his hands. The heat from his body steamed in the damp air, and his wet work boots had rubbed his ankles raw. When the five-o'clock whistle blew outside and echoed faintly through the corridors, he was too tired to care if the J.W.s would be waiting for him above ground or not.

The afternoon sunlight was bright on the poplars and red maples across the hollow when he rode out of the hole in the string of cars with the rest of his crew. He shielded his eyes until they adjusted to the light.

The cool wind in the shadow of the mountain blew on his face, and he felt his sweat dry against his skin. He cleared his throat and spit the coal dust taste out of his mouth, and breathed in the good smell of the summer air. The mountains were green and blue in the distance, and he could see white water rushing over rocks in the stream beds. Strips of purple rain clouds had formed across the horizon, and the slanting rays of the sun struck like gold on the white oaks along the ridges of the cliffs.

The industrial referee from the National Labor Relations Board had set up two tables by the company office for the election, and the lines of blackened men waiting to vote already stretched back to the mine entrance.

Perry went to the water faucet by one of the tool shacks and turned it on full force. He took off his hat and shirt, knelt down on his knees, and let the water pour over his head. The coal dust ran off his hair and face onto his T-shirt and trouser legs. He found a used bar of soap and tried to scrub the grime out of his pores, but he knew he could never get it all off even with a wire brush. He turned his palms upwards under the tap to wash the pieces of cotton lint and grit out of his broken blisters, then he dried his face and arms on the inside of his shirt and walked back to the voting line.

Each man was given two slips of paper, one of which stated 'union' and the other 'open shop.' The miners were told to fold one and place it in the ballot box as they passed, but many of them could not read the words on the paper, and the U.M.W. agent went down the lines with a union ballot outstretched before him in his fingers until the industrial referee said that he was trying to influence the vote and ordered him to stop. There were six more company deputies on duty, each with a pistol and blackjack on his leather belt, and although they didn't speak to any of the miners, they walked up and down the lines and often looked hard into a man's face. The scabs and strip-mine workers stayed in groups to themselves, and as Perry glanced at the faces around him, many of them unfamiliar, he wondered if the union would have enough votes to carry the election. He had heard that if the mine went nonunion, the scabs would receive all the jobs, along with a pay raise, for staying loyal to the company, and no man with a union card would be allowed down in the hole. Some of the union miners rolled cigarettes, cut slices of chewing tobacco with finely honed pocketknives, and talked in voices loud enough for the scabs to hear:

'I heered they shot a couple more scabs over in Letcher. Somebody cotched them on a road at night and blowed them all over the side of a rock house. They say you couldn't even tell who they was by looking at their faces.'

'They say a scab down at Sterns stole so many chains he couldn't swim across Cumberland Lake. They couldn't find him for three days until somebody waved an association check over the water and his hand come up a-looking for it.'

'What about that feller that got burned up on the tipple at the Blue Belle? There wasn't enough of them charred pieces left to fill up a Bull Durham sack. That fire must have covered him up like he'd been soaked in gasoline.'

'I don't figure nothing like that could happen in this hole. Every man here looks like he knows which way to vote if he don't want to worry about walking on the street after dark.'

Once, a fight broke out in the line between a scab and a union miner. They rolled in the dirt, clubbing each other with their fists, and before they could be separated by the company deputies, the union man picked up a flat rock and knocked the scab unconscious. He lay still on the ground, his mouth wide open, with a large skinned lump above one eye. After two other scabs had picked him up and carried him between them to the water tap, the industrial referee climbed on top of a wooden chair and said that he would close the election if there were any more fights or if any deputy or union agent even came near the lines.

Perry waited his turn to drop his union vote into the box, then he began the long walk up the mountain road in the evening twilight towards his cabin. There was a car headed up the gravel in his direction; but Perry saw both of the J.W.s in the back seat, and he waved the driver on when he slowed to give him a ride. 'We'll see you in the hole tomorrow morning,' Little J.W. said out of the back window. He spit into the wind stream as he passed.

As Perry walked along and looked at the dust of the car he thought of the next day and the one after that and the endless weeks to follow. Every day in the mine would be the same. The J.W.s would always be somewhere near, with their threats and hatred, the fear would lie cold in his stomach every time he went back down the dark entrance, the dust would coat the inside of his mouth, his boots would be hard and stiff from the pools of water on the corridor floors, and each day the cracks along the ceiling would look wider from the tons of rock crushing down overhead. He thought of Cincinnati in the spring sunlight, the rows of maple trees in front of the narrow, German houses, and the beautiful sweep of the steel bridge above the river. He wondered if he would ever get back there, away from the mines, the slag heaps, the smell of men crowded together deep underground, the boredom of work that never changed from day to day, and the fears inside him that he could never admit to anyone. There was no way to tell how long it would take him to find the men who murdered his father, and after he did, he would probably be faced with years, or even death, in the state penitentiary. It's like you don't have nothing to say about the way any of it turns out, he thought. The law and the company and the J.W.s got you between them, and there ain't nothing to do about it except run, and you can't do that. So you got no choice about any of it.

On Friday night all of the election votes were counted, and almost every major mine on the plateau, including Perry's, had gone union. The association was forced to sign contracts, pay union scale, allow safety inspection teams to visit the mines, pay into a welfare fund for injured miners, install ventilator systems in shafts where there was gas, and guarantee time and a half pay for work over forty hours. Hundreds of miners had come into town directly from their jobs to hear the vote count read in front of the union office, and by ten o'clock all the bars and poolrooms were filled with drunken men, many still covered with dust from the mines. Those who had no money borrowed from the union agent on their next check, and the sheriff had to put on four extra deputies to protect the scabs, who were often shouldered off the sidewalks, knocked about in the saloons, or had their automobile tires cut on the streets. Men broke bottles on the concrete, windows were shattered, a miner was shot in the leg by a prostitute inside the jenny-barn, and the sheriff's jail was crowded before midnight. Men staggered along the sidewalks from one bar to the next, and a moonshiner from Rachel's Hollow sold clear whiskey in half-pint bottles on the street. Five scabs were forced to leave a cafe by union men, and as they tried to drive out of town, their car was surrounded by drunken miners, who at first made only insults and threats; then they began to rock the car until the underside of the body was hitting the pavement. One man spiderwebbed the driver's window with a beer bottle, another cut the air valves off the tires, and someone poured dirt into the gas tank. The men's faces inside were strained with fear. They pulled away from the windows and held onto the dashboard and seats. The driver got the engine started, and the car lumbered down the street on its metal rims while the tires split into ribbons. The union men laughed and threw more bottles against the back window and trunk.

Perry had also come into town to find out if the union had carried his mine. He had intended to return to the cabin early, but as he stood in the crowd of men in the velvet light before the union office, he took a drink from Bee Hatfield's bottle, then another. The whiskey was warm inside him, and it took away the long day in the mine and the dull fatigue in his body. He bought a bottle of corn liquor from a bootlegger who was selling out of his truck cab, and in a short while Perry was as drunk as any of the other men in town. The clock above the bank read ten o'clock, and he promised himself that he would start home by eleven. It seemed as though he was watching the time constantly, but then it was suddenly midnight and he couldn't remember what he had been doing for the last hour. There was a half-empty bottle of cheap wine in the side pocket of his field jacket, the fiddler and banjo player on the platform in the barroom were playing into the microphone, and Bee Hatfield was standing next to him, waving a full beer bottle in the air and yelling at people around him. The foam splattered on the floor. Bee's eyes were red, and his voice rasped above the hillbilly music.

'By God, every union man's a-making twenty-two dollars a day,' he said. 'The union come through for us, boys. We beat them scabs and strikebreakers, and the association ain't ever going to step on us again. Goddamn, let's have another drink.'

Perry upended the bottle of wine and passed it to his uncle. A man collapsed over a table filled with drinks, and one of the sheriff's deputies dragged him by the arms across the floor to the doorway.

'I been a-working for the union all my life, and I always knowed one day we'd lock this coal field up,' Bee said. 'There ain't going to be a scab left on the plateau Monday.'

'There ain't going to be no live ones,' another man said.

'Bring them goddamn drinks down here,' Bee yelled.

Perry steadied himself and looked at three men who were drinking at the end of the bar. Through the drunken haze he saw their brutal faces grinning at him. Their expressions were like death above their jiggers of whiskey. He had seen them many times in his dreams, and he knew that these were the men he had been searching for. He could smell their rotted breath and the acrid odor of exploded dynamite that still clung to their clothes. In the reflections of their eyes he could see the school building roaring in flames at night on top of the mountain. His elbow knocked Bee's bottle of beer over on the bar.

'You got to take me home to get my pistol,' he said.

'What?' Bee said.

'That's the ones that done it.'

'What are you talking about, boy? Done what?'

'Them three at the end of the bar blowed the schoolhouse.'

'That's the Caudill brothers. They're a-working in the same hole you're at.'

Perry's breath was coming hard and something was trembling inside him.

'I know the Caudills. You drive me home.'

'Set down in that chair. You must have bought some real bad moon this evening,' Bee said.

'I'll take them with my knife if I can't get my pistol.'

'You hush up. I ought to taken that corn away from you. Everything they sell out of Rachel's Holler has got bleach poured in the mash.'

'Who's he talking about cutting up down there?' one of the Caudill brothers said.

'He's drunk. He don't even know where he's at,' Bee said.

'By God, it sounded like he was talking about us,' the same Caudill brother said. His whiskey-inflamed eyes looked out from under his hard hat. His sleeves were cut off at the elbows, and he had tattoos of nude women on both arms.

'You goddamn murdering company sonofabitch,' Perry said.

'Buddy, that was the wrong thing to say,' Caudill said. He rose from the bar stool and walked around the side of the bar towards Perry.

'You stay where you're at,' Bee said. 'He don't mean nothing against you all. He thinks you're somebody else.'

'That don't matter. He ain't talking to me like that.'

'I'm a-taking him out. His daddy got killed and it don't ever get off his mind. He just got too much of that bad Rachel whiskey tonight.'

'He's a-staying till I say he can go.'

'No, sir, he ain't. Don't try to do him no harm, either, or I'll have your union card tore up by tomorrow morning.'

'Goddamn, they're the ones that–'

'You shut up and don't open your mouth again,' Bee said, and pulled Perry past the Caudill brothers. Perry knocked over a chair and stumbled into a table before Bee could get him outside.

'I got it under my bed.'

'Get in the car,' Bee said. He pushed Perry into the front seat and slammed the door.

The neon lights above the bars glittered off the broken glass on the sidewalks. A miner was passed out on the curb, and a girl from the jenny-barn was bargaining with two men in the doorway of the only hotel in town. Perry rested his head on the dashboard and felt the blood spinning in his brain. The car pulled out on the street and headed for the gravel road outside of town. His head rolled back and forth on his arm, and he thought the motion of the car was going to make him sick. The wind blew through the open vane into his face. Bee coughed as he drove, and wiped the spittle off his lips with his shirt sleeve.

'Ain't you got enough problems without fooling with the Caudills?' he said.

Perry tried to speak, but his mouth wouldn't work and in his mind he still saw the three grinning faces at the end of the bar. The moon was blue over the trees on the mountain, and the shale road stretched out white under the headlights as they drove through the limestone hollows and over the hills. He fell sideways against the door and his head banged against the window jamb. Then the darkness of the hills seemed to enclose about him as though he were dropping down through the shaft into the bottom of the mine.

Two weeks later Perry received his first union scale paycheck. As the men filed out of the hole, the timekeeper called each man's name and handed out the brown envelopes. Perry noticed that the timekeeper seemed nervous and avoided looking directly into anyone's eyes. The sun was warm on Perry's back, and the light was yellow above the line of shadow on the limestone cliffs. He planned to use part of his money to take his mother on the bus the next day to see Irvin and his two sisters at the state children's home in Richmond, and he wanted to get home and scrub the coal dust off his body in the stream behind the cabin.

'What the shit is this?' a miner next to him said. The man had opened his pay envelope, and he held a slip of mimeographed paper in his hand. He stared at it as though he didn't understand the words.

Perry was too exhausted from the day's work to pay any attention to him, and he put his own paycheck in his back pocket and buttoned the flap down on top of it. He slung his field jacket over his shoulder and started through the groups of men toward the road.

'This says I ain't working here no more,' he heard the miner say. 'Who the hell put this in my envelope?'

Then Perry saw that other men also had slips of paper in their hands, and their faces all had the same dumbfounded expressions. He took out his envelope, tore it open across the end, and looked at an identical slip clipped to his check. It read, *Due to the introduction of new machinery in your mine and a cut back in production orders you are temporarily discharged.*

Until there is a request for an increase in the work force your membership in the United Mine Workers of America is also temporarily voided. We regret that circumstances have brought this situation about – U.M.W. *Local 442.*

'Where's that goddamn timekeeper at?' a miner said.

'What's it mean?' someone else said.

'They're canning us,' Perry said, still looking at the paper with the same disbelief as the others.

'We got our contract. They can't fire us.'

'Get that goddamn timekeeper out here,' the first man said.

'This didn't come from the company. It's signed by the local,' Perry said. 'They're a-taking our cards away.'

'They can't take no union man's card away. Tell that timekeeper to get his ass out of the shack.'

The miners who had not been laid off walked towards their automobiles. Most of them looked at the ground and didn't speak to the angry men forming in groups.

'Some of them scabs has still got their jobs, and we ain't,' a man said.

'They ain't running me off this hole. I waited four months for it to open up. My family ain't going hungry no more.'

'I'm going to tear that shack down unless that goddamn timekeeper gets himself out here. You hear that, you sonofabitch! Come outside and tell us we're fired!'

'Lay one of them bricks through his window.'

'I'll do you one better than that, buddy. I'll drag him outside and stomp his head good.'

The door to the company office opened and the timekeeper walked out with two uniformed company deputies behind him. He had taken off his tie, and his shirt was damp under the arms. There was fear in his face as he looked at the fifty men who stood before him. The deputies had unsnapped the leather holding straps on their pistols. One man wadded up his layoff slip and threw it at the timekeeper's feet.

'You tell me to my face I ain't a-working this hole no more,' he said.

'The layoff is temporary. We might have full crews back on in a few weeks,' the timekeeper said. His voice almost cracked when he spoke.

'That's a goddamn lie. You're bringing in more machines to take our jobs because we're making scale now.'

'He looks like he's fixing to turn his britches brown, don't he?' another miner said.

'I work here just like you men,' the timekeeper said. 'I don't have nothing to do with laying anybody off.'

'I seen you get union men fired before we got our contract.'

'You people have been laid off before. You know you always get work again,' the timekeeper said. His voice was strained and his hands were awkward at his sides.

'This says our union cards is cancelled,' Perry said.

'The association don't have anything to do with that,' the timekeeper said. 'That came down from the business agent at your local.'

'The union don't turn against its own people. You sonsofbitches are behind this shit,' another man said.

'Go find your agent and ask him who took away your cards. You wouldn't have this trouble if you'd stayed with the company.'

'Why don't we take him down to that last flooded room and teach him how to swim?'

'Them deputies look pretty dirty, too. I know a deep hole they might fit in at the bottom of the second level.'

'You can't blame the company for what happened to you,' the timekeeper said. The deputies had set their hands on their revolvers. They shifted their weight and looked uncomfortably at the crowd of miners. 'This mine can't stay open and at the same time pay scale for all you men. The company just ain't got the money. You can work a dollar and a quarter forty hours a week and put a paycheck in your pocket every Friday night, or you can get nothing at all. The union didn't hire you, and the union don't make out your check. See if that business agent is interested in your problems now. They carried the election, and they don't need you all no more. Your card ain't worth a bubble gum wrapper down at the hall.'

'You lying bastard. You all had this planned since the hole opened.'

'Let's see the agent,' Perry said.

'I think we ought to fix this feller first.'

'That won't do no good. He ain't nobody. They wind him up every morning and tell him when to open his mouth and when to shut it,' Perry said. 'We been a-paying our dues to the union, and the agent's got to answer about taking away our cards.'

'That's right, by God. This sonofabitch can't tell us nothing. He's too scared now to know what he's talking about.'

'Everybody get in your cars and meet down at the local,' someone said.

'We'll see you at the first shift tomorrow morning, timekeeper,' another miner said. 'Them deputies of yours ain't going to keep us out of the hole, neither.'

The miners crowded into their battered old cars and

pickup trucks, and some men stood outside on the running boards, with their arms wrapped around the window jambs. The cars headed down the shale road through the hollow and a cloud of white alkali dust rose above the treetops. Perry sat between two other men in the back seat of a Ford coupe. The rocks rattled under the fenders, and the dust from the other automobiles poured back through the open windows. One man opened a bottle of corn whiskey and passed it around, and as each man took a second drink, some of the fatigue seemed to leave his face, and his eyes became more bright and intent. The cars reached the bottom of the hollow and turned onto the blacktop towards town. The old Ford and Chevrolet engines roared through broken mufflers off the surface of the road, and some of the cars careened around the curves at the base of the mountains. The men on the running boards were bent down inside the windows, their arms pressed tightly against the door panels.

There was already a line of cars double parked on the main street when the men from Perry's mine pulled into town. At least a hundred miners were standing on the sidewalk in front of the union office, and others were walking towards the office from the side streets where they had left their cars. Some of the men still had their discharge slips in their hands. The late sun reflected off their tin helmets and head lamps, and perspiration glistened through the coal dust on the backs of their necks. There was a rank odor in the air of men pressed against one another, and as Perry worked his way into the crowd he could smell the sweat, the hot tar on the street, the slag smoke in their clothes, and the cheap whiskey and wine on their breaths.

The door to the union office was locked and the shades were drawn across the windows.

'There's somebody in there. Beat on that goddamn door till they come out,' a man yelled from the back of the crowd.

'We been a-waiting for the agent a half hour.'

'Maybe they shut down early when they knowed we was coming.'

'They ain't gone nowhere. They're probably hid out in the back.'

One man walked up the concrete steps to the entrance and knocked on the door. When there was no answer, he hammered on it with his fist.

'A couple of you fellers up front kick it open. We ain't standing out in this sun no more.'

'Tear it right off the frame. They're a-making their salary right out of what we pay them, and they ain't locking no doors on us.'

Two other men climbed the steps and began kicking the door with their steel-toe work shoes. A wood panel splintered out of the bottom.

'Stand back, boys, and I'll put that sonofabitch right through the back of the building,' one man said. He set himself, raised his foot, and slammed the sole of his boot into the wood. The door flew back on its hinges and crashed against the inside wall.

The union agent and a man dressed in a business suit stood just inside the entrance. The agent's name was Bert Ramey, and he always wore starched khaki workingman's clothes and a Lima heavy equipment badge on his watch fob, although no one had ever known him to work on a construction or mining job. He was short and overweight, and his head was bald through the center of his hair. He wore a brown rain hat whenever he was outdoors, and there was a line of faint pink sunburn across his forehead. The man in the business suit was a stranger to Perry. His thin, graying hair was oiled and combed straight back, and he wore a silk tie with a gold pin through his white collar. His manner was relaxed and confident as he looked out over the heads of the men in the street.

'I been on the phone talking long distance, boys. You all didn't have no need to kick my door in,' Bert Ramey said.

'We don't care what you been doing. Who had this slip put in our envelopes?' one miner said.

'We can explain that to you if you give us time,' Ramey said.

'You better start doing it pretty fast, then.'

'Mr Hendricks here is from the main office in New York, and he's got a statement to read,' Ramey said.

'Goddamn, we ain't stood out here this long for no shit like that. What about our cards?'

'This thing ain't happening just here in our county,' Ramey said. 'They're a-cutting back men all over the plateau and in West Virginia, too.'

'You ain't said nothing yet. Who sent out these slips?'

'The association's putting in new machinery in every big mine around here, and there just ain't that much work for everybody no more,' Ramey said. 'The union don't want to drop you, but they can't send men out to jobs where there ain't none.'

'Our welfare cards ain't no good, either, then.'

'The welfare fund's been broke a year,' Ramey said. 'You all know that. There's more men drawing disability now than we got money for.'

'I been in the union sixteen years, and I ain't giving up my card,' the miner who had smashed the door open said.

'Every man here has walked pickets all over Kentucky for you,' another man said.

'I done two years in Frankfort penitentiary for the union, and by God I don't figure the U.M.W.'s going to tear up my card now.'

'Look, it ain't me that done it,' Ramey said. 'The order come down from New York. I've worked with all you fellers on every strike around here, and I don't like to see none of you get dropped.'

'You taken our dues out of today's check. You're a-drawing your money right out of our sweat.'

'It ain't that way. They might drop me just like they done it to you,' Ramey said.

'That's why you and this New York feller had yourself locked in the office together.'

'I can't tell you all no more. None of the locals around here would have taken your cards away. We just didn't have no say about it,' Ramey said.

'You made a deal with the association. You carried us till all the mines was union, and then you locked us out.'

'That ain't true,' Ramey said.

'Shit, it ain't. You better have your ass out of this county tonight.'

'As Bert told you, the union doesn't like to reduce the labor force, but there's almost a quarter million dollars of new machinery going into every major mine in the association, and there is no way to stop automation and its effects on labor,' Hendricks said. His clean-shaven cheeks shone in the sunlight.

'Who the hell are you, anyway?'

'I represent the southern region of the U.M.W. You men have seen this cutback coming for a long time. All of the miners out here can't do the work of three new

233

auger drills. We don't like it, but there's nothing the union can do about it.'

'Why don't you shut that smooth Yankee mouth? There wasn't nobody talking to you.'

'I bet you ain't ever been in the hole.'

'This isn't doing any of us any good,' Hendricks said. 'You men have to understand that we had no other recourse.'

'I spent thirty years underground, and you're a-telling me I can't work no more.'

'We can't do nothing now except scab or work truck mines for eight dollars a day.'

'My family lives in a company cabin, and they'll put us out just as soon as I miss one month's rent.'

'Our charge ain't no good at the store unless we're working.'

'That don't bother you, does it? You're a-staying in an air-conditioned motel down in Richmond, and tomorrow morning you'll have your airplane ticket back up North.'

'You men stay back. Hurting me won't help you,' Hendricks said.

'You think you can tell us we got to scab for a living?'

'We been on the picket six months waiting for this election. You ain't a-taking away what we won.'

'All of you stand away. This won't change your situation,' Hendricks said.

'Pull that sonofabitch off there.'

As the crowd pressed forward, the union agent ran for the back of his office. A big miner in a hard hat and overalls, with no shirt on, pushed Hendricks off the steps onto the sidewalk. The crystal on Hendricks' wristwatch broke, and his coat sleeve tore at the elbow. The walk was covered with tobacco spittle, and there were brown stains on his trousers and the palms of his hands. He got to his feet and backed against the wall of the building. 'It won't restore your jobs. You'll just have something to regret tomorrow,' he said. His collar had broken loose, and his oiled hair had fallen down on his temples. Someone threw a wine bottle through the office window, and other bottles crashed inside the doorway. The miner with no shirt shoved Hendricks to the pavement again, then knelt beside him and ripped his coat up the back. 'I don't reckon you'll come down here again and tell us we ain't got jobs,' the miner said. The white sun reflected off the pavement, and the miner's eyebrows were heavy with sweat. He pulled Hendricks by the shirt into a sitting position and threw him back against the wall. A siren echoed off the building fronts at the end of the street. The miner looked over his shoulder as the sheriff's car braked to a stop at the edge of the crowd, then he stood up and stared down at Hendricks. 'You're a pretty lucky sonofabitch, mister,' he said, 'and you can think about that all the way back to New York.'

chapter eleven

The late July heat settled on the plateau and shimmered on the ridges in waves. There was no breeze in the hollows, and the hardwood trees remained motionless in the humid air. The creeks and streams went dry, and the sandy beds were covered with swarms of sweat bees. Copperheads and rattlesnakes slithered through the burnt grass looking for water, and the tobacco in the fields began to wilt and turn yellow under the sun. In town unemployed miners who had hoped to get work cutting tobacco sat under the canvas awnings in front of the saloons and pool halls, cursing the heat and wiping the sweat off their foreheads onto their shirt sleeves. No one could remember when drought had lasted so long on the plateau, and as the weeks passed and the plowed rows began to harden and crack, the farmers marked off their crops as lost. The corn stalks withered and rattled dryly in the fields, and crows fed off the new ears lying parched on the ground.

Perry worked one or two days a week at a strip mine, where he had to report every morning at seven o'clock before he could find out whether or not he had a job for that day. He sat hours at a time in the Richmond employment office, only to have the window closed at four-thirty without his name being called. He applied for work cleaning out bars and filling station rest rooms, washing cars, scrubbing the insides of oil drums, and picking chickens for a nickel apiece on a poultry farm. In the afternoons he walked aimlessly around town and listened to other men talk about their unemployment claims that had been disallowed, the work to be had in Ohio, the ten-dollar-a-day jobs in the truck mine, and the county welfare allotment that was never enough to feed a family.

For two weeks the company cut off Perry's credit at the store because he hadn't paid last month's bill and was no longer employed. There was nothing in the cabin that could be pawned or sold except his pistol; and the manager at the finance company in Richmond wouldn't even accept his application for a loan. His mother made corn bread from the powdered milk and meal given out at the federal surplus food center, and in the early morning Perry killed rabbits by the red pools of water in the bottom of the creek beds. He cleaned and skinned the rabbits and hung them upon the front porch to let the heat and blood drain from their bodies in case they carried summer fever. At night his mother boiled them in a stew and poured it over pieces of old bread that the store sold at half price. At breakfast they ate the same stew again, but the grease and fat lay thick on their plates, and the stale bread was harder to chew and swallow. Then there were fewer rabbits in the creek bed as the remaining water evaporated or seeped into the dry cracks, and some days the James family ate three meals of grits mixed with powdered milk.

Perry thought about transporting whiskey for old man McGoffin again, but the A.B.C. had caught seven more runners in the last three months, and all of them had received at least a year in jail. Also, the federal agents had smashed stills all over the plateau and had sent several moonshiners to Atlanta. Even the bootleggers in Rachel's Hollow were afraid to move their whiskey, regardless of the high prices paid by the syndicate in Detroit. There were more men each morning at the strip mine shape-ups, and eventually Perry was not able to get even one day's work a week. Finally, he applied for relief at the welfare office.

The waiting room was crowded and hot, and the air was heavy with smoke that drifted towards the single window fan in back. Women sat stiffly on the straight-back chairs, holding crying children in their laps, while their husbands spit tobacco juice on the wooden floor and ground it into the grain with their boots. There were only two social workers to interview all the people in the room, and a family usually had to wait five or six hours before it was called to one of the desks. The toilet in the rest room was broken, and often a woman took her children across the street to the filling station and returned to find that her name had been called and she would have to wait until everyone else had been interviewed. At noon the social workers and the typist left for an hour, but the people in the waiting room ate sack lunches of fried potatoes and pork chops rather than chance losing their place in line. By mid-afternoon the air was fetid, the floor was littered with paper, orange peels, and cigarette butts, and children slept stretched out on the chairs, their faces flushed from the heat.

Perry sat on the back row and wiped the sweat off his neck with his cap. A child on the chair in front wet his pants, and the urine ran down his legs onto the floor.

'It ain't right to make us wait this long,' a man next to Perry said. He was a miner, and there was still a pale line around his eyes where his goggles fitted. A boy of about four slept in his lap. There was a damp imprint of perspiration on the miner's shirt where his son's head pressed against it. 'I been in here six hours and the boy ain't had nothing to eat.'

'How much can you get on the welfare?' Perry asked.

'We come down here three times, and they ain't give us nothing but a two-dollar grocery order so far. We had to go all the way to Richmond to cash it because the company stores don't take them.'

'I ain't ever done this before,' Perry said.

'I never had nothing to do with these sonsofbitches, either. But I ain't worked in a month, and the union's got us locked out clear over to old Virginia. My welfare card ain't no good, and I had to give our last thirty dollars to some shithead doctor in Richmond when the boy was sick. If they don't give us nothing today, I'm going to pull that feller over his desk and stick his head in that broken toilet.'

At four o'clock one of the social workers called Perry's name. She was a thin woman, and she wore her straight black hair on her shoulders with a ribbon in it like a young girl. Her face was covered with white powder, and across the desk Perry could smell her perfume and the odor of cigarettes on her breath.

'Are you applying just for yourself?' she said.

'It ain't for me. I come here because of my mother and the kids.'

'Are they here?'

'I didn't see no reason to make them set in this office all day.'

'Your mother will have to sign an affidavit of need,' the woman said.

'What's that mean?'

'It's just a rule the agency has.'

'I been in that chair since seven-thirty this morning.'

'I'm sorry, but you'll have to come back with the rest of your family.'

'There ain't no food in our house, and my mother ain't up to setting in a hundred-degree heat for seven hours,' he said. 'We ain't ever asked you all for nothing before, and I wouldn't be here now if I could go anywhere else. But by God I ain't spent all this time for nothing and I ain't leaving till I know the kids are going to have something to eat besides grits every day.'

The woman looked at the clock on the wall and lighted a cigarette. She blew the smoke out and coughed, holding her hand over her mouth. A child began crying loudly in the waiting room.

'Let's fill out this form and I'll have a social worker make a home call at your house,' she said.

'What's that for?'

'It's the only way your case can be certified.' She wrote Perry's name on the top of the welfare application. 'How many people are there in your family?'

'Seven besides me, but three of the little ones are in the state children's home,' he said.

'You should have told me that before. You probably already have an ADC case opened.'

'I told you I ain't been here before.'

'If anyone in your family is receiving state aid, we have a record of it,' she said. 'I'll have to pull your case history tomorrow.'

'When can I get something for the kids?'

'The social worker will be out next week, and then we can make a determination.'

'They can't wait a week. There won't be nothing left to eat by then,' Perry said. 'We can't get no more surplus food till the end of the month.'

'There's not much more I can do. You'll just have to manage the best you can.'

'What are the kids supposed to eat till you all get finished fooling with them papers?'

'I'll arrange a home call for next Thursday,' she said. 'That's the earliest I can make it. Have all of your family at home that afternoon.'

'This place don't help nobody,' he said. 'People wait in here all day so you all can tell them to go home and wait some more.'

She turned sideways in her chair and dropped his application into a metal file drawer. Perry put his cloth cap on his head and walked back out through the waiting room. The broken toilet had overflowed onto the floor and cigarette butts and paper wrappers floated in the water. Some families still sat on the hard chairs, hoping that their names would be called before the office closed in five minutes. Perry stepped outside into the bright sunlight and felt the moisture on his face dry in the hot breeze.

Two days later Perry received a government check in the mail for the remainder of his Job Corps savings. He paid his charge at the company store and gave the clerk twenty-five dollars for credit on next month's account. He bought screening for the windows on the cabin, to keep out the mosquitoes that swarmed up in clouds from the creek bed at night, and he spent five dollars on shoes for the children at the secondhand store in town. After he paid for the patent medicine nerve tonic that his mother had been charging at the drug store, almost all of his money was gone and he still needed to buy new work gloves and boots for himself in case he caught a day's work at the strip mine.

The days passed into August and the heat continued.

Perry sat on the front porch in the stillness of the twilight evening and looked off at the purple haze above the mountains. The crickets and cicadas were loud in the breathless air, and occasionally a bullfrog croaked at the bottom of a stream bed. The children played on the broken wagon in the dusty front yard, and Mrs James sat in her rocker, gazing at them with no expression on her face. Perry felt the tedium of the long evening begin to settle upon him. But he had no money to shoot pool in town or buy whiskey from Rachel's Hollow, and it was too hot to sleep. His mother seldom spoke, except to ask if he or the children were ready for their dinner, and their evenings were usually spent in listless silence. Tomorrow he would go to all the strip mines again, then he would stand on the street corner for a couple of hours in town until he had to return home once more and sit on the porch and listen to his mother's rocker creak back and forth on the wood boards. Mrs James' head nodded on her chest and her hands went limp in her lap. Her grey hair was wet around the temples. In the distance Perry saw an old coupe driving fast up the road, with a cloud of white dust behind it. On the turns the car showered rocks into the hollow far below. The rusted fenders and running boards shook and rattled, and wisps of steam rose from the engine. He must be drunk, Perry thought. He's going to put one of them pistons through the hood or go over the cliff.

'Who's that?' Mrs James said. She raised her head up abruptly from her chest. Her eyes were dazed with sleep.

'It's Bee Hatfield.'

'What's he up here for? He don't come by except when there's trouble. The last time I seen him he took your daddy to the union meeting at the schoolhouse.'

Perry watched the car slow into second gear on the last curve and stop at the foot of the hill.

'He's probably drinking. I'll go talk to him,' he said.

'You tell him he don't need to stop by here no more. We already had our share of his kind of trouble.'

Perry stood up and walked down the trail towards the road. The dirt was dry and hard under his bare feet. Half of the red sun still showed above the ridge, and the dark shadow of the cliffs fell across the treetops in the bottom of the hollow. All the windows in the coupe were rolled up and filmed with dust. Perry could smell the hot odor of the tires and engine. He stepped out softly on the rock road as Bee rolled down the driver's window. He wore a cloth, duck-bill cap and a soiled, striped shirt, and his face was beaded with perspiration from the heat inside the closed car. Perry could smell whiskey on his breath.

'We got them. Go get your gun,' Bee said.

'Got who?'

'All three of them. Hurry up and get that pistol.'

'Wait a minute. What do you mean you—'

'Goddamn it, boy, we ain't got time to wait.'

'Where are they at?'

'Listen, I didn't almost pile this junker up so I could come out here and argue with you. You been talking about getting them three men ever since they blowed the schoolhouse. Now if you want to go back and set on the porch, that's all right with me, because I'll let the others finish it for you.'

'What others?' Perry said.

'I'm starting this engine, boy. You better move it if you're a-coming.'

Perry headed back up the trail in a half run. The sun had set lower behind the cliff, and over the mountains the early moon was pale in the fading light. Mrs James had fallen asleep in her chair. The magazine she used to fan herself lay at her feet, and her flat breasts rose up and down with her heavy breathing. Perry opened the screen door quietly and went into the bedroom. He slipped his shoes on over his bare feet and took out the long-barreled, Buntline special revolver and the box of magnum shells from under his mattress. He unwrapped the oil cloth from the pistol, pushed it down inside his work trousers, and covered the butt with his shirt. The metal was cold against his body. Two of the children began fighting in the front yard, and through the thin board wall he heard his mother's rocker scrape on the porch. He stuck the box of shells in his pocket and went back outside.

'Why is Bee still down there?' she said.

'He knows about a job in Jackson.'

'I don't want you going with him.'

'I ain't going to be long. Go inside and lay down. It's cooler now.'

'He don't have a job for you, son. He ain't been around work since he come out of the penitentiary.'

'I got to go. He's a-waiting.'

'Turn around here. You got that pistol under your shirt.'

'We might jump a rabbit along the road.'

'You ain't telling me the truth. I can see it in your face.'

'Don't fix no dinner for me. I'll eat in Jackson.'

'Woodson would have never let you keep that gun in the house. I ought to have throwed it down the holler. Now you're going to use it on someone. You're acting just like all the Hatfields, and I can't take it no more, Perry.'

'I'm going now. Drink some of that tonic and go lay down.'

He worked his way back down the trail to the road and got inside Bee's car. He pulled the pistol out of his trousers and set it and the box of cartridges beside him on the seat. There was a layer of white dust on the dashboard. The last slanting rays of the sun struck the front of the cabin, and he saw his mother motionless and small in her chair. Bee put the car in first gear and roared off down the road, spraying rocks against the fenders. There was a half-empty bottle of whiskey in his lap.

'All right, where you got them?' Perry said.

'Down by that flooded shaft at the far end of Rachel's Holler.'

'How'd you find them?'

'You know that company deputy that looks like he's half nigger? He was drunk in the barroom, and he was telling them whores he'd educated some union men in a schoolhouse. We got him outside in the alley and sweated him good till he told us who the other two was. We found both of them upstairs in the jenny-barn. One of them was in a room with his pecker out when we grabbed hold of him.'

Perry opened the loading gate of his revolver and inserted the shells into the cylinder. His heart was beating fast and his hands felt uncoordinated. He eased the hammer back into the safety position on one empty chamber and snapped the loading gate shut.

'Who all's with you?' he said.

'The J.W.s and some others that's been waiting to catch them sonsofbitches.'

'They got no part in this.'

'They figure they have. They wanted to kill them three and throw them off the ridge soon as we got out of town. But I told them not to do nothing till I got you.'

'I already had it out once with Little J.W. I warned him about fooling in my business.'

'Look, you'll get your chance at them men. They're locked up in Big J.W.'s trunk, and there ain't nobody going to bother them till we get there. All you got to do is line them up and finish it. Just leave the J.W.s alone. I don't feel like pulling you out of no more trouble.'

Bee drove with one hand on the top of the steering wheel and drank out of the whiskey bottle with the other. They neared the bottom of the road as the last light faded in the hollow. The car bounced over a wooden bridge that spanned a dry stream bed and the dark trees and cliffs rose up ahead. The road through Rachel's Hollow was corrugated and baked hard as concrete by the sun. There were a few clapboard shacks and log cabins set back in the trees, and occasionally a cigarette glowed in the shadows on a front porch. The car banged over the ruts, and the whiskey in Bee's hand spilled out on his shirt. They drove deeper into the hollow, and the maples and white oaks towered above the road like a canopy under the moon.

'I didn't want nobody else in on it,' Perry said. 'You should have come for me when you first heered that deputy talking in the bar.'

'Boy, everything can't be like you want it. You'd have never cotched them men without us helping you. Goddamn this heat. There ain't no air at all down here.'

'What do the other two look like?' Perry said.

'They probably don't look like much at all after riding ten miles in that trunk. It must be two hundred degrees in there.'

'I didn't want it like this.'

'Are you backing out? By God, if you are I'll set you on the road right now.'

'I ain't a-backing out of nothing. You just get me there and keep them J.W.s out of it.'

Perry's breath became more rapid. He unbuttoned his shirt and let the hot air from the vane blow against his chest. The gun metal on the pistol was warm in his grip. He put a plug of tobacco in the side of his jaw, but his mouth was so dry that he could not chew.

The road ended at the base of a limestone cliff on the far end of the hollow. Bee turned off into the trees and followed an abandoned logging trail through the dense scrub brush and briar thickets. The beech trees were white in his headlights, and water ticked out of a rock house and glistened on the grey boulders at the foot of the cliff. The night was strong with the smell of the woods and of the dead leaves piled around the tree trunks. Then the undergrowth began to thin, and ahead Perry saw a clearing where a Coleman lantern burned on the ground beside a parked car. The shadows of six men grouped in a circle stood out in the light. One figure raised something in his hand above his head and slashed it down murderously, then someone screamed out in pain.

'Let's get it over with quick. That whiskey's making me sweat like a whore,' Bee said. He braked the car on the edge of the clearing and cut the headlights.

Perry got out and stuck his pistol down in his trousers. He felt the muscles tremble in the back of his legs as he walked towards the lantern's white glare. Three men lay on the ground, and Perry wanted to turn his head aside after he had looked at them. They had been beaten with chains. Their faces were swollen and streaked with blood, and their shirts had almost been ripped from their backs. Two of them had their arms over their heads, and the company deputy's shoulder sagged as though his collarbone were broken. His eyes were glazed with fear, and his mouth shook convulsively when he tried to speak. His hair was matted with sweat and dirt, and his exposed, soft stomach bulged out over his trousers. He tried to push himself away from the group of men, but his arm folded under him and he fell against his bad shoulder. One of his shoes had come off, and his sock had slipped down over his hairless, pink ankle.

Perry had seen the other two men before in the poolroom. They were both sallow and thin, their hair was uncut, and they had crude tattoos on their arms. They made their living shooting dice, hustling the pool tables, and sometimes driving company coal trucks through union picket lines. Their sharkskin slacks were torn at the knees and covered with grease from the trunk of the car. Little J.W. stood above them with a double length of chain in his hand. He wore his tin hat at an angle on his head, and his denim shirt was rolled up neatly over his short, muscular arms. His jaw bone was tight against his cheek. He let the chain swing loosely against his pants leg, and he chewed on a match stick in the corner of his mouth. Perry looked at the other faces reflected in the lantern's light. Big J.W. stood tall and lean by his brother, with a hand-rolled cigarette between his long, yellow teeth. Next to him was Foley Rankin and three of his cousins, all of whom had belonged to the Ku Klux Klan when it had existed briefly in southeastern Kentucky after Negroes from Alabama had been hired to scab in the mines. Perry remembered the story his father told about how Rankin had led a caravan of cars filled with men in peaked hats and bed sheets to the company shacks where the Negro workers lived. One cabin was burned, several Negroes were forced to kneel in the dust, and a company bus was turned over into the hollow.

Rankin walked behind the car and picked up three heavy cement cinder blocks and dropped them by the three men on the ground. His narrow eyes glinted, and the blood had drained from his lips. He pulled a coil of thin rope from his back pocket and cut it into three sections with his knife.

'You know what this is for, boys?' he said. 'I'm going to tie them blocks around your neck, and in a few minutes you're going all the way to the bottom of that hole.'

The deputy twisted his neck and looked at the flooded mine opening set back in the trees. Broken timbers were scattered around the sink hole, and rotted twigs and leaves floated on top of the stagnant water.

'I reckon it's a hundred feet straight down,' Big J.W. said. 'I hope you fellers can hold your breath a long time.'

'Maybe they might find somebody down there to talk with,' Rankin said. 'Didn't somebody throw a nigger in there once?'

'That's the one that swole up till he floated all them bricks to the top,' one of Rankin's cousins said.

The deputy put one hand over his eyes and began to cry softly. His fingers trembled on his forehead.

'He looks like he's going to piss all over himself, don't he?' Big J.W. said.

'I just drove. I didn't know they was going to blow the schoolhouse when anybody was there,' the deputy said. His breath came in spasms.

'You was bragging on it in the bar, you sonofa-bitch,' Little J.W. said. He raised the chain and whipped it down on the deputy's back with all his weight three times. The deputy writhed in the dirt under each blow. His eyes protruded from his head, a dry scream caught in his throat, and his body arched backwards as though his spine had been broken. 'Here, you want some more? I can do it all night if you want to open your mouth again.'

Good God, Perry thought. *Not like this*. The heat seemed to gather in the clearing like steam off a forge, and he felt the perspiration run down his face and neck onto his shirt. He smelled the stagnant water in the mine shaft, the dried sweat of the men around him, and his head began to spin. The cruel faces in the light and the figures on the ground didn't look real to him. Heat lightning flashed above the ridge, and he heard a clap of thunder echo in a distant hollow.

Rankin tied a section of rope through the hole in a cinder block, then knotted the other end in a loop. He swung the weight back and forth in his hand to test the strength of the rope.

'Let's get on with it,' he said.

'They ain't in no hurry. Sweat them a little more, baby brother,' Big J.W. said.

'We spent too much time on this trash already,' Little J.W. said. 'Throw that little one in there first. We'll save something special for this loudmouth deputy.'

One of the poolroom hustlers dragged himself backwards and tried to get to his feet. Big J.W. kicked him hard in the small of the back and knocked him into the dust.

'Don't do it, mister. Please,' the hustler said. His face had gone white, and a line of spittle ran from the corner of his mouth. His puffed eyes were dilated with fright. Then he began to shake all over.

'He's a yellow sonofabitch, ain't he?' Big J.W. said.

'Please, for God's sake,' the hustler said. 'You beat us enough already. Don't kill us.'

'Tie it tight around his neck and shut off his air,' Little J.W. said.

Rankin knelt beside the man on the ground and tried to force the rope over his head. The man curled into a ball and clenched his arms across his face. Rankin pulled him upright by his hair and struck him in the mouth.

'Hold your head up straight, you bastard, or I'll take your eyes out with that chain,' he said.

'Wait a minute,' Bee said. 'Let Perry finish it. I reckon he's got more right than anybody else.'

'It don't matter to me,' Rankin said. 'I don't like putting my hands on them, no how. They all smell like piss.'

'Just do it and let's get moving. It's too goddamn hot down here,' one of Rankin's cousins said.

'You figure that boy's got it in him?' Big J.W. said.

'He don't look too good, does he?' Little J.W. said. 'In fact, he looks just like he did when we run him out of the hole.'

'Goddamn, throw them in the shaft and let's get back to town,' Rankin's cousin said.

'Lay it on them, Perry,' Bee said.

Perry felt the veins grow tight in his head, and the line of treetops seemed to shift against the mountain's dark outline. His shirt was soaked through. The pulse pounded in his wrists, and his eyes filmed and burned in the light.

'Let them go,' he said. His voice almost broke when he spoke.

'What did you say?' Little J.W. said.

'Get that goddamn gun out, boy,' Bee said.

'We ain't going to kill them,' Perry said.

'Why'd you bring this little sonofabitch down here?' Big J.W. said.

'You listen, Perry. Them men never give your daddy no chance,' Bee said. 'Now, you get that gun out quick.'

'Get him out of here,' Little J.W. said.

'No, by God. He's going to finish it,' Bee said.

'I ain't going to do it. Nobody is. I told you all before not to mix in it.'

'I ain't a-waiting on this kind of shit,' Big J.W. said. 'Pull the rope over the little one's head. If he fights back again, I'm going to cut his throat.'

He opened his knife blade against his trousers and stooped his long frame over the man on the ground. He held the point of the blade under the hustler's chin while Rankin widened the loop in the rope.

'Stand away from him,' Perry said.

'You shut your face,' Little J.W. said.

'I ain't fooling. Turn loose of him.'

'Rap him across the head with that chain,' Big J.W. said.

'I'm just about to do it, and once I start I ain't stopping,' Little J.W. said.

'You ain't going to do nothing.'

'I been putting up with you too long, boy,' Little J.W. said. His words were slow and measured.

'You and your brother ain't no better than a pair of shithogs,' Perry said. 'You ain't good for nothing except burning people out or beating a man to death while you hold a gun on him.'

Little J.W. raised the chain over his shoulder and came towards him. He breathed heavily through his nostrils, and his eyes looked insane. Perry pulled the revolver from his trousers and pointed it at arm's length directly into Little J.W.'s face. He cocked the hammer back with his thumb and felt the cylinder click into place.

'It's got magnums in it. They'll tear half your head off,' he said.

Little J.W. stopped, his mouth tight, and remained motionless. There was no sound in the clearing except his hoarse breathing.

'Throw the chain down,' Perry said.

'Your life ain't worth nothing now. You won't ever get out of this holler.'

'Throw it down, or I swear to God I'll kill you where you're at.'

Little J.W. released the chain and let it drop to the ground. Perspiration rolled down through the rings of dirt on his neck.

'You do this against union men?' Bee said.

'Stay out of it,' Perry said.

'We cotched them for you, and you pull a gun on us,' Bee said. 'I told you to keep clear of it.'

'You ain't no kin of mine. I wouldn't let you in my back door.'

Perry moved out into the light by the three men on the ground and kept his pistol pointed at the J.W.s. Rankin stepped back from him and tripped on one of the cinder blocks. The hard lines in his face had gone slack, and he rubbed his fingers up and down on his trouser leg.

'You three sonsofbitches get up and run,' Perry said.

'I can't make it. They broke something inside me,' the deputy said.

'Buddy, your luck's pretty good right now. Get moving.'

'I won't have no chance.'

'I ain't going to give you long. Pick him up,' Perry said.

The other two men rose slowly to their feet, watching the circle of faces in the shadow. Their legs were weak under them, and they couldn't straighten their backs. They stumbled forward, off balance, and lifted the deputy up by his arms. He winced in pain at the pressure on his bad shoulder.

'Goddamn you, run,' Perry said.

'Take us out with you, mister. They'll find us again,' one of the hustlers said. He swayed on his feet.

'Then you just ain't got no more luck. I'm a-turning them loose in about one minute, and you better start finding a rock house to hide in.'

The three men stepped backwards across the clearing, still watching the J.W.s; then they turned and crashed into the briar thickets. The thorns scraped across their faces and tore their skin; they slashed at the branches with their forearms, tripped over rocks and dead logs, fell to the ground, then plunged forward again.

'How do you figure on getting out of here?' Little J.W. said.

Perry heard the thrashing in the underbrush grow more distant.

'You don't worry about it. You ain't even going to move,' he said. He edged around the group of men, reached inside Big J.W.'s car window and pulled the keys from the ignition. He threw them as far as he could into the trees.

'You're going to sweat harder than them others for that,' Big J.W. said.

'I'm taking your car, Bee,' Perry said. 'You can pick it up in front of the courthouse.'

He kept the gun pointed in front of him while he

254

retreated towards Bee's coupe. His knuckles whitened from his grip on the pistol.

'Kick over the lantern,' Little J.W. said.

'I'll dump all six shells right in the middle of you,' Perry said.

'He can't hit nobody in the dark. Kick it over, Rankin. He ain't going to walk away from us like this.' But no one moved.

Perry opened the car door and steadied the pistol across the window jamb. He leaned inside, flipped the gear stick into neutral and turned the ignition, then depressed the gas pedal and floor starter at the same time with one foot. The engine throbbed under the hood, and he eased into the seat sideways, with the door still open and the pistol leveled across the window. He waited a moment for any movement from the J.W.s, then he threw the pistol on the seat beside him, shoved the car into reverse, and popped out the clutch. The coupe spun around in a half circle, the tires whining on the hard earth, and the door sprang back on its hinges into a tree trunk. For an instant he saw the group of men break up in the light and head towards him. He double-clutched the transmission, slammed the gear stick into first, and pressed the accelerator to the floor. The car roared through the brush and weeds, and he heard the muffler hit a rock and tear loose from the frame. A tree limb smashed the right front window. He turned on the lights and wound up the transmission in first until the gear lever was shaking in his palm. He swerved around the chuck holes in the road, bounced across logs at thirty miles an hour, and scraped the entire side of the car against a white oak tree.

He could smell the tires and engine burning when he turned out of the woods and headed back through the hollow. He had knocked the front end out of alignment, and the car swayed from side to side over the ruts. He knew that it would take the J.W.s only a few minutes to cross the wires on their ignition, and then they would be down the road after him. He was breathing fast, as though he couldn't catch his wind, and he wiped his face with the front of his shirt. Heat lightning flickered above the ridge again, and a black thunderhead had begun to move across the moon. Up ahead he saw lights in a cabin through the poplars, and the road became more even and started to climb towards the far cliff.

The exhaust fumes from the broken tail pipe rose up through the floor boards and made his eyes water. He worked his shirt off his shoulders with one hand, rubbed it over his chest and neck, and opened the air vent on the hood. He watched the rearview mirror for any headlights behind him, but the road was empty and the bottom of the hollow was dark. As he climbed higher, a thin breeze began to bend the treetops and the air felt suddenly cool. Then he saw the moonlight on the wood bridge across the stream bed and the limestone boulders in the dry sand.

He kept the car in second gear up the gravel lane along the ridge. Below him he could see the flat expanse of black-green trees, the dry washes, and the logging roads pale and yellow under the moon. More clouds had formed on the horizon, and gusts of wind swept across the cliffs and spun dead leaves through the air. He heard the pines creak in the breeze, then a bolt of lightning ripped through the sky in a brief, crooked white line and struck a mountaintop in the distance.

Perry felt spent inside, as though all the fury and heat in his blood had been drained from him in a few minutes' time. The strain and violence of the last hour had left him exhausted. His hands were thick on the steering wheel, and the skin of his face felt dead to his touch. In the beating of the air stream through the window, he thought he could still hear the voices of the J.W.s and the screams of the men on the ground, then he forced them out of his mind and looked ahead at the ragged line of maples on the ridge, the steep cliffs, and the black clouds that rolled and twisted over the hollow. A solitary raindrop struck his windshield as he turned onto the blacktop towards town.

The store fronts in town were darkened, the streets almost deserted, and the wind blew the dust in clouds along the worn brick paving. He could hear the banjo and fiddle music in the tavern and the drunken laughter that always continued until early morning. There was a smell like scorched copper in the air, and a garbage can rolled loudly down a sidewalk. The light in the sheriff's office fell out on the courthouse lawn. Perry parked the car at the curb, unloaded the revolver and stuck it in his belt. He put on his shirt, without buttoning it, and walked across the grass to the courthouse entrance.

The sheriff sat behind his desk with an electric fan blowing in his face. His brown uniform was rumpled and stained darkly around the collar, and the papers under his huge arms stuck to his skin when he moved. There was a pitcher of ice water by his elbow. He stopped writing and looked up at Perry, then dropped his eyes to the revolver.

'You must have lost your goddamn mind,' he said. His breath wheezed down in his throat when he spoke.

'Them three men that killed my daddy are at the back of Rachel's Holler. They ain't going nowhere, either.'

'By God, I warned you what would happen if you–'

'I didn't do nothing to them. The J.W.s worked them over with chains. They're hid out in a rock house somewhere.'

The sheriff stood up from his chair, opened his drawer and took out an automatic pistol and a blackjack with a spring handle. He slipped one in each of his back pockets.

'Get in the car,' he said.

'You don't need me for nothing. Just drop this gun at the pawnshop and tell Mr Mac to give the money to my mother.' Perry pulled the revolver from his belt and set it on the desk top.

'Where are you going?'

'I ain't got to stay here no more.'

'Wait a minute.'

'I'm gone, Sheriff.'

Perry left the courthouse, crossed the street, and walked past the coal bins to the edge of town. He followed a dirt road lined with clapboard shacks and junker cars, then climbed through a barbed wire fence into a meadow, and headed toward the C & O railroad embankment on the far side. The wind was blowing harder now, and he could smell the rain in the distance and the ferns in the stream beds. The moon had turned blue overhead. Cows were bunched together in the field, and he heard them chewing at the grass and dandelions in the dark. He jumped across an irrigation ditch by the water tower and climbed the railroad grade to the track. Weeds grew between the gravel and wooden ties, and the rails stretched off between two black mountains where the grade made a bend.

He followed the track to the curve and sat down on the edge of a tie. The rain began to fall evenly on the mountaintop, and a white mist moved through the hollow and settled in the base of the trees. Then he felt the rail vibrate under his palm, and a train whistle echoed on the other side of the ridge. A few moments later the headlamp on the engine swept around the bend, and he saw the rain spinning in the light and the line of freight cars that stretched back a half mile. He slid down the embankment and waited as the locomotive drew closer. The chains on the couplings banged and sparked against the gravel, the earth trembled from the weight of the cars, and the weeds along the side of the road bed were knocked flat by the blast of hot air from the wheels. The engine thundered past Perry, and he began running over the rocks in an even line with the string of box cars and tankers. The train was starting to pick up speed again at the end of the curve. All of the doors were locked and sealed, and none of the flat cars had handrails on them. He was running short of breath, and over his shoulder he saw the green and red lights on the caboose coming up behind him. He leaped upwards and grabbed the iron rung on the side of a refrigerator unit and pulled his legs up over the wheels. For a moment he thought he would lose his grip and be sucked under the car. The ties and road bed sped by below his feet, and when the train made the curve he had to hook both of his arms around the iron rung. The rain beat in his face, and the mist between the mountains was so thick that he couldn't see the tree trunks. He climbed to the top of the car and sat on the wooden walkway with his knees pulled up in front of him and his back to the wind.

In a few hours he would be out of the Cumberland Mountains, rolling through the bluegrass country towards Lexington. Then he would hop another C & O freight to Cincinnati, and by dawn he would see the great bridge across the Ohio River, the white paddle-wheel pleasure boat churning in the current below, and the sunlight on the narrow, German buildings and trees along the boulevards. He'd find a job somewhere, and on Sunday afternoons he would go to the ball games and drink beer and eat sausage at Crosley Field. In the evening dusk he would walk along the water-sprinkled streets, and maybe, if he had enough money, he would go out to River Downs where the best thoroughbred horses in Kentucky raced. The train gathered speed as it roared down the grade on the far side of the mountain, and he held onto the walkway tightly with both hands. The purple silhouette of the hills stood out against the sky when lightning crashed into a hollow, and he could smell the sweet odor of wet earth in the tobacco fields and meadows. Part of the moon shone from behind a cloud, and the rain in his hair reflected like drops of crystal.